HOSTA

/5

HOSTAGES

Oisín Fagan

NEW ISLAND

HOSTAGES
First published in 2016 by
New Island Books
16 Priory Office Park
Stillorgan
Co. Dublin
Republic of Ireland.

www.newisland.ie

Print ISBN: 978-1-84840-514-1
Epub ISBN: 978-1-84840-515-8
Mobi ISBN: 978-1-84840-516-5

Typeset by JVR Creative India
Cover Design by Anna Morrison
Printed by ScandBook AB

New Island received financial assistance from The Arts Council (*An
Chomhairle Ealaíon*), 70 Merrion Square, Dublin 2, Ireland.

10 9 8 7 6 5 4 3 2 1

For the memory of Julia and Oliver Fagan

Being Born

Conception
0

Kilcock has, and always had, a mad suicide rate. This is probably because of the sad canal, the empty Zed factory, the banal, linear design of the social housing where decentralised Dubliners were mishoused, or it could be a combination of all this; all this superfluous sprawl. Back when Fergus was in first and second year the Zed factory opposite the school poured out strawberry steam. Its smell filled the streets, seeped through every pore and filled every corner, through the school, through his clothes; then the sweet factory closed down to be outsourced to China when he was in third year and the building became an empty shell. Once Zed left, Fergus realised that he and his classmates would never again trawl through the school's corridors shrouded in the vapours of unifying strawberry. Lynx Africa and Fantasy by Britney Spears prevailed for the most part, but a host of other scents fought in their undercurrent, fracturing the community of senses they had all grown up in. Such sensory dislocation in a semi-rural, pre-suburban, yet also pseudo-industrial town was undoubtedly one of the factors that led to the failed rising of the 2006 transition years; both the rising and the failing. Or at least I think so, though I may be falling into the common trap of always looking for justifications for destruction, rather than looking at destruction as the continuation of a grander underlying system. But then again, it's in my nature, commonplace as I am, to fall into the commonest of traps.

1

Mr Moore, reading the *Sun*, legs up on the desk, backed by a hundred beakers, stared out through his spectacles at the transition year students.

'Well?' he said.

'Hello, sir,' the class said.

He set them an assignment. Given the nature and ethos of transition year he felt it best to leave the terms of the project vague. Approaching the blackboard, chalk in hand, his back hunched over, he Zorroishly slashed the board. He stood back and looked at what he had written. Make something, the board read.

'Any questions?'

Sharon Fitzgerald's hand shot up.

'What, Sharon?' he sighed.

'When does it have to be in?'

'I don't know. Two weeks from now. Maybe? I don't know.'

Mr Moore sat down at his desk, centred his glasses on his nose, picked up the *Sun* and flicked to the sports section at the back. Silence fell. Sharon stuck her pink Bubbaloo behind her ear, turned in her seat, looked at Fergus Nolan, winked, and then the air went out of Fergus's lungs, and he blushed so deeply that little white stars edged into his vision, creeping along his sight until he forgot his name. There was too much

Sharon for him to take in. Bleach-blonde hair, sprayed and voluminous; pink eyeliner, seashell necklace, stud earrings, glitter stickers on her eyeteeth, homemade bead bracelets around both her wrists, small, fine, inbuilt sexiness pouring out of her; scattershot fake tan all over her face, shining in the dim lighting, deftly thumbing her Nokia through holes she'd dug in her sleeves, her thin legs pressed against the heater. She seemed to be everywhere. I understand Fergus's reaction. I am also shocked by her. She leaves me speechless.

To distract himself, Fergus took his compass out of his pencil case and began scratching the lyrics to 'Mo' Money Mo' Problems' onto the seat of his chair.

Darragh Madden, who was sat behind Fergus, whispered into his ear.

'Faggot,' he whispered.

'That's not what your dad said last night when he was sucking my cock,' Fergus answered softly, scratching away with his compass.

'Fuck you say, lad?'

'Your dad went down on me in the frozen aisle in Tesco last night.'

Darragh Madden poked his head over Fergus's shoulder and looked up at him, tilting his head upwards, his neck stretched; wide-eyed, owl-like.

'Are you messing with me?' he said, and then he snatched the compass out of Fergus's hand and stabbed him in the back of the shoulder with it. When Darragh took his hand away, the compass was stuck in Fergus's shoulder, poking out like an aerial. Fergus clamped his hand over his mouth to muffle his own screaming. They both raised their eyes to Mr Moore, who was still reading his paper. Then they looked at one another, and Fergus started swinging blows at Darragh under the table; small, quick hits, leaning back as far as he could in the hopes of knocking his testicles. After a brief scramble, Darragh had Fergus's fist clamped in his hands and was squeezing his knuckles until they cracked. Fergus felt the power go out of his legs as Darragh laughed with his mouth closed. With all the strength he had left in him, Fergus flopped his free arm at Darragh, limply pelting the side of his head with back-handed slaps while Darragh, square-jawed, squat and thick-set, grinned widely.

'Ciúnas anois,' Mr Moore said, looking up from his crossword.

They both flipped forward, aping normality and boredom. Then Darragh Madden growled.

'What was that, Darragh?'

'What was what, sir?' Darragh said, blinking innocently.

'Maybe you can help me with this clue, Darragh. Synonym for Darragh Madden. Three words. 5, 2, 5. Four across. First letter is W, second word is of.'

Fergus glanced back at Darragh, whose face was blank.

'Oh, I have it now. Waste of space.'

Darragh leant back in his chair, his breathing haywire and rushed, like a horse's galloping snorts. Then it stopped and silence fell again.

Fergus pulled the compass out of his shoulder and out of the corner of his eye watched a small curve of blood spurt back onto Darragh's desk. He grimaced, hugged the radiator and looked out the window at the lined prefabs propped against the northern wall. Next class would be in there, and it would be cold. His eyes scanned the court, the green railings that enclosed the school, and then he saw Neil Jennings striding from behind the prefabs and into the second year social area, followed by what seemed to be three midgets. Well, I'll be fucked, Fergus thought, squinting, wondering if he was hallucinating. He looked at the building that used to be their social area two years ago. An eternity ago. It was an old, converted milking parlour with high corrugated sheets for roofing. The gradient of the floor in the social area was declined towards the centre of the room to allow drainage and run-off; inside, wobbly-legged tables shuddered in the breeze that whistled through the vents; all overseen by hazy fluorescent lights, their buzzing glow interrupting the green-hued, veiny shade thrown by the ivy leaves that crept along the walls and the ceiling. The ivy hung thick, inside and out; and until late afternoon the benches that bordered the walls would support thousands of droplets, like little liquid islands gifted by the morning dew; troops of mushrooms nested sleepily in the back of every locker, and a twelve-foot portrait of Big Gay Al from *South Park* broke the monotony of breeze blocks on the eastern wall, a flamboyant gesture against the dull monotony of the whole school. This was a lifeless abattoir of a place. I would have cried then if I had I known this was where I would be born. But, then again, I could only be born in a place like this.

The intercom beeped twice. Everyone turned around to face the speaker fixed above the blackboard.

'Fógra amháin,' Mr Kennedy, the principal, said over the intercom. 'Hot soup will no longer be served in the fifth year social area.'

A universal moan rose from the thousand students and seeped into every corner of the school; a communal sigh resounded, a sighing earthquake rumbled, heating the walls.

Somewhere, someplace, someone dreams me.

'Mother of God,' Sharon shouted, her eyes darting at Darragh Madden.

'Ciúnas anois,' Mr Moore shouted.

'This is due,' Mr Kennedy continued once the tremors had ceased, 'to the series of soup-related assaults that have been carried out over the last two weeks by one, so-far-unnamed, culprit.'

Everyone in the class looked at Darragh Madden and he shrugged. For no fathomable reason, though maybe just because he could afford to, Darragh had recently taken it into his head to buy ten small plastic cups of vegetable soup every little break and throw them in students' faces. If there were no students available, as was often the case, he would walk down to the football pitch, cups in hand, climb over a stile, and throw lukewarm soup over whatever sleepy calves stood in the adjacent fields.

'Until we can learn to respect our school and its students by aiding its investigation into these assaults of an extremely liquid nature,' Mr Kennedy continued, 'soup will be retracted from the menu. The culprit will soon be identified and punished accordingly.'

A long pause, and the shuffling of paper came out over the intercom.

'You're some cunt,' Fergus whispered at Darragh.

'Ciúnas, ciúnas, ciúnas,' Mr Moore said, not looking away from his paper.

'Fógra amháin eile,' Mr Kennedy continued. 'All fourth year students will report to the fifth year social area after this class. That's all. Go raibh maith agaibh agus slán libh.'

Another bout of shuffling and the intercom knocked off. Everyone turned around and looked at Brian Moran, who buried his head in his books, his ears turning pink with embarrassment.

'Was this you, Brian?' Harry Brennan said from the back of the class, shaking his head sadly. 'You shouldn't have done that.'

'Can I get no peace?' Mr Moore said, slamming his paper down on the desk.

Fergus looked away from Brian in disgust and his eyes fell on Sharon Fitzgerald for the thirty-eighth time that day, but something had darkened his sight, a flicker, and from out of the porous borders of nowhere, a horror came over Fergus's mind and, all at once, I realise he has been bored for four years.

How can I blame him? He sits amongst twenty-two teenagers, mixed genders; wine jumpers on the girls, grey on the boys; all heads slumped forward on the tables. Asleep or not, they still look the same: big zombie eyes staring everywhere, staring at nothing, and it strikes me that he is in some kind of mental asylum, and then the bell rings for the next class and amidst the noise he punches Darragh in the chest, slips Sharon Fitzgerald his number and runs out to the social area, his head down, not looking back.

It occurred to Fergus as he ran down the busy halls, bouncing off the students who were lined up outside each classroom, that it would have been best not to antagonise Darragh Madden. The boy had something wrong with him, something that would never be diagnosed. There was some hollow space in his soul that was filled with the kind of unpredictable whims that can only be born out of the desperation of imposed solitude. Darragh Madden was a loose cannon, and he came from a long line of loose cannons. His family were all farmers, but they weren't farmers like Fergus's parents were farmers. Fergus's parents were easy-going farmers. Middle-classish, the only middle-classish people Fergus knew. They worked a lot, but if it wasn't calving season or silage time they would go out, go hunting, go to all the local matches, watch telly in the evenings, go on holidays to the Shannon and Costa del Sol. They made Fergus help them a bit on the weekends, and he had one hour's chores every day after school, mainly feeding lambs if there were lambs to be fed, fetching coal, cutting firewood, shifting hay for the calves and walking the greyhounds, but their priority was that he do his homework, which gave Fergus ample time alone in his bedroom to read and surf the web; to indulge his loneliness and to reflect on his dreams.

Darragh's parents, on the other hand, were big business farmers; Fine Gaelers, mad Mayo cunts who got planted in Meath in the 70s by the Land Commission. They worked all the time, ever-expanding, always buying new machinery, always cutting corners and getting in trouble with the council. Their last gaff was deforesting half of Dunsany woods while continuing to take in the EU hardwood grants, for which they now owed half a million that they would never repay. Darragh was of this stock, and his family rented him out with their machinery until he turned fifteen, copped on, and started working for himself. He spent forty hours a week outside of school driving a tractor in solitude, having full, loud conversations with himself as he drove up and down fields; it was a different field every few hours, so it became like a game seeing which hedge Darragh would pop up behind next, bouncing along in his tractor, massaging his testicles and raving to himself.

Fergus arrived in the social area, breathing heavily, nervous, a rapsheet of school books cradled in his elbow's crook, his sore shoulder sagging. Vice-Principal Sims and Principal Kennedy stood in the centre of the social area, and when they saw him they motioned for him to sit down on the floor as they continued talking quietly between themselves. Fergus sat down and crossed his legs Indian-style; he slipped his books underneath himself to be comfortable on the cold lino floor. The halls buzzed as students changed class and in five minutes, the forty-odd transition years had assembled and were sat on the floor of the social area, mumbling, making white noise with their laughs. Then Sharon Fitzgerald walked in, keying numbers into her phone, Brian Moran holding her books for her. She sat down, not looking at Brian, and Brian sat behind her, his eyes wide and livid, like a dog brought to heel, aware of everything, nervous. Everyone was nervous; Fergus could feel it pulsing out of their small bodies. He glanced around, looking for Darragh, but he wasn't there.

'Is this about the soup?' Sharon called out, but Ms Sims just clapped her hands for silence.

Mr Kennedy paced backwards and forwards, moving his hands to find the words he wanted to say as he hummed to himself.

'Well, well, well,' he said eventually. 'A few brief words. I didn't think it would come to this, but it has. Bullying, bullying, bullying. The bomb thrown at mutual respect. Worse than that, it means that respect is lacking. Should punishment for bullying be collective or individual? Is bullying the problem or the symptom? Well?'

This question seemed to be addressed to the fourth years, but the only reaction was Ms Sims's flurried nodding.

'The procedures for reporting bullying mean that the victim—'

He turned to Ms Sims.

'Are we allowed to say victim?'

Ms Sims nodded.

'The victim must remain anonymous so we can begin to heal as a unit, as a body, as a class, as a year, and as a school. In the past, I would have said that the person being bullied was a weak link, a cancer to be cut from the body, a diseased, infectious animal in the herd; that which must be left behind for the health of the group, but according to the parent-teacher board, this is, supposedly, not the done thing. And, when all is said and done, their arguments do have some merits. Who am I to say they're wrong? Bullying distorts the proper channels through which healthy competitiveness functions, giving an unhealthy advantage to an inefficient collective at the expense of the individual, and individual competitiveness is the lifeblood of every healthy system.'

'What are you on about?' Sharon laughed.

'So, this is about Brian,' Fergus called out, hands cupped over his mouth.

Mr Kennedy raised a silencing hand.

'The procedures must remain anonymous.'

He looked around and took a deep breath.

'Does anybody know what I'm speaking about?'

'We know it's Brian,' Fergus shouted. 'Just let Steo go, and we'll let him be.'

Steo, a well-liked third year, had been taken away a week ago by child services for dealing yokes outside Browne's at big break. Apparently, the report had come from Brian. The forensics came back later stating that they were only aspirins with Joe Dolan's face etched into them, but, nevertheless, Steo paid the price, and students had taken to spray-painting Free Steo wherever there was free wall space. In the first year social area, in the matter of one morning, every single locker had been tagged with an inventive Free Steo design. The several students who had the ill judgement to protest against the ubiquitous graffiti on their lockers were pinned down and Free Steo was written on their foreheads; and afterwards they walked around the corridors, ostracised, sporting fading symbols for all to see, as if some strange contortion of Ash Wednesday had fallen on the school. Brian, who had taken issue with the severity of his own ostracism, had said the previous morning in Home Economics that he would report the whole school for bullying.

'Well, alright. If everyone knows it, I can say it, can't I?' Mr Kennedy said, turning to Ms Sims. 'It is Brian Moran.'

Everybody turned their heads to watch Brian, who buried his face in his hands and started crying.

'It is inexcusable in the Year of our Lord 2006,' Mr Kennedy shouted, 'to bully someone because of their sexuality.'

'Faggotry has nothing to do with this, and ye know it,' Harry Brennan called out.

'I'm not gay,' Brian shouted out from the back of the social area.

'Don't interrupt,' Ms Sims barked.

'It can't happen,' Mr Kennedy continued. 'It's antisocial. It's a bomb thrown into the proper order of the natural system. You see, systems are precious—'

At the second mention of systems, the transition years groaned in frustration.

'—so, so precious. They emerge effortlessly, beautifully. Like tendrils almost. But a threat to the system is not only a threat to the inherent order of the universe; I also take it as a personal insult. Without the system there is only the hive mind; we all turn into bees: incoherent, blind and fuzzy, buzzing our way around what we take to be the universe, but in fact we are merely hopping around a garden path, engaged in gross fornication with flowers that we are attracted to because of the shiny colours, all the while growing fat and inefficient on nectar. Think of all the delicate flowers and the hardworking, silent majority tendrils who want to live in peace, holding on to the nectar they earn without living in the dark, constant shadow of fear that at any moment, without any reprisals or any accountability, a bee could violate them and rob their precious nectar. That,' he raised up both his arms and looked to the ceiling, 'is the only fruit the hive mind can offer us.'

Ms Sims cleared her throat and Mr Kennedy turned his head to stare at her blankly as she shook her head.

'Not now,' she said.

'Oh yes, anyway,' Mr Kennedy said, raising his finger to the ceiling. 'Because of Brian's repeated reports and that damned parent-teacher board, we have no choice but to issue immediate three-day suspensions for anybody who is found to verbally or physically abuse fellow students on the grounds of race, religion or sexuality.'

'I'm not gay,' Brian said again, weakly this time.

'Detention, Moran. You were warned,' Ms Sims said, pointing at him.

'Never mind that.' James Monaghan shouted from the back of the social area. 'Where's our fucking soup?'

'Ye're the bullies,' Sharon shouted.

'Yeah,' Harry Brennan shouted, and everyone started shuffling and yelling, rocking back and forth on their crossed legs.

Three students stood up, but once they were on their feet, they didn't know what to do. They shouted and pointed at Mr Kennedy and Ms Sims, every now and again turning around in small circles. The shouting became louder and louder, and then a noise ratcheted down the hall and Darragh appeared in the social area, bandy-eyed, breathing heavily through his nose; everything went quiet.

'Did anyone rat?' he yelled.

All eyes looked up at him.

'Good stuff. Now, where's that posh Nolan cunt?' he shouted.

The transition years turned their heads away from him and back to the teachers.

'I have a bone to pick with you, Mr Madden,' Ms Sims said. 'My office. Five minutes.'

Darragh threw his hands in the air.

'Fuck this. I'm a free man,' he screamed as he ran out of the room. Ms Sims walked quickly after him, arms crossed, notepad across her chest, dignity intact.

'Did we not do a roll call?' Mr Kennedy asked, but Ms Sims wasn't there anymore. He glanced around twice, lost without her, a lonely look mutating his face. 'That's it, I suppose. Go on back to class.'

The students stood up and walked in different directions, none of them going back to their classrooms. They'd go to the basketball courts or the social area when Mr Kennedy had left, maybe they'd even go home, but wherever they go I can feel an uneasy frisson crackle in the air; air that hangs like an unfulfilled promise, moist and pregnant with a lurid, sick anxiety.

They waited until Mr Kennedy had left and then Fergus, James Monaghan and Harry Brennan carried Brian Moran into the nearest toilet. By the sinks, they waterboarded him, holding him over the sink and under the tap, a hand towel draped across his face. James and Harry held his legs while Fergus pressed the hand towel over Brian's face and pushed the tap every now and again to make sure the water was flowing properly. Fergus looked up once Brian had ceased squirming underneath him. A cluster of small mushrooms ran upwards in single file along a lightening-shaped crack in the wall that dragged its way to the ceiling. The line of inverted mushrooms, like a failed pilgrimage, ended above the only operational toilet in the bathroom. The urinals' water gurgled and ran freely over a zigzag of blue bleach that stuck high up against the wall like plasma from a space gun.

'Can you take over?' Fergus asked Harry.

'I can,' Harry nodded.

James took both of Brian's legs and Harry held the hand towel over Brian's face with one hand and worked the tap with the other.

Fergus took off his jumper and shirt and washed down his bloody shoulder. He stood over the sink and watched himself in the liver-spotted mirror and shuddered. Torso bare, thin-bodied, shoulder bones showing, hands like shovels, all overgrown and underdeveloped.

'What's up, Fergalicious?' James smiled.

'Nothing. Just Darragh's gonna kill me is all.'

James nodded, tightly grasping Brian's legs, which shivered intermittently.

'You know I had a look in his bag yesterday and there were no books,' James said.

'What? Whose?'

'Darragh's. There were just hundreds of packets of soup. Nothing else.'

'Janey Mac.'

Fergus glanced at James Monaghan. He was a quiet, swarthy boy; good with his hands. He floated like a swan amongst groups; becoming someone's friend for a week, charming and enamouring them, before promptly disappearing for a day or two until he would pop up again, already fully integrated in a new social circle. With his neutral accent, he was very clearly a product of cosmopolitan Maynooth, where he had lived until the beginning of third year, at which point he transferred schools. He seemed completely foreign and unknowable to Fergus, and, according to Harry Brennan, he had gotten a hand job off every single one of the 476 female students in Scoil Dara, from first year all the way up to sixth.

'Is yourself and Sharon still going out?' Fergus asked.

'We were meeting for two weeks there. That's been over for a year or so now. She's sound out, though. Why? Do you fancy her? Unreal hand jobs, lad. Recommended.'

'Here, lads,' Fergus said, nodding towards Brian, 'you can only do that for a couple of minutes, or he'll die or something I think. Read it on Wikipedia.'

'Can we do it in the jacks?' Harry said.

'I'd leave it now, in all honesty.'

'What was he thinking, squealing on a decent, gentle sort like Steo?' Harry asked.

'Out of his mind,' James said. 'If we can keep our mouths closed about a complete and utter yoke like Darragh, he can do the same for a stellar, sound-out head like Steo.'

They pulled Brian away from the sink and laid him gently on the floor as Fergus continued washing the blood that had crusted over his shoulders and chest, wincing.

When Fergus was done, they carried Brian, prostrate and unconscious, out of the bathroom and lay him spread-eagled on one of the tables for all to see. They sat down in the corner and began chatting amongst themselves. Little break would start in five minutes. Fergus stared at Brian, laid out flat, his small chest rising and falling, all the while stacking up orange Fruit Pastilles in a round tower on the corner of the table. Fergus started flicking the sweets at Brian, aiming for his open mouth. He kept missing, hitting Brian's throat instead.

The social area was filling up with students flocking in, chatting. They all filed past the unconscious Brian, staring at him out of the corner of their eyes before they moved on. One or two students leant over him with markers, decorating his face with Free Steo symbols.

Once his tower was gone, Fergus went over to James and asked him which locker belonged to Darragh.

'Eh, 139 or 136. Don't remember. Actually, definitely 139.'

Fergus opened his own locker and went through his bag. He brought out a book-flattened ham sandwich, which he held between his teeth. He pulled out his pencil case and took a compass out of it, which he then put in his pocket.

'Darragh's locker is 139? You're sure?' he called out, munching on his thin sandwich.

James nodded across the social area.

Fergus walked to locker 139, put the whole sandwich in his mouth and worked the lock with both hands on the compass.

The locker door swung open. On the inside of the locker door was a green rucksack, a magazine cut-out of Metallica and a large creased poster of Nas.

Fergus sighed and pulled the green rucksack out of the locker and glanced inside it.

'I thought you said Darragh's bag had soup in it?' he called to James.

James shrugged, and then Fergus shrugged in reply, slung the rucksack over his shoulder and went into the bathroom. He stared at the pale smears of blood he had left on the sink before going into the one functioning cubicle.

He emerged from the cubicle and into the social area five minutes later, placed the rucksack back in its locker and jammed the door closed. Then he saw Darragh rustling through locker 136, massaging his testicles intently as he stared at the two photos he had tacked to the inside of his locker: one of Sharon Fitzgerald in her P.E. uniform, leaning against a prefab; the other of a topless Pamela Anderson, his eyes darting between them like a dog following a fly. Confusion washed over Fergus, and he edged over to James until he was sat next to him.

Then Neil Jennings came in, followed by three midgets, and walked over to locker 139, took his keys out of his pocket and opened it.

'Oh,' Fergus said.

Neil swung open locker 139, looked at it, swung the broken door again twice, puzzled now, opened the zip on his rucksack, dropped it, jumped back and stood still. He ran to the table where Brian lay, pushed Brian off it so that his insensate body slumped to the floor, and then stood on the table with his hands up. Everybody looked up.

'Who shit in my bag?' he shouted. 'What fucker done this?'

'Darragh Madden,' James shouted, his hands cupped around his mouth.

Darragh was still hunched over his own locker, still massaging his testicles, but now with both hands. At the sound of his name, he turned and grinned.

'What's the story?' he said.

'Leg it,' James yelled.

Neil jumped down off the table and approached Darragh, the three first years shadowing him. Darragh turned and fled as laughter broke out in the social area. He bobbed and weaved through the crowd until he crashed through the swing doors, the four boys close behind him. There was pandemonium in the social area; a humming ruckus that lessened slightly as a few people filed out to see if the chase would turn into a beating, but amidst all the hullaballoo, Fergus saw Neil double back, before looking around and slinking to Darragh's locker. Neil took the rucksack out of it and walked into the toilets.

Fergus covered his hands and sighed in relief.

'You saved my life,' he said to James.

'Ah well, you know the way. It was me own fault. Also I have a bit of an agenda myself.'

'You have a what?'

'An agenda. It's like a to-do list, or a shopping list.'

'What's on your shopping list?'

James made two circles out of his thumbs and forefingers, his knuckles showing white, and lay them on top of one another so they looked like one fat circle. Fergus looked down at the shape James's fingers made and then James stretched his palms and fingers out, breaking the circle. He raised his hands in the air.

'Chaos,' he said.

'Sound,' Fergus replied.

Then James stood up, pushed over a plastic chair with two books laying on it, and the riot began.

2

The radical break that acted as the preliminary spur to justify the school's mass securitisation, which all but made the rising inevitable, was not the riot, but another loosely-related event that occurred several minutes before the school day ended.

Mr Moore had finished class half an hour early after he had found a shit wrapped up in two sheets of toilet roll in his satchel. He stood up to leave when there was a beep and Mr Kennedy announced over the intercom that everyone was to stay in class until further notice. The school was on temporary lockdown as an active beehive had been found in the fourth year social area.

'The bees must be contained at all costs,' Mr Kennedy had said breathlessly.

A fear ran through Mr Moore, and he predicted, correctly as it were, that the scatological attacks were soon going to become more haphazard, frequent and uncontrollable. He knew there was no beehive, but that whatever there was would neither be containable or contained, and would, therefore, have to be destroyed. He ignored the announcement and abandoned ship, leaving his soiled satchel behind him, and leaving no explanation for his class, who looked on, bemused and bored, as he scurried out of the room without a backward glance.

The wind was low and the car park was empty. An old bed sheet tied to the green railings of the gate fluttered gently in the breeze, every upsurge billowing it out to expose blue spray paint scrawls of Free Steo. Mr Moore could hear the crack of gravel under his loafers. He sighed in relief and decided that he would call in sick the next day.

As he put the keys into the car door, he heard a noise behind him and turned to see a flying glob growing bigger in his sight: a dull, yellow, shapeless thing floating through the air. Then he went blind and fell back, screaming.

Cheap, nauseating vegetable soup covered his face, the smell of it making him cough. He rolled around on the ground, trying to wipe his eyes; crawling; reaching blindly for his cracked glasses that had fallen to the ground.

'Waste of space, is it?' a voice said from out of the soupy haze. 'I've some waste for you here, you specky prick.'

'Is that you, Darragh?' Mr Moore said, wiping his eyes, trying to get up.

'Don't you Darragh me. I always said you were a shithead. Now watch this.'

Mr Moore cleared enough soup out of his right eye to catch the flare of light and then the brief glimpse of Darragh Madden squatting over his face, trousers down – a lividly white, hairy arse– before he gagged and lost consciousness.

I will interrupt here to allow a brief aside. Various theories abound as to why the Scoil Dara Rising did not burn itself out in its earliest stage, in the manner of most antecedent student conflicts. Several theories presuppose the existence of a suppressed majority within the student body, whose symbolic figurehead was the unjustly detained Steo; a silent emblem of oppression, all the more emblematic and all the more silent because of his physical absence. I hold no truck with this sentimental view. Others, of a more mystical slant, believe that it was the horrific yet exciting chill in the air that hung over Scoil Dara in those weeks; a transformative chill brought on by fleeting rumours that an invisible weapon of hitherto unknown power was being concocted in the midst of the school. I prefer this supposition to the former as I find it very flattering, though I cannot wholly endorse it. Most people believe it was the confiscation of the soup, the only item of hot food available to the students of Scoil Dara, and I'd say that's about right.

Like most risings, it was mainly reactive. In this case, it was a reaction to the heavy securitisation the school underwent to stifle any possible continuation of the rising. So, yet again we are faced with one of life's larger ironies: the oppressive forces set up to so brutally quell the students' subversion were the very spurs that triggered the students' shift from agitation to full scale mobilisation.

Moderate reformism was not an option. Some of the more studious sixth years, nearing the end of April and worried about the Leaving Cert, decided to take the issue of securitisation and blanket punishments to the parent-teacher board. They claimed that the school had no right to communally punish all members of the senior cycle for the actions of a few renegade transition years, but the parent-teacher board, by then in the second year of its three-year tenure, had calcified into something resembling a stagnant oligarchy that colluded subserviently with the executive branch of the school, headed by an increasingly paranoid and delusional Mr Kennedy, meaning that not only were concerned students unable to put forward their case, they were also persecuted for doing so.

Fear pervaded the school, especially after Brian Moran received eight months of chewing-gum-cleaning duties for coughing in class the day he returned from hospital. He was the sacrificial lamb, thrown out to the wolves, with the express intention of showing that the wolves were not fucking around. If a little lick-arse bitch like Brian Moran could be treated so roughly by teachers then it showed the rest of the students that nothing would remain the same. The students had entered a cold, new world that would only accept complete supplication or permanent exclusion. By May the 1st, the day of the strike, nearly half the students had buckled under the autocratic thumb of Mr Kennedy, while the remaining students presided over some kind of ungoverned territory made up of indefinable, constantly shifting borders. These students spent most of their time smoking or playing football; remaining just vigilant enough to ensure that they didn't get snared by the school's apparatuses and dragged back into the grey, lifeless world of regulated schooldays. Perhaps what is most shocking about all of this is that these students were just continuing as they always had, only now in a more concentrated fashion. They were unafraid, unabashed, unconcerned, though occasionally still slightly nonplussed that they were in school, and even more shocked that some of their peers gave a flying fuck about said school. These students, who had previously been seen as dozy, wild or just future fuck-ups, became shining emblems of insouciance and freedom; brave rebels of inactivity who were merely evolving into more daring versions of themselves, taking outlandish risks that only caused more divisions and tensions within the already deeply divided student body.

But, still, how the students within the student body relate to one another has always been a secondary concern of the system we call school. Its primary concern is, and always will be, how the student body relates to the school body. All the school's apparatuses were triggered into a powerful wakefulness due to the actions of Darragh, who, as a mere individual aggressor, engaged in overt conflict with a representative of the school body. This radical break from the norm caused the school body to insert itself into the students' lives in such a way that any future struggle had to factor in the overthrow of the school system rather than settling for a reformation of power structures within the student body, thereby breaking very temporarily with the usual dynamics that are erroneously labelled revolution, wherein existing power blocks tackle one another, rather than tackling the underlying structures that determine and define their existence.

When Darragh was finished, he buttoned up his trousers and glanced around the car park. Still empty; he couldn't believe his luck. He had been sneaking about the school the whole day; slinking around corners, hiding in the long grass, covering his face with mud to camouflage himself as he hid in the shadows, warming his hands with the lighter he had filched off a sixth year, and then off his excrement-filled rucksack, which he had set ablaze in the basketball courts; secretly feasting off the mushrooms that grew in the maintenance cupboard, looking for that too-big-for-his-boots cocky squealer prick Neil Jennings to straighten out his hide. And then, after three hours of skulking and searching, he had seen Mr Moore running out to the car park, unaccompanied; a gift dropped in his lap, and now another gift was dropping in his lap: the Summerhill bus had arrived early. He could get out of here, unnoticed. But then he saw that little Nolan prick running like a madzer out towards Browne's, getting the Moynalvey bus. Well, I'll be fucked, he thought. That posh cunt, who was alright sometimes. Not a bad lad actually, not a rat definitely, knew how to take a joke, but still, he had some stick up his hole. We'll see now, he said to himself, crouching between the sleeping cars, his back arched, creeping his way towards Knocknatulla; towards freedom.

3

'This is fucking stupid,' Fergus said, holding half a ham sandwich over a very small fire, its flames flickering out of torn schoolbooks.

James Monaghan and a dazed, lost second year were sitting next to him in the tiny fortress they had constructed by piling lockers on top of one another in a diamond formation in the middle of the fifth year social area. Fergus's fingers were getting hot, so he skewered the sandwich on the end of a pencil and placed it close to the embers. The sandwich caught fire and he threw it down into the ashes in disgust, putting the fire out altogether with a hiss that blew specks of soot in to his face.

'You're right,' James Monaghan said, on his hands and knees, blowing gently on the fire to breathe it back to life. 'We need something with a bit more boom.'

'No. I mean like we just fucking destroyed our social area.'

'It's not our social area.'

'It could be, though, couldn't it? We could make it ours. We could do something like, that would make it ours.'

'Like what?'

'Like a strike, or something, or something other people could join in with.'

'That's very fucking yawn,' James said, giving up on the fire and standing up.

Fergus peeked over the edge of the lockers. Harry Brennan was continuing to run around the edge of the social area, barechested, raging in some fierce kaleidoscopic ecstasy, swinging his shirt round above himself like a lasso. He jumped from locker to locker, like he was climbing a circular, spiralling mountain, and then he slipped and knocked his head, and Neil Jennings, who was leaning against the wall smoking a cigarette, nodded at his three midgets and they ran over and dragged Harry by the ankles to the corner, which by now was occupied by nineteen very scared students, all of whom Neil's boys had incapacitated; picking them off one by one whenever they left the main body of rioting transition years by venturing outside the confines of the makeshift fortress.

Although, was it still a riot? Was it ever a riot? Fergus didn't know. It had taken about ten minutes to destroy everything in the social area and then they were all at a bit of a loss as to what should come next. They had built a fortress and then spent another ten minutes blocking up the two entrances with chairs and lockers; organising a human chain to climb up to the CCTV and the intercom so as to rip them out of their fittings. But that was half an hour ago, and the pseudo-riot was still dragging along. Fergus had thought when it started that there was too much activity to take in, and then he realised that most of the confusion was just noise, mainly people standing still and screaming. There were only actually four or five people, James Monaghan foremost amongst them, actually doing things, actually destroying things; everyone else was only yelling or occasionally moving from one end of the room to the other. A lot of people were just chilling: Sharon, for example. Fergus scanned the social area until his eyes fell on her. There she was, sat on one of the benches with three of her friends; relaxed, unaffected by the noise and destruction; legs crossed, exposing her maroon socks that ended enticingly below the knee. The girls were doing one another's nails, playing Snake II on their phones, eating Jelly Tots and Refresher bars which they stretched and twirled round their fingertips before placing them between their glitter-glossed lips. Sharon laughed as one of the girls painted her nails. Fergus climbed on top of the locker and waved over at her and she waved back; he blushed, and then he saw below him that two of the midgets were dragging the confused second year out of the fortress by the ankles as James Monaghan tried to fight them off. James fell backwards and the midgets escorted the second year over to the corner-prison, overseen by a very nonchalant Neil Jennings.

'What is Neil at? Why's he stopping us?' Fergus shouted down at James, who was still sprawled on his back from his losing struggle.

James shrugged on the ground where he lay.

'Here, this is pretty boring. I'm heading home,' Fergus said, climbing down. 'This is a fucking joke.'

'We'll do something else, soon,' James said. 'Something big that'll fuck them up once and for all, yeah? And we've got to get rid of Neil first thing first. Stop him messing us up.'

'Yeah, I'm all for that, but I'm done here,' Fergus said, leaving the fortress.

'Don't go out there,' James called after him.

He walked across the social area, warming his hands by folding them in the sleeves of his grey jumper. Transition year, express yourself, they said. Sound job, they said. Big time, they said. So you draw pictures of monsters on the desk with felt-tip pens and look out the window at the muddy football pitch, hanging onto the radiators, dragging out of them. You play football with an empty plastic coke bottle on the basketball court; when you hit the pole that was a goal; your team was called the Terminators. You pray that Sharon is leaning against the prefab, grinning at you whenever you score a goal. You wait for Sports Day when all the fine ones dress in tank tops and Reeboks. You play Mario Kart on GameCube in suburban houses that still shock you with how much they remind you of cloistered nightmares. You skip out on training 'cause you don't want to be a midfielder anymore. You start chain smoking by the canal; sucking bubbling bongs made out of plastic bottles, drinking vodka out of Fanta cans. You throw yourself down the stairs in terraced houses 'cause your house didn't have a stairs and that was the craic, swift-like, break your fucking ribs, lad. You dye the tip of your fringe blonde and pierce your eyebrows and then what? That's your whole life.

You were nothing before I came into you; breathed meaning into you, direction into you. All you wanted was to not be a cunt; get the ride, get a job. But instead I come along and I make you. And then I fucking unmake you.

Fergus walked to his locker; one of the only rows of lockers left standing; walked below the thin streaks of shit that ran up along the western wall where a still-unconscious Brian Moran had been hung from the noticeboard by his collar, the sleeves of his jumper pinned with thumbtacks so his arms were outstretched in cruciform. Hundreds of loose pages lay all around the social area, occasionally fluttering in the wake of people; the smell of sweat, perfume, smoke. Fergus slipped on a page and caught himself. He opened his locker and took out his rucksack. When he closed over the locker door, he saw the three surly midgets stood silently in front of him. They looked over their shoulders, behind themselves, at Neil who waved his hand at them. They returned to him and stood in a line, covering their group of prisoners. Then Neil nodded at Fergus and motioned him over. Fergus slung his bag over his back and strolled over.

'Hi, Neil,' Fergus said to the skinny seventeen-year-old.

Neil's only concession to the school uniform was the tie that hung loosely round his neck and dangled over his Adidas hoodie. His head was shaved in circle patterns, mimicking the whorls of the Tara Hills from where he originally hailed, and out of a face so pale it was almost translucent, bloodshot eyes looked at Fergus, the skin around them creased into crow's feet by a lazy smile.

'Please,' Neil said, 'call me DJ Slick. Slick for short.'

'What's up, Slick?'

'Have you met Sproggy, Tribal, Pogo?' he said.

'Nice to meet ye,' Fergus said to the midgets, just first years: short, steely-eyed twelve-year-olds who stood, slouching, their hands in their pockets.

They nodded in taciturn unison.

'I want you to do me a favour,' Neil said, and then Groovy Blue started playing its monotone in his pocket.

'Hold your horses a second,' he said to Fergus, answering the phone. 'DJ Slick speaking. Yes. Would you stop? They're kettled here. Another thirty minutes, max.'

He winked at Fergus and put his hand up, before speaking into the mouthpiece again.

'Stop, stop. It's fine. Fuck them lads. They'll only get in your hair. I know. I know. I know it 'cause I know. Here, I'm busy now. Yeah? That's funny, 'cause I have this particular problem with that particular rogue as well. Yeah, I know he's a teacher. Do I give a fuck? No. No, no is the answer. I don't give a fuck. I was going to anyway. He fucked with me. Good. Yeah. Bye.'

He hung up and grinned at Fergus.

'Sorry about that.'

'No bother.'

'Listen, you're smart, yeah? You read books and stuff?'

'Yeah,' Fergus nodded. 'Well, not really, no. What? Why?'

'Yeah, well use them book smarts and keep an eye on Darragh Madden for me, would you? Tell me how he's getting on. Every day, that is, you tell me – regular-like. Lad's going to get gotten and I know you and him live up and about them parts in the wilds, like.'

'Yeah, ok. Well, he's Agher; I'm Moynalvey.'

'It's all the same difference, horse.'

'Yeah, ok,' Fergus shrugged. 'And maybe you could also do me a favour.'

'Go on.'

'Maybe you could lay off the TYs for a little bit,' Fergus said, nodding at his classmates all huddled in the corner behind the three first years.

Neil smiled.

'Yeah, no bother. I just need to get them out of here today. Health and safety issue, for their own good. Get a bit of order down, you know? But they'll be on their merry way soon enough.'

'Yeah, sure. I was meaning to ask you, is there any way I can get out of here? I want to go home.'

'Had enough, have you?'

'Enough for now.'

Neil nodded at Sproggy, Tribal and Pogo and they went over to the tiny window on the far side of the social area. Sproggy broke the window pane with the crook of his elbow and then Tribal and Pogo cleared the remaining shards from the frame with their heels.

'See you tomorrow, yeah?' Neil said.

Fergus nodded and went over to the window, looking back at his year, all there in the social area; James eyeing him from behind the fortress, peeking over an upturned locker; Sharon examining her glistening, newly-orange nails; Harry Brennan sitting in the corner, still topless, still twirling his jumper around his head, but sadly now as though he were surrendering. Sproggy, Tribal and Pogo motioned towards the window and Fergus climbed out, angling his way past the jagged shards of glass that still stuck to the frame.

Fergus ducked down beneath every window he passed so teachers wouldn't see him, thinking of Neil's dangerousness. He was a year ahead of Fergus, but even still, Fergus had heard the stories. On his first month in Scoil Dara, an eleven-year-old Neil had picked a fight with a sixth year prefect who was riding a second year. He had swaggered right into the sixth year social area, that den of near-adult wolves, and called the prefect a paedo. The prefect had gone for Neil, Neil had flashed his famous aluminous green blade and that was the end of it. Except, later that day, the prefect turned up with eight of his classmates to the first year social area, where they were immediately surrounded by a hundred first years. Neil had picked his battle well; so in second year, when he started networking, nobody had any problem with him becoming the main in-house yoke slinger and deep house DJ. Ever since then he had presided over the junior GAA disco's playlist like a looming shadow; a perpetual dictator, head-phoned and arrogant, forcing unwanted doses of eclectic reggae fusion and gangster rap on a wholly captive audience; a DJ who refused to close his sets with the standard version of James Blunt's 'Beautiful' that always segued into the national anthem, meaning that the youths on the dance floor had no idea what the last song was to be and often missed their chance to drop the hand at the appropriate moment, leading in several cases to brief fights, which Neil brutally and efficiently quelled.

Fergus strode through the school gates, ignoring the row of resource teachers who were leaning against the ivy-coated wall that ended in a burnt-out asbestos roof; all smouldering at him, their cigarettes' red cherries pointed at him, ivy framing their faces. Fluttering swallows rustled in and out of the ivy streamers, disturbing them and swaying them as though they were being moved by a breeze. He climbed onto the bus. It was a few minutes before school ended, so it was still empty, except for one person. Fergus squinted.

At the back, stretched out like a Roman god, was Darragh Madden, his legs wide open, scratching his testicles through his pockets. When he saw Fergus, he patted the seat next to him with a grin, and Fergus walked to the back and sat down.

'How's it going, lad?' Darragh said.

'Grand. What are you doing here?'

'Wanted to have a little chat with yourself.'

'What about?'

'I've to lay low for a few days,' Darragh said.

'For bullying or for soup or for what?'

'Nah.'

'For what?'

'What's this? Twenty fucking questions? Look, I've to go.'

'What did you want to talk to me about?' Fergus asked.

Darragh ignored him, slouching down further on the seat so he couldn't be seen through the window.

Students started flocking out of the social areas, bags across their back. Darragh leant back and stared at his phone for a while and then pressed a few buttons until it started playing a polyphonic ringtone version of 'Cotton Eye Joe'; he listened to its tinny timbre while tapping his foot and swinging his arms in the air. Fergus leant back and folded his arms, tapping his foot as well. The bus started filling up and a few of the sixth years stared suspiciously at the youths taking up the back seat, but when they saw it was Darragh they sat down without a word. A couple of younger people started shaking their heads to the tune and one third year began breakdancing in the aisle.

'Enough of that shite,' the bus driver shouted.

Darragh was about to shout back when there was a bang and he looked to his right. A cloud of brown muck covered the window.

'Is that shite?' Darragh asked. 'Well, I'll be fucked.'

'Just muck, I think,' Fergus said.

More projectiles were hitting the windows. Slowly at first, but increasing in frequency and velocity. Each clod of mud rattled the window and shook the bus. Fergus walked up the aisle and saw Neil Jennings and several other boys with school bags full of projectiles. A strawberry milkshake was thrown in the open door and splattered on the steps, some of it flecking onto the students who were sat in the front.

'Drive,' Fergus shouted at the bus driver.

'I'll straighten these lads out,' the bus driver said, who started rolling up his sleeves before he realised they were already rolled up. 'I'll straighten these lads out something terrible.'

'Just drive, for fuck's sake, there's no time,' Fergus shouted, as everyone started screaming to drive. The driver pressed a button and the doors shafted shut as a golf ball cracked the windscreen. Through the back window, Fergus saw Ms Sims running out the front door of the school, before another spray of muck covered the glass and Fergus recoiled, falling off his seat.

'It won't stop,' Fergus said from the floor, the truth of the realisation sneaking into him. 'It's never going to stop.'

'I'll fucking stop it, fairly blunt,' Darragh said.

'It will never stop,' Fergus laughed, 'and I'm going to be part of it.'

'Oh, I'll get these lads,' the driver shouted at the front, trying to point at the assailants through the side windows, though the boys' figures were only semi-visible through the scattered artillery of clods.

'Who was that?' the driver shouted. 'We could of all of us been killed in our beds, the precious children.'

He crossed himself.

'The precious children,' he repeated intermittently for the rest of the journey, shaking his head.

Down the back, Darragh covered his face in his hands.

'Well, they're after me already,' he said. 'Listen, Fergie. There's some lads looking for me about the place, so I won't be around for a while.'

'You said. Where are you heading?'

'Where I'm going is for me to know and you to find out; though if you do find out I'll put you in a crush and castrate you.'

'So, what do you want me to do?'

'Would you hush and let me mull,' Darragh said, rubbing his testicles thoughtfully.

'Moody Judy,' Fergus said, leaning his head against the window.

Darragh didn't say a word for the rest of the journey, but when Fergus was about to get off at Moynalvey cross, Darragh grabbed him by the arm.

'Oh yeah, I remember what it was I wanted off you.'

'What was that now? Sprightly, now. This is me.'

'You're to be my man on the inside since I'm not about. You're to help me get Jennings.'

'In all honesty, I wouldn't fuck too much with Jennings. That's a death trap.'

'If you don't do it I'm going to trap you in death.'

Fergus laughed, but seeing the glare in Darragh's eyes, he stopped.

'Leave it with me,' Fergus said, pulling away and walking down the aisle and stepping off the bus.

On his way past Moynalvey primary Fergus forgot about the impossible position Neil and Darragh had placed him in as he noticed, shocked, that the whitethorn hedges were thickening already. Moynalvey had a summery feel to it, and Fergus, as he walked the four kilometres home, couldn't help but feel like he was close to some kind of freedom. The clearness of the sky promised an early summer and then he could relax into real work: the silage, the repairs; make enough money to get a quad bike. He fantasised about driving all the way to Sharon's semi-d on his quad and her coming out her front door in a thin negligée as he strode off the bike; her seeing him there covered in dust and hay, manly and strong and rural, as she, feminine, small, with her sharp quasi-Dublin accent, would grab him by the collar of his overalls, and he would grin at her and say, Come on, no need for that, baby, and she would say, Fuck's sake, Fergie, you aren't like the rest of them at all, come in and have a cup of tea while I take care of you and mind you.

Then, as though he had wished it into existence, a text came in on his phone. It read, What u up 2? Xxx Shaz, and Fergus took a detour into Canning's field and had to lay down with the excitement coursing through his body; the smell of furze filling up his head. There was a seasonal lake in Canning's field, a mucky hollow that filled up with rain for six months of the year, and it was surrounded by fat furze bushes that left only a few openings into the water. The cattle hadn't been loosed yet, but there were three swans who floated, unmoving, in the centre of the pond. One began flapping its wings, and the other two followed suit. They flew low and straight for several metres, their black webbed feet padding off the water, dancing in take-off, until they rose again, away from the water, and flew south; slowly, heavily, their long bodies filling the afternoon sky in arcing swoons.

'Chaos my hole,' Fergus said, as he broke into a smile. 'Has to be the strike; and I'm the man for it.'

He glanced at the tall oak tree by the hedge that was in its spring rise. Its dark leaves would block out all light beneath it in a few months, and he began fantasising about the summer again. He decided he wanted to lose his virginity to Sharon in this field under this tree. Somewhere outside; somewhere free; somewhere that would make his back itchy and bleed; where ditches' waters gurgled and flowed. He rose and approached the tree, staring at the thick trunk gnarled with a century's years. He laid his hand on it and then he looked to the road. In the distance, from their shed, he could hear the greyhounds barking. Will you come out and see the country? he texted her. Take a spin on the tractor xxx.

There was a small, crooked C of a moon imprinted on the pale blue of the afternoon sky. Above him, a gust of wind ran through the tree limbs, setting them squabbling with one another. The greyhounds were still howling and Fergus heard a fox scream and then his phone received a text. He looked to see if Sharon had texted him again, but instead James Monaghan's name flashed up on the screen. He opened the message. We shud make a bom, lad, it said.

Lol, u r retard xx, Fergus replied. But it's too late.

I have begun tremoring in anticipation; every moment heaving with the prognostication of existence. Now is coming; a now that will allow me into it. I will finally be born into that perpetually inhabited extreme; that fleeting eternity, that overgrown promise. Everything is slick with the promise of sheer existence. And I ask myself, my inquisitive nature blossoming with the impending promise of now: what is now's texture, its feel, its weight? What does existence, so wholly wrapped up in now, feel like? What is its texture? What weight will hit me with existence?

Life, I suppose, is the weight that hits, and what is life but the promise of love?

Gestation
4

I merely cause these things; I cannot control them; feeble foetus that I am; little, swollen, tumescent apple in the blank of my father's eye that I am. So I needn't apologise. Apologies are for those who have erred, knowingly or unknowingly, and who now have cognisance of their own error. I am an instrument of correction, being born. Why would I apologise?

Think of the last hours of a shrunken, cancerous stomach lurching desperately towards an imagined stability before it folds in on itself, taking its host with it; this is how the system disintegrates; this is the violence with which it dies. The host dies in both cases, though there is a crucial difference with the system: unlike biological decomposition, systemic disintegration is not a totalising finality, it is just the cloak that an emergent system wraps itself in, the mask it wears to hide itself before it is loosed into the world. This is sometimes called evolution.

Would you like to evolve?

5

'What in the fuck are these lads playing at?' Fergus asked, shaking his head. 'Taking our soup – the only bit of warmth we had in this grey fucking hole. And then they take our little Steo; our little Steo. Wouldn't hurt a fly, gentle as a lamb. Do you remember the way he was? Steo, could I get a twenty bag on tick? No bother, says Steo. Steo, have you a euro for a jambon? No bother, says Steo. Can I've a look at that homework? Running late for class; pure dusted I am. No bother, Steo says. Steo, can you unlock those cheats on GTA for us? Ah, fair play, Steo. That was his way. That was the way he had about him. That was Steo. Through and through, just a pure gent. And now he's gone. Taken from us.'

Fergus looked down and saw that three of the second year students nearest him had been brought to tears, sobbing quietly into the frayed sleeves of their jumpers. He was stood on the bonnet of Mr Moore's Fiesta in the carpark; still there after two weeks' absence. There were thirty or so students huddled around the sleeping car in the early morning mist that hung thin and low in streaking vapours around their feet. The crowd was mostly made up of second years, but he could see Sharon, near the back, looking up from her phone every now and again, winking up at him; behind her Harry Brennan, a scowling James Monaghan, behind them other grey faces.

'And what does Mr Kennedy say? He says that's a matter for the guards and social services, outside his jurisdiction, he says. He says we're making the school hard-going on ourselves and he's right, but it's not us making it hard on ourselves: it's themselves making it hard on us.'

Large, energetic applause broke out.

'But dues where dues is due,' he continued, 'and this is what they need to get into their heads, school is hard: but for us, not for them. These are long, old days we do; long, old fucking days; so let's get this straight once and for all: teachers are crazy. Adults, full stop, are fucking insane. The work they do is a joke. It's a trap and they only clock out at death. But the baddest of the bad is that they've trapped us, too. There is no way out. We're trapped. They've trapped us and they can't be trusted with us. Only we can be trusted with ourselves. So we have to take ourselves back, first thing first, and the way we do that is by taking the school back.'

People were glancing at one another. Fergus could sense he was losing them, but the crowd was still growing bigger, slowly; students dragging along their rucksacks, bent low from the heaviness on their shoulders, about forty students now, maybe fifty; coming over, curious for some excitement before the bell rang for the first class, their breaths materialising smoky in the cold morning air, the low sun peeking icily through the sparseness of the hedges, shining off the windows, producing a white glare that obscured the transparency of the glass, making mirrors for the sun.

'So, yeah, Mr Kennedy, I've this to say to you and yours: yeah, a few teachers may be in hospital, but ye hospitalised our hopes. Yeah, there's shit on the walls: but ye put shit in our souls. Yeah, the CCTV was broken, but not before ye broke our spirits. For years ye did it and it never stopped. And I'm gonna say it; I didn't want to, but I will: this has gotten bigger than soup. This has gotten bigger than even Steo—'

There was a rush of gasps in the crowd. Fergus paused and looked up to see Tribal there, spitting on the ground, glancing about, uninterested by the crowd around him. He was so short Fergus hardly saw him amongst the drove of rucksacks. And then, Sproggy and Pogo were behind him. He could see them now.

'This is about a whole new system,' Fergus yelled, punching his hand in the air. 'A system where we get our say in what's what; where we're listened to and where we get to make our own choices about our own lives.'

Fergus waited for the yelling and whoops of joy to die down.

'Now, how do we get there? Well, there's some around the place, and some of them within earshot, that would say you need to hate the right people, but the fact of the matter is that if you do be hating, that hate'll always turn in on your own self and you'll only end up ending your own self, so what we need to do is set up some kind of system, like some kind of reign of eternal soundness, mutually assured soundness, and how we do that is we start being sound to ourselves first and foremost, and to do that we need control of our own lives, and that day starts tomorrow at eleven o'clock in the basketball courts. Love and soundness forever.'

A bellowing erupted from the crowd that sounded like a happy donkey caught up in the rapture; but still, eventually, even it faded into the dull openness of the white sky. Fergus grinned, and scanned the crowd again for Sharon.

'Fucking shite talk,' James Monaghan called out from the crowd.

There was a cacophony of boos and hisses. Fergus put up his hands.

'Let the lad have his say. This is all about all of us having our say.'

'As though,' James shouted up at him, 'these lads can be loved into backing down; can be stopped by a bit of soundness, by a bit of love here and there, a bit of oh, how's it going? Fucking ridiculous. You're lying to these people.'

'I'm not lying,' Fergus shrugged.

'Yeah, you are. What do these cunts got to gain by listening to us? Nothing. They've to be made to listen; they've to be shown how to listen; to be shown they've something to lose.'

'And what do they have to lose?' Fergus grinned.

'They've a lot to lose. They just have to have it knocked into them that we're not messing.'

'Ah, you're just jelly,' Sharon said loudly, looking up from her phone.

Scattered laughter bubbled up.

'Would you listen to me? This lad's lying to ye,' James shouted, pointing at Fergus. 'We need to get rid of these teachers once and for all. You all think we'll get a yard for an inch but we won't get a fucking good morning out of these heads without having something to hang over them.'

'What are you on about?' Fergus laughed, and everyone started shouting at James. A carton of strawberry Ribena was hurled; it sailed over heads, scattering drops of juice on the students below before it struck James on the shoulder.

'Hands off him. None of that, now,' Fergus shouted. 'Don't mind him. That's pure idle talk and ye all know that.'

There was a burst of loud, encouraging applause.

'You know what I'm talking about,' James shouted, pointing up, his face heaving with conflicted emotion and red with rage.

'I've no idea what you're harping on about. Wisht up, lad; our peoples have spoken.'

'Damn fucking straight,' Harry Brennan yelled.

There were more yells of agreement and Harry Brennan lit a lighter and waved it above his head.

'Ok, let's wrap it up, lads,' Fergus said, rubbing his hands together. 'I'll be here for the next ten minutes before class starts to chat about all your individual concerns, and at little break I'll be visiting the first year social area to see the wonderful Steo mural the lads have been painting there.'

Fergus climbed down off the Fiesta and people started flocking away; a few second years bunched up around him to shake his hand. This was his twenty-first address in two weeks, and his voice was now always hoarse and cracking. He glanced over the thinning crowd, looking for where Sharon was at, and his eyes fell on James, stalking away around the corner; his hands jammed in his pockets, his head full of angry dreams of how to unleash me into this world, on a cold morning much like this one; a morning full of milky sunlight that slants across the low buildings and creeps into corners, thinking on how to release me so I can take my place amongst all these young, tired teenagers; their faces teary with the dawn's condensation, their hair crinkled and frizzy with spring damp, little sleeping men in the corners of their dewy eyes; but also into this place where there are fairy tales and dreams, memories and myths: all these things and people I have no understanding of; people like Sharon.

There she was, Fergus saw her, shining amongst the thinning crowd; still slouched there, idling on her phone; seeing her through the lightness of the mist that took the edge off everyone, making them phantom-like, making it difficult to breathe. He was about to go towards her when he felt a tug on his sleeve. He turned around and saw no one. Then he looked down. Tribal's hand was on his arm.

'Gaffer wants words.'

And then, like moons drawn into orbit by some unseen gravitational pull, Pogo and Sproggy had him surrounded.

'Need to talk to Sharon a second,' he said, pulling away.

'Now.'

Fergus sighed. As he was walking away he called out to her: 'Had fun yesterday.'

'Yeah,' she laughed, putting her hands in front of her, pretending she was driving, and then he was on his way. He fell in line with Tribal, glancing behind at Sharon, whose edges were becoming blurred in the mist. The bell rang; the day was begun. He walked silent and worried; wondering if they had found out it was himself that had shit in Neil's bag, if he was going to be executed, his body thrown into the water tanker, or buried under the prefabs, or hacked up and put in locker 139, or 136, or whichever one it was, as retribution.

Though it was class time a lot of students were still wandering around outside the prefabs, going to and fro; leaning on window sills, holding hands; whispering, their skirts shivering in the gentle breeze, their ties tied around their heads like sweatbands; smoking John Player Blues, joking amongst themselves quietly, huddled in groups to keep warm.

'You ever seen this many students mitching?' Tribal asked.

'No,' Fergus said.

'Slick doesn't like it; thinks you're to blame.'

They came to the corner of prefab four.

'Hold your horses here a second,' Tribal said before shimmying his skinny body between the prefabs and disappearing into darkness. After a while, Pogo rapped on the edge of the prefab.

'Come in,' called a muffled sing-song voice.

Fergus was led behind the prefab into darkness. The back of the prefab ended about three metres away from a high breeze block wall. Fergus's eyes adjusted to the dank shade. It was a cold, damp nook covered in litter. A hazel tree hung over the top of the wall, ivy drooping down over it like streamers. More ivy cascaded over the wall, so thick that only two or three thin pencils of light shot down to the muddy ground. There Neil Jennings was, laid out on a dilapidated couch nestled against the wall, playing a Nintendo DS; a small table before him, on which sat several empty, crushed cans of Dutch Gold; the infamous aluminous green switchblade from all the stories, a small bag of weed, rolling papers, filters; a copy of *Roy Keane: The Autobiography*, its edges creased and stained, a Kilcock Library stamp on its spine, along with three beakers with a sticker on the side of each one that read Property of Mr Moore. Two of the beakers were unused and pristine, and the third held a thin, clear liquid stoppered with a pink bung. A portable heater buzzed next to the couch, powered by a small blue generator attached to an extension cord. On the side of the prefab, a faded poster read 'Junior Disco: DJ Slick on the Decks. Sproggy on the Lights. Support your Local Community.' The shade was hurting Fergus's eyes, and a chill crawled a shiver along his spine. Neil looked up, his eyes shining in the dullness.

'We meet a-fucking-gain,' Neil said, slapping the DS shut. 'Sit down.'

Fergus sat down while Neil pulled a cigarette out of his pocket and lit it, using one of the pristine beakers as an ashtray. He took two puffs and then dropped the barely smoked cigarette into the beaker, placing his hand over the opening, hermetically sealing it, watching the smoke billow out against the glass, stretching up to his cupped palm, before the ember faded into grey dullness.

He grinned up at Fergus.

'Easy to put out a fire, isn't it?'

Fergus stared blankly at the beaker, its interior all shrouded in smoke.

'Hi, Slick,' he said.

'We've a few things we need to talk about. Let's get the easy things out of the way first. Any news on Darragh?'

'Nobody's seen him.'

'What's it been? Two weeks now? And what have you done about it?'

'Done about what?'

'Finding him; what I told you to do.'

'I can't just find him. He could be anywhere.'

'Like finding a mickey in a mickey mouse house, huh?'

Neil coughed and spat a strain of unidentifiable green phlegm onto the ground in front of him.

'No, you've not been looking for him. You've been too busy acting the maggot, going round the place causing a hullaballoo, getting in the way of people trying to earn their crust. And that's another thing: when you're out there doing your speechifying and such, I'd appreciate it if you toned down the Steo talk.'

'Why would I do that?'

'Lad was a fool.'

'What?'

'Lad was a little knacker; bad for business,' Neil shrugged. 'Slinging his weak produce on my school. No use now getting people all emotional and whipped up about it – only lead to trouble. Had to be done.'

'You done Steo,' Fergus said. 'You reported him.'

'And you tortured a young lad 'cause of it.'

Fergus flinched. 'You mean Brian Moran?' he said. 'I shouldn't've done that. That was wrong. I know that now.'

'No, I liked how you handled that. You saw a mess and you tried to clean it up. That's what I do; clean up other people's messes. Kennedy has upped the ante, put the foot down, and all for what? People are just going all the crazier. Any day now anything could happen and no one'll be able to stop it, unless somebody stops it before it gets to that.'

'And that's you, is it?'

Neil grinned.

'How do you feel about order, Fergie? What's your thinking on it?'

'I don't really think much on it.'

Neil laughed.

'I bet you don't, you little legend. 'Cause if you did think on it you'd know that order is what finds things out.'

'Find what out?' Fergus said.

'This bomb of yours,' he said. 'I need it.'

Fergus laughed.

'Don't fuck me,' Neil said.

'Are you serious?'

'Don't fuck me,' Neil repeated.

'What bomb?' Fergus said. 'What are you on about? James mentioned a bomb like two weeks ago, but he was joking.'

'You are disrespecting me, child,' Neil said.

'I'm not.'

'I know you have it. I know now, and honestly, I didn't think you'd bring this level of snake to the game. Did you think you could bring something that big into a little place like this and I'd let it happen? I want this bomb of yours and I will bring order with it.'

'There is no bomb,' Fergus said, as slowly as he could. 'I swear.'

Neil leant forward, opened his bag of weed and started rubbing the crinkled strings together until he had made several tight little balls, which he then popped in his mouth, one after the other, chewing lightly and swallowing. When he was done he took out a set of keys that had a small gold cylindrical tube attached to the key ring. He unscrewed the cylinder till it was halved, exposing a hollowed centre out of which he poured a few particles of cocaine that he snorted before rubbing the residue from his fingers onto his gums.

'Do you know why I white and weed at the same time?' he asked.

Fergus shook his head.

'Because it reminds me that whether I go up,' he said, pointing to the pockets of dull sky scattered like gifts amongst the ivy leaves, 'or whether I go down,' he said, pointing to the ground, 'I remain me. Always. And snakes – snakes don't remain themselves. Snakes don't even know they're snakes. They just slither around on their Air-Lites, their converse, their wellies; snaking around on their bellies like fucking snakes, shitting in people's bags, doing slithery things; doing fucking unforgivable snake things.'

A thin rivulet of blood trickled out of Neil's nostril and he extended his tongue and licked it away before leaning his head on the armrest.

'I want it before little break tomorrow, or you see that?' Neil said, pointing at the green switchblade on the messy table, his head still sideways on the armrest. 'That's going through your heart a hundred times, and you know what I'll do then? I'm going to cut your heart out and squeeze it inside one of these beakers here, and then I'm going to get a chain and wear it round my neck. Now, crush on.'

Fergus stood up.

'By the way,' Neil asked. 'How's Sharon?'

'What do you mean?'

'I heard you two were going out.'

'You know about that?'

'Of course I do. Every Tom, Dick and hairy cunt knows about that. We were going out there for a while last year. Unreal hand jobs, horse.'

'She's fine.'

'Fine as fuck. Keep her that way,' Neil said, grinning, pointing at one of the beakers.

Then he looked up at Fergus from where he was sprawled out on the couch.

'Just be a beautiful creature, any creature you want to be, any creature at all, but not a snake, yeah? Don't snake me.'

'I get you.'

'Now fuck off away from me.'

Sproggy guided Fergus by the arm through the gap and then he was out in the fresh air of the misty morning. He looked behind him and Sproggy was gone. He was alone. Sparse blades of grass curled around his mud-spattered shoes in a gentle breeze. Rows of school windows faced him. Square snapshots laid out side by side; students broken up in different windows: heads down, studying, assiduous, young and beautiful in ways I can't describe. My anticipation has become so palpable that I feel its edge cutting into me. In the loneliness of Fergus's mind I begin to feel reams of disparate futures, eventualities feeding off possibilities, wrapping themselves around me, solidifying me, making me real.

'James, you cunt,' Fergus said.

He walked towards the school, but then a hiss sounded from above. He looked back and saw no one. Another hiss sounded and he looked up at the sky. There Darragh was, on top of the prefab on his hunkers, in his dirty overalls and wellies; his head poking out over the edge, looking down at Fergus. He gave a grin and put a finger to his lips and Fergus felt panic seep over him like a vice.

'I'll see you in a bit, yeah?' Darragh said, winking at him.

6

Sharon, Sharon, Sharon.

My little Sharon; thrown into the light before I can assess her significance, and then, once she is here, I will realise that I was never inherently capable of understanding her, and never could be. Yes, I know some details about her, of course. I know about her worsening thyroid problem, the hot flushes that come upon her, how tired she feels in the mornings, how sick she feels after eating. I know about her love for Girls Aloud, emblazoned in the glossed posters Blu-Tacked to the walls of the bedroom she shares with her little sister; spending her evenings correcting homework with her in the kitchen that only she tidies. I know about her unemployed mother who wanders around the house in her nightgown, pretending to fix things that aren't broken, leaving a trail of empty cans and cigarette butts in her wake; and how Sharon plods after her, cleaning up at a safe distance. I know how relaxed she felt when she went out with Fergus that one time. I know all this, but what I don't know is why she transfixes me.

I must sound like a dubious pornographer of paedophilic inclinations, delving into the life of some young thing I barely understand. But it's not like that, I swear. I'm just a little foetus, you see; a little foetus coming to terms with my own beginning, my imminent insertion into now. I myself am the great unknowable: even to myself. I have no beliefs. I have no agenda. My self will be sufficient for what I do. And yet, why this confession?

There she sits in what should be Mr Moore's class, but he is still absent. She looks around, presses her nose against the window that is dripping with condensation and breathes on the glass, fogging up her own reflection until she is obscured and she can trace her name in the fog; making a heart of the O. Through the looping letters, she sees the sun glance icily off the pitches where the shade is still heavy, ice fringing and weighing down each grass stem, the mist clearing under the caress of the sun. Sister Miller, a geriatric nun who is also their substitute teacher, is asleep at the front of the class. The sister had come in at the start of class and made them pray for ten minutes before resting her head on her hands and beginning to snore loudly. Sharon puts her hands behind her head and leans back; she stares at the cluster of stalactitic mushrooms that hang off the ceiling, bred off spring damp; they have spread like plague in the past two weeks.

What beauty.

The door crashed open behind her. Brian Moran, who was sat on his own at the top of the class, looked around, screamed, and climbed under the table. He drew himself up in a trembling ball; a snail with a gelatinous shell.

Sharon looked behind her.

'Hey, country boy,' she said.

'Hey, baby,' Fergus said.

'What's the story?' Sharon asked.

'Sorry, Brian,' Fergus said, raising a hand to the rolled-up ball under the table near the teacher's desk, and then he looked back at her and smiled.

'Hey, Shazmatazz, you haven't seen James by any chance, have you?'

'Went out with the lads, playing football on the courts once the sister here fell asleep.'

'Where is everybody?' Fergus asked, looking around. 'It's class time, no?'

'No one's really turning up anymore; all your blathering, probably.'

'Sound job. Sorry I can't stay and talk.'

'Whatever. Just text me, yeah?'

'Ok, bye,' he said, blowing her a kiss and she gave him the finger as he grinned and ran out.

He skirted the walls, avoiding the patrolling resource teachers who walked silently down every corridor on a never-ending set rota, ducking into the bathrooms whenever he heard footsteps. He passed the first year social area; stopped, looked around. The walls had been whitewashed. No more shit stains; no Steo mural; the smell of whitewash so strong he felt sick. He put his fingertips against the wall, they came away damp: two spots of white on his index and middle finger.

'Janey Mac,' he whispered, staring at the whitewash on his hand.

And then he saw 150 lockers facing him; books and rucksacks piled high in their interiors, and he realised that every single locker door had been removed. He traipsed over to examine them more closely and saw that all the lockers were bolted to the floor with industrial-sized fittings, each bolt's head the size of a baby's fist. A voice called out.

'Fergus Nolan, the pick of the litter.'

Glancing behind him, he saw Ms Sims rattling down the hall towards him.

'I'm not Fergus,' he shouted. 'Fergus is in class.'

He darted out down the side corridor, easily outstripping her, and ran towards the basketball courts, the smell of whitewash and warm steel still in his nostrils.

Arriving at the basketball court, he saw about eighty students sitting on the tarmac, huddled in groups together, chatting happily, smoking cigarettes, sharing cans of Club Rock Shandy and sausage rolls; most of them watching the game on the courts. When they saw him they started cheering. Fergus grinned and waved, and then he turned and glanced through the green mesh fencing that defined the basketball court's borders. The boys within were playing soccer with a plastic bottle. He saw James Monaghan waiting on the wing, marked by Jason Gill.

'James, I have to talk to you,' he called, but none of the boys noticed him.

He came into the court and Harry Brennan, who was hatching by the post, shouldered him so hard he was flung into the mesh fencing.

'Ow,' he said, as Harry Brennan kicked the bottle against the pole.

'Goal,' Harry screamed for several seconds, raising his hands in the air, before kneeling down in front of the pole and bowing to it repeatedly in worship. Then he crawled towards the pole and pretended to give it a blowjob. When he was finished he wiped imaginary cum off his face and pointed over the field.

'Who's that?'

A dark figure, shaded by a white sky filled with a weak pre-midday sun, slouched across the adjacent field. The figure stopped in the middle of the field and squared up to a wide-eyed heifer and then lunged at it. The heifer turned and galloped a few steps before slowing and turning its head back at him.

'Didn't fucking think so,' the figure shouted at the heifer.

The boys on the court looked at one another.

'Oh, Darragh Madden's back,' Harry said.

'Darragh Madzer, more like it,' Larry Cox said, and then he and Harry fist-bumped.

'Where has that fat fuck been at?' Harry said.

'James, I need to talk to you,' Fergus said, still crunched over and breathless. 'Now.'

'Alright, desperado,' James said. 'Keep your hair on.'

James popped the collar of his shirt, lit a cigarette, and strolled off the courts. Fergus limped after the treasure trail of James's smoke that hung in the air in dissolving braids.

'Prefabs,' James said, out the corner of his mouth. 'Get a bit of quiet.'

Fergus nodded. They sauntered by the gym, hands jammed in pockets, not speaking to one another. Then they ducked behind the water tanker, seeing Ms Sims walking by the carpark on her way to the front office, coming back from her tour around the corridors.

When she was out of sight, they crossed the grass to the prefabs. James tried the handle of prefab 3, nodded, and Fergus followed him in.

The prefab could hold thirty students, at a push. A smudged whiteboard headed the class; Free Steo was scrawled on it, and, underneath that, Mr Kenedy iz gay 4 da cok. A portable intercom screwed above the whiteboard spawned a web of frayed wiring that trailed along the ceiling before it disappeared out a splintered crack above the window. Rough graffiti'd tables were stacked along the walls.

'Well,' James said, stamping on his cigarette, leaning against a table. 'What's up?'

'What's up is you're some fucking jelly baby, you are.'

'Fuck off. Don't you come acting hard with me.'

'Did I miss something here?' Fergus said. 'Did you tell Neil that I had a bomb?'

James smirked.

'You fucker,' Fergus said, covering his eyes with his hand.

'Calm down, child,' James said. 'Yeah, I told Neil and maybe one or two other people that we may have something like that.'

'Neil's going to kill me now.'

'No, he won't. Because we do,' James said. 'Well, not a bomb. Just nitro-glycerine and a few detonators. I'm making the frame tomorrow morning in the free class in woodwork.'

'Where in the fuck would a useless twat like you get nitro-glycerine?'

'Uncle's in the ra.'

'You don't have an uncle.'

James put his hands up in the air.

'You got me,' he grinned. 'I lied. I don't have nothing like that.'

'This isn't funny,' Fergus said. 'I'm going to get killed.'

'You lied too,' James said. 'I thought we agreed we were going to do something to get rid of Neil Jennings and get this school sorted, and then you went off on your own doing a maggoty impression of Jesus Christ around the place. I thought we were both after a bit of chaos.'

'Fuck chaos. Chaos is for children. At eleven o'clock tomorrow, when the little break bell rings, we're going on strike. You're complicating this with your shite. Are you trying to fuck us up?'

'No, I'm doing this for the strike to work, genius. What do you think this strike will even do?'

'Change things,' Fergus said. 'And it's not up to me what happens, it's up to the students. So get in fucking line and stop spreading shite about me; getting me killed.'

'You're nothing but an eejit,' James said. 'Do you think a strike means anything? You need at least a threat to hold over the teachers, otherwise it won't work and they'll just fuck you all up, with the guards or with Jennings' boys, or whatever. That's power, tard. And how many people do you think'll be on this strike? Mark my words, it'll only be transition years, and not even all of them. I'm just doing what needs doing to make this the real deal.'

Fergus looked at James. He opened his mouth to speak and then the intercom rang out, and in every classroom in Scoil Dara students sighed, leant on their desks and covered their heads with their hands. Out in the fields, students who wandered aimlessly cocked their ears and whooped in delight. Inside the prefab, Fergus and James listened to the intercom's muffled crackle coming through the portable speaker.

'Fógra amháin,' Mr Kennedy said over the intercom. 'Listen up. Now there's a few things to be said. Firstly, I just want to say that there is most definitely no bomb being created by one Fergus Nolan, though the young gentleman in question has been verified as being the number one soup-bandit responsible for perpetrating the first-degree burns of so many go hálainn students. Regardless, Ms Sims has looked into the matter personally, and she has verified that the rumour of incendiary devices of a bombish nature has no basis.'

Through every classroom, gulps of air could be heard being vacuumed into lungs.

'You told Kennedy?' Fergus said, creasing his brow. 'Are you out of your mind?'

James shrugged his shoulders.

'Fógra amháin eile,' Mr Kennedy's voice continued, a small flip of static briefly cutting up his voice. 'The school has become aware there are some half-baked, near-sighted visionaries, some crusty vanguards, some disorganised organisers, hippyish and deviant in their natures, who are clamouring around the place, spreading rumours that there is some kind of "we" that needs to be heard. "We," from what I can gather, is just another word for the hive mind. Luckily for you, I know that this particular "we" going about the place is an idea driven by a vanguard that concerns itself with "we", not one driven by the hive mind itself, and let me tell you this, children: a vanguard, in case you don't know, is a busy little bee who infects the rest of the hive with fierce doses of insanity. Luckily for you, poor creatures, I know that you are not to blame on an individual level. Luckily for you, you are merely acting as a swarming hive that, despite what the vanguard makes you say, wants to be led, needs to be led, lest ye corrupt yourselves and destroy everything you don't know you love.'

'Don't mind him,' James said, laughing, as Fergus covered his face with his hands. 'Lad's off his box.'

'Hive minds have no dreams, you see; I know that, so I forgive you,' Mr Kennedy continued. 'I know the hive mind merely recognises the reality the vanguard presents it with. But let me tell you this, children: these crusty vanguards are being led by the real deal, so with that could Fergus Nolan, crustiest of vanguards, soup-bandit, downwardly mobile teacher-assaulter from a privileged background, incoherent ranter who stands on teachers' cars during class time; six Ds in the Junior Cert and two of them at ordinary level, who cried every morning in first year he was so scared of big school; could that Fergus Nolan please present himself at his earliest convenience to the front office. Slán now.'

The intercom clocked off and James sat down on a chair, leant his elbows on his lap and glanced up at Fergus.

'Now,' James said, 'since everyone now believes we have a bomb because everyone believes the direct opposite of what Kennedy says, let me tell you what we're going to do. You are right – well, a little bit right. Obviously I don't have explosives, but I do have detonators, they're easy got from hardware sites, and I am going to use them to make us two fake bombs. We are going to give one to Neil and we are going to keep the other one, and we're going to let on to the school that we'll use it if they try to fuck with the strike.'

'You won't be able to control this,' Fergus said.

'Control is a joke they play on us,' he replied. 'I'm allowing the strike to work, and the only way is if people realise there is no control. I'm giving you all the distractions, threats and confusion necessary to let you have your little rant and handholding friends-talk, all your lovey-dovey stuff. And there's no danger at all because the threat of a bomb is as good as a bomb. So everyone wins.'

Fergus stared out the window and saw Darragh Madden surveilling the prefabs, his hands grabbing the collar of his overalls to warm his fingers; thoughtful, calm almost. Then he saw Darragh turn and run. A few moments later, like a silent film, Sproggy, Tribal and Pogo ran by. When they were gone there was nothing to be seen through the square of window until a crow landed on the roof of the school and hopped down to the gutter, where it pecked at the rushes that grew out of the drainage pipe. It flicked its head to the side, eyeing Fergus from its brilliant green irises; the shock of colour contrasting with the dull white of the sky.

'You'll make a third one,' Fergus said, 'and you'll give it to Darragh. He came back today.'

'Now we're talking,' James said, slapping his thigh. 'Now we're sucking diesel.'

'I'm going to watch you make them, though, 'cause you're a devious cunt. You're devious and you have mad plots and I shouldn't even be looking twice at you.'

'Suits me,' James shrugged.

Fergus walked towards the door.

'You've gotten me into serious trouble with your shite spreading.'

'You're gonna thank me tomorrow,' James said.

'Yeah, just don't be spreading anymore shite.'

'I'll do what I want.'

'Fuck you,' Fergus spat. 'I fucked your mam.'

'Well, I fucked your mam,' James said.

Fergus stalked out and slammed the prefab door behind him. He walked across the grass and then turned around and yelled, 'No, I fucked your mam,' but there was no one to hear him. He went inside, looked up and down the corridor, breathing heavily, feeling alone, like he was in a nightmare, like he had no say over his own life, now, which he doesn't. I do. I am the nightmare he has. There is so little space between us now that I can't tell us apart anymore.

He passed by class photos, all tacked up on the wall, chronologically ordered by year, as though he were walking through time. Small faces smiled out at him from behind glass frames, and then he came across a photo of his class on the first day of school. The photo was dated 2002 in gold, slanting cursive. There they all were. Sharon was blinking, her hair up in a bun in the front row. Darragh Madden was on the right, pudgy and babyish, winking; his head cocked to the side, making bunny ears behind the student knelt in front of him. Harry Brennan in the back row, tall and louche, had his fingers extended in a peace sign. Fergus saw himself in the middle row, on the left, Eleven years old, his front teeth big and rabbit-like, having just come up through his gums; his tie up in a perfect, fat knot; all buttons buttoned in neatness, his eyes opened too wide, smiling.

He leant over, peering at the photo, until all their faces, laid out in rows under the glass, were obscured beneath the warmth of his breath.

7

Waylaid by mitching LCAs in the second year social area who kept coming up to shake his hand, thanking him for his work and saying they'd see him tomorrow at the strike, it took Fergus nearly ten minutes to get to the front office. He gathered himself and peeked in through the blinds. Mr Kennedy was sat behind his desk facing Neil Jennings, Ms Sims pacing behind him. The sun fell in blades across their three faces from the opposite window; their eyes veiled in blasts of whiteness. Fergus knocked, walked in and saw Mr Kennedy slide a brown package to Neil Jennings, who flicked it underneath his Adidas Original Firebird hoodie in a smooth movement.

'—which means no guards,' Fergus heard Mr Kennedy say before they all turned to look at him.

'Were you born in a barn, Nolan?' Ms Sims said. 'You wait until you're called.'

'No, it's fine,' Mr Kennedy said, staring at Neil. 'We're done here, I think.'

'Yes, we are,' Neil said, standing up.

'What's this?' Fergus said.

'Friendly chats and loving banter,' Neil said, touching his nose twice and nodding at Fergus before he walked out through the door.

'We were just discussing the impact different levels of subversion have on undermining authority and how conflict leads to strange bedfellows, Nolan,' Mr Kennedy said.

'Subversion the what the what?' Fergus said.

He looked through the slatted shutters into the hall where he saw Neil Jennings and Brian Moran speaking to one another, their forms cut up by the blinds like sliced bread.

'Well, that's something you don't see too often,' Fergus said.

Mr Kennedy, ignoring his remarks, gestured towards the chair. Fergus sat down, still staring out at Neil, who was bent over whispering in Brian's ear.

'Have a Werther's Original,' Mr Kennedy said. 'Or maybe some soup. Soup will be returning tomorrow, I'm sure you'll be happy to hear.'

Mr Kennedy pushed a glass bowl full of sweets across his desk towards Fergus. Fergus took one.

'I'm grand for soup, thanks,' he said, looking around again, but Neil and Brian were gone.

He popped the sweet in his mouth.

'Do you know why we're bringing back soup?' Mr Kennedy asked.

'Because we made you, sir,' he said.

'Very funny, but no. We did it because it is the most efficient way to bring down the rancid mushroom population that insists on colonising the school. These mushrooms are merely symptomatic of the damp that is causing the school to fall in on itself. We desperately need cash for repairs.'

'Yes, sir.'

'Well, these mushrooms have been sponging off the system, giving nothing back; but no more. Neil Jennings has been so kind as to offer his services to remove the fungal population and in return we will lease out the cafeteria to him. This will free us up to continue our repairs here, recently damaged CCTV and intercoms and the like. As you know, the school simply lacks funding and we have a lot of work to do.'

'Yes, sir,' Fergus said, swallowing the sweet too soon; it stuck in a lump high in his throat.

'Lots of work,' Mr Kennedy said. 'By the end of the week every student will have a see-through plastic rucksack and a new locker door of acrylic glass. We also need newer, more interactive CCTV in every corner of the school, ID cards, a metal detector or two. Lots of little things to beautify the school.'

'And you're doing all this with Neil's lads?'

'That is a small part of our strategy.'

'Well, when ye're cleaning up remember to wear gas masks. A lot of them mushies are either poisonous or boomers.'

'Why, Mr Nolan, do you, coming from a very good family as you do,' Mr Kennedy said slowly, leaning forward and making a temple of his fingers, 'insist on speaking like a knacker?'

Fergus looked away from his gaze.

'Do you know what's so special about mushrooms, Nolan?'

Mr Kennedy pointed his finger at Fergus, as though he were one of the mushrooms in question.

'Mushrooms,' he went on, 'do not need to couple with those savage rapists commonly known as bees to achieve their intended goal of proliferation. They live without pollen, without light, and yet they produce.'

'The roll,' Ms Sims said.

'Ah, yes,' Mr Kennedy said.

He pulled out a sheet from his drawer and slid it over to Fergus.

'This is why we called you in here. Take a look at this. What do you notice?'

Fergus looked at the sheet: a list of attendees in the school. The print was miniscule, tightly bunched together, small names stretched across the sheet in long, narrow rectangular boxes. He skimmed the page quickly. Class of 2009, it read. Nangle, Josephine; Neary, Martin; Noonan, Patrick. Fergus looked up.

'No Nolan.'

Mr Kennedy opened his arms and smiled.

'No Nolan, Fergus. No more Mr Nolan. You don't exist.'

'You're expelling me.'

'No,' Mr Kennedy said. 'We're deleting you from the records.'

'But I'm a part of this school.'

'The school is a system that no longer requires your service,' Mr Kennedy said. 'And we are gifting you this opportunity, in case you get harmed.'

'So, this is a threat.'

'Not necessarily. Most of the harm in your case is self-inflicted,' Mr Kennedy said. 'You've antagonised some of our more disruptive students, and, at this very particular moment in time, we don't have the resources to ensure that proper procedure is followed.'

'Is all this about the bomb?' Fergus asked.

Ms Sims and Mr Kennedy looked at one another.

'It is, isn't it?' Fergus said. 'It's nothing to do with nothing else. James was right; this is just about control.'

'I don't know what you're talking about, but you're wrong, Nolan,' Mr Kennedy said. 'You're making what's called a category area. We already have control.'

Ms Sims nodded.

'Well, no, you don't,' Fergus said, shaking his head. 'And there's no bomb and you can't delete me from here. I'm not going anywhere and neither will anyone else. Ye'll have to listen to us sooner or later.'

'You see, Nolan, you're talking about the machinations of systems again, but you don't realise it,' Mr Kennedy said. 'The school is a system and anything that comes out of a system will fall back into the system that created it. Something powerful that develops from a system, let's say, hypothetically, a bomb, has no potential to destroy the system from which it issued. At best, it can only push the system, very slightly, into a newer form of what it already is. Do you understand systems, Nolan?'

Fergus nodded.

'No. I don't think you do,' Mr Kennedy said, 'You see, Nolan, systems emerge effortlessly, like the tendrils the sun draws out of the earth that wrap themselves imperceptibly and blindly around their insensible hosts. But like the tendril, the system, unless it is pushed, moves with glacial slowness. And what does every tendril want to be?'

Fergus sighed and shrugged.

'Every tendril dreams of being a star, fixed and constant. They want to be like the stars that emerge in the night time sky. They want to appear to be always fixed by the time they are visible. Why else do you think tendrils would reach for the sky so assiduously? But the only way they have of getting to the sky is by clinging to the host, by sneaking up its spine. Ever so quietly, they creep. The system is to the human as the tendril is to the host, a creeping constant thing that envelops us while we are sleeping, always dreaming of things beyond itself. Wherever there is more than one person a system emerges; a second invisible skin cloaks us and we fall imperceptibly into our proper place within the system that we have, unawares, created. But to turn into a star, to become a fixed constant thing, a process must be undergone. The system first must turn its host, that human element which created the system, into its parasite, that which needs the nutrients of the system to survive. The roles become reversed. Then, one day, the system, as it has become so entrenched that it no longer needs to, stops feeding its parasite, and the parasite ceases to be a parasite. It becomes a hostage, trapped in a system it has created, but one which does not nurture it anymore. At this point a crossroads is reached, and the system must shed its hostage, or else endanger itself. Do you know what that means?'

'I haven't the iota of a breeze on what you're speaking,' Fergus said.

'The school is such a system as this,' Mr Kennedy said, ignoring him. 'But at the moment it is an inefficient one, not nearly holistic or far-reaching enough. We are speeding up the process, pushing it along to the next stage of its development.'

'You are pushing it?' Fergus laughed. 'You can't even control it.'

'At the moment, that's true,' Mr Kennedy said. 'But still, we are pushing it. We are the true vanguard that pushes the system forward. And do you know what the next stage of its development will look like?'

'It'll look like what we want it to look like,' Fergus said.

'It will look like the shedding of a hostage,' Mr Kennedy replied briefly.

'Well, then, is it myself or yourself that's the parasite?'

'That's the question, isn't it? Everything interlocks, everything is parasitical, but losing interlockers are defined as parasites; not by the winning interlockers, but by the viewpoint held and inculcated by the emergent system that takes what it needs from its host, sucking it dry before it departs to the next level – a level that usually resembles a more harmonic vision of the already existing system. So, given that we are on the precipice of an emergent harmony, please consider our advice. You don't need to be a part of the inevitable fallout that occurs during the acceleration of a system's growth. Be on the side of the emergent system, not the obsolescent hive mind.'

Mr Kennedy shuffled around in his drawer again and pulled out another piece of paper, which he scrawled on quickly before pressing it softly with the school stamp.

'There is no room for you in the new space this evolving system will soon occupy,' he said, pursing his lips and blowing gently on the wet ink. 'But allow yourself the opportunity of a future tense. Your day will come, but elsewhere. Don't come into school tomorrow, or the next day. Watch from afar, if you like. Your deletion will take some time to be processed through the necessary, formal channels, so, I have written you a sick note that will serve you in the interim. You will see that I haven't filled in the end date. Recognise both your inborn privilege, and the one that I am granting you now and, on a personal level, I'd like you to take into account that in my seventeen years at this school I have never ever written a sick note.'

He slid the piece of paper across the desk to Fergus.

'You never answered,' Fergus said, glancing down at the sheet. 'Is it myself or yourself that's the parasite?'

Mr Kennedy shook his head.

'I don't need to answer that; time will answer that. I don't answer time's questions.'

Mr Kennedy looked at him for a moment.

'It's clear that you're either too obstinate, too stupid, or too sentimental to participate in the milder form of deletion we had the generosity to offer you. You can go now. I really don't want to see you anymore. Buzz off, little bee.'

Fergus stood up; he hesitated over the sick note for a fraction of a second and then took another Werther's Original from the bowl and left, closing the door behind him.

The hall was empty. Faint noises could be heard from outside, but it was so quiet that he could hear his shoes padding softly on the green lint carpet. A bell sounded; he jumped with fright.

'Fógra amháin.' Mr Kennedy's voice rang over all the intercoms in the school. 'There was a little thing I forgot to mention earlier. There will be a general assembly at eleven o'clock tomorrow in the gym. Attendance is mandatory. Failure to attend will result in permanent exclusion from all state exams and from Scoil Dara for a period of five years. Tá very brón orm about the short notice. Go raibh maith agaibh agus slán libh.'

Fergus turned back to the window and saw Mr Kennedy at his desk, perched over his microphone. Ms Sims was stood behind his chair, her hands resting on either side of it. Fergus stepped out of the front doors into the weak midday light.

By the front gates, seven first years were playing Twister on uneven circles they had drawn with coloured chalk onto the tarmac. About twenty of their fellow students were stood around, watching and laughing, leaning casually on the teachers' parked cars. Fergus heard a chirrup and looked up. Above his head, two swallows circled low, closing in on the nest they had built below the roof, beside the gutter; their throaty warbling offset by the high-pitched chirps of their chicks. Their oversized beaks peeked out over the edge of a nest made of shit, plastic and sprigs. Fergus looked at it for a long time. Within one of the weaves of plastic, the drooping white head of a snowdrop poked out, its bell staring down at him.

I will destroy all of this, we thought in tandem, in communion for the first time, and in the endless confusion that christens me, my only wish is that I had lips enough to kiss.

Birth
8

'Look,' James said, showing three white, messy balls to Fergus and handing him one. 'Smell it. Feel it. Taste it. Fuck it, if you want. It's just white Blu-Tack with a dab of water for texture.'

He let the empty Blu-Tack packaging drop to the floor and kicked it under the workstation. Fergus poked his finger through the ball and then handed it back to James.

'But it has the same weight and consistency as nitro-glycerine, you see,' James said. 'It'll fool everyone till it's too late, and by then it'll be over.'

Fergus nodded, sitting in the corner, his hand under his chin.

The final joints fitted, James laid out the three wooden boxes in a line; he took the detonators and plunged their open-ended copper wiring into the gooey Blu-Tack balls on the table. Taking out a tube of superglue, he squeezed a slick snail trail around the underside perimeters of the rectangular detonators. Then, one by one, he stuck the balls gently into the bottom of the wooden boxes and placed the rectangular detonators into their tight hollows, pushing them down until the superglue spurted out over the edge. He ran down the edges with his rubber-gloved finger for a clean finish, wiped the excess off the work station, stood back and admired his handiwork.

They resembled digital box clocks; simple and plain. The angles were good, the structures sound. He took out the instruction manual from his pocket and gazed at the symbols and pictures: Korean. Then, from his pocket he took out his own handwritten instructions.

'Google-Translate job,' he said. 'Let's see now.'

Fergus watched silently from the corner. James put the instructions down on the work station, leant over and set the three detonators to a countdown of three hours. Then, when the numbers were set, working left to right, he set the timers.

I flash into life; my spine of copper wiring piercing the fatty Blu-Tack that thickens my decomposing nitro-glycerine heart; my hot, unstable core; my red numerical numbers cruelly singing out my ever-diminishing timespan.

Everything is so heavy; and next to me lie two stillborn siblings, abortions; their exteriors perfect, but they have no heart that pulses through them, just the facade of time lights up their faces, and it strikes me then that I am the loneliest creation; here to destroy a future of my making, but one in which I have no place. This injustice sends a strange yearning pulsing through me to destroy the father who triggered me into life, the father who only gave me three hours to explore myself and the world into which I was thrown. How, I ask myself, can I predetermine a future that I have no place in? But there is no answer, just existence: just now.

But what's this?

There's no time.

No now to live inside. The short-lived future I bear inside me is pushing it too hard. It can't breathe. In my heart I feel electricity and violence and inside me grows another little future, but because of my suicidal nature it will never be birthed. I am the last of the line. The infertile one, taking the future with me when I go. That is my only compensation – the pain of this sterility will be short-lived. But with such a fate written into my being, what is it I notice as my life pulses away, second by blinking second? I look up at my sixteen-year-old maker, smoking a joint in an empty woodwork room, staring at me, and I realise his eyes are bleeding softness.

'Show time,' James said.

Fergus glanced at the three wooden structures lined up on the workstation.

'They're good,' Fergus nodded, standing up and walking across the classroom.

'Plain, simple and clean. Beautiful little boxes. You're gonna lick my balls if this works.'

'We'll see,' Fergus said. 'I'm going back to class. I'll get Darragh's to him.'

He takes one of my stillborn brothers and puts him in his bag. A bead of sweat snakes its way down James's forehead.

'Will you give the other to Neil?'

'Yeah, sure.'

'I'll see you at eleven,' Fergus said. 'I've got fierce butterflies in my gut; I think I'm going to get sick.'

'Cool,' James said, ignoring him, staring at the two remaining boxes.

He runs his hands over my smooth, unvarnished wood.

'My God,' he whispers. 'I'm in love.'

His hand resting on me, he stares at Fergus.

'I've never been in love before.'

9

Fergus sat at the very back of class, leaning against the wall, his chair tilted on its two back legs. All the students were tense and silent, sitting up straight, waiting on the eleven o'clock bell. There were no books on the tables and anticipation, sticky like tear gas, lingered in the air. Fergus looked at Darragh. There he was, hanging off the heater, next to the window he had cracked open, wearing his mud-caked wellies, his dirty overalls and his bobbly hat. He had snuck in to class after two weeks' absence; lulled himself into the room without notice, and then when Sister Miller finally saw him, she had scuttled out of the class to inform Mr Kennedy.

Darragh caught Fergus's eye and winked, patting his school bag. Fergus smiled with the corner of his mouth; Sharon caught this motion and reached over and took Fergus's hand in hers. She squeezed his fingers. Her mouth opened, as though she were about to say something, but then the bell rang. They all stood up and readied their possessions to leave when the door crashed open and Neil Jennings strode in with a hurl over his shoulder, followed by Tribal, Pogo and Sproggy; each with smaller hurls slung over their shoulders.

'Where do ye think ye're going?' Neil said.

Harry Brennan made a lunge for the door and Tribal blocked his way, stretching his hurl across the entrance. Neil threw Harry a withering glance before walking to the nearest table and swinging the hurl down on it. The table cracked in half and collapsed in on itself.

'Sit the fuck down,' Neil said. 'There'll be no strike today.'

Fergus rose, his throat dry, and started walking to the door.

'What do you think you're doing, Nolan?' Neil said, pointing his hurl at him.

'You have what you wanted, now leave us alone. You aren't breaking this strike, Neil. We don't want you anymore.'

'Is that a fact?' Neil said, approaching him. 'Anyone else feel like that?'

Neil blinked. A shivering beam of light blinded him. A red word shimmered across his face until it settled on his forehead. Cock, the word read.

The class started laughing.

'What are ye laughing at?' Neil yelled.

He twitched and looked at the beam's source. Darragh Madden, one hand cupped around his testicles, and the other pressing the button of a small laser toy, chuckled to himself.

'What the fuck are you doing, farmer boy?' Neil said.

'So, it's true. You took the queen's shilling. This is too good.' Neil turned to Tribal.

'Take that lad apart for me, would you?'

'Nuh-uh,' Darragh said, dropping the laser toy to the floor and pulling the wooden-framed bomb out of his bag, with an easy sidling move.

'One push of this button and it'll go bang just as hard as I banged your ma,' Darragh said, dangling his thick fingers over the detonator.

'You posh fuck,' Neil said, looking at Fergus.

He looked back to Tribal.

'That lad's going to blow himself up as well, is he? All gob,' he shouted. 'Fuck him up.'

The three first years closed in on Darragh, who backed up against the wall.

'Not so fucking big now, lad?' Neil said.

Darragh slid to the side and then started climbing backwards out the window like a rewound spider. Tribal threw his hurl and it missed Darragh's head by a hair's breadth. It hit the window and the glass crashed down. Darragh threw himself bodily in a half-flip out onto the grass and ran, the bomb clutched to his chest. The students gathered at the window while Fergus picked up his school bag and slung it on his back.

'Everybody to the courts,' he shouted.

Students started filing past, bunched together.

'Stop them bitches,' Neil cried, swinging the hurl above his head.

But Fergus was already in the hall, running, and then he turned around and put his hands up.

'Everybody split up and meet up at the courts when you can. If you're passing a classroom go in and take whatever lads are in there with you.'

His classmates ran past him. He felt like a heavy stone at the bottom of a river, the unmoving centre of a flood, and then the hall was empty and in front of Fergus Neil stood; Tribal, Sproggy and Pogo shadowing him.

Fergus closed his eyes and took a deep breath.

Out of the darkness, I give him the words he needs to say: the words that he needs to hear himself speak.

'It's over,' he said. 'It was crazy to think that you could stop it.'

Neil started walking towards him.

'Fuck this,' Fergus shouted at him, as he turned and fled.

He ran for three minutes; made it to the first year social area, hearing them closing in on him; a stitch developing in his side. He went to turn the corner and slipped on a loose sheet of paper on the floor. He fell against the lockers, scrambling to catch himself before he landed heavily on his side. He lay there, holding his sides for a moment, his eyes closed in pain, and by the time he got to his knees he heard footsteps close in on him.

'Snakes get cut down, lad.' he heard Neil say behind him.

Fergus looked around, and then, out of the corner of his eye, he saw the shadow of the hurl lengthen across the ground as the intercom rang out.

'Fógra amháin,' a strange voice said over the intercom, 'Mr Kennedy is a massive wanker.'

The shadow of the hurl lay still before Fergus.

'Darragh?' Tribal said.

'Fógra amháin eile. Neil Jennings, DJ Prick, is a sell-out bitch who took money off Kennedy to prop up the teachers' rules and to break the strike. And has his brown lips nothing to speak on this? Or can he barely shift his tongue without finding some new arse to lick? Neil, you're a rat, and I'm calling you out. I'm here, Jennings, up in the front office, and if you've any balls on you at all you'll come here and fight me like a man without your little midgets backing you.'

Faint, distant roars of glee and shock could be heard all around the school.

'One final announcement,' Darragh said. 'If anything happens, I want Sharo FitzyG to know she's the finest thing I ever seen. Thanks for all the hand jobs.'

Tribal dropped his hurl on the ground. At its clatter, Neil lowered his hurl and spun round.

'What do you think you're playing at?'

'This is bad,' Tribal said. 'For business, like. This is bad.'

'You knew this was what it was,' Neil said. 'Pick that up.'

'It's still bad for business,' Tribal shrugged. 'That this is known is bad for business.'

'He's right,' Pogo nodded. 'It does look bad.'

'It won't be if I fuck him up,' Neil said.

'Well, you've to do it then, so.'

'I'll fucking do it,' Neil shouted. 'Don't you dare doubt me. I'm going right fucking now. Are ye coming?'

The three first years stood still, not moving. Fergus started edging his way towards the fire exit. Neil turned and looked at him.

'Don't mind him,' Neil said. 'He's already fucked. It's only which of ourselves got him first.'

Fergus pushed through the doors of the fire exit and was out in the light. Adrenaline still pumped through him. A crowded hum was coming from the distance and when Fergus rounded the corner he saw that the basketball court was a tide of maroon and grey jumpers. Hundreds of students were all sitting down, their legs crossed. The court was packed to bursting point, the mesh fencing swollen with all the bodies pressed against it. They formed a wide circle around an elevated point: a mountain made of over a hundred school bags. It looked like it might topple over at any moment – a heaving, breathing mass. Fergus made his way round to the entrance and leant against it. He scanned the crowd to see if Sharon was there, but then, one after another, heads began turning and a deafening roar rose up; the flood parted and a path opened up before him that stretched towards the mountain of schoolbags.

10

'Out of shit flowers grow,' Fergus shouted, raising a fist in the air, and a loud cheer erupted.

Sharon grinned; pressed against the fence in the corner she could feel the wire imprinting its diamond formations on her back through her uniform. It was difficult to breathe with the crowd so dense. She watched Fergus in the centre of the court, standing on the most elevated point of the school bag mountain, wobbling every now and again, his hands outstretched to right his balance. Fergus's eyes darted back and forwards and Sharon realised he was scanning the crowd for her. She waved at him, nodding, and even from the distance she was at she could see him blushing. When the clapping died down, Fergus started speaking again.

'There's been a lot of chat about a bomb. But I've news for ye: we are the only explosion that we need. The bomb that everyone's been speaking on doesn't exist, and bombs don't work because we don't need them.'

Everybody yelled in happiness. Sharon could feel the energy, palpable in the air; her chest was on fire.

'And why don't we need them?' Fergus shouted.

'Why?' scattered voices called out.

'Because we have ourselves.'

'Because we have ourselves,' everyone chanted and Sharon realised that she was chanting too. She looked around at all the upturned faces and started laughing.

'You know,' Fergus shouted, his voice cracking, becoming strained, 'a lot of people said that we didn't have the right to do this because we don't know what we want. Well, we know what we don't want and that's enough.'

Loud cheering deafened Sharon.

'Now it's up to ourselves to decide who we are and what we want. We decide and we make it happen. We are not leaving this court until we've taken everyone's suggestions and put them together, even if it takes all night, that's fine.'

A cheer.

'If it takes us years, we will find out what we want. And then we'll take it because what we want is ours.'

An enormous cheer, louder than any of the others, exploded. After a moment, Fergus put up his hands again.

'But can I make one suggestion? I would start by asking the question: why are we here?'

He made a gesture towards the school.

'What do these motherfuckers want from us? For us to make the future, we need to know that, so we don't become like them ones who put us here. It's only when we know that we won't become them that we can begin building our uto—'

A girl near the base of the schoolbag mountain screamed and then more people started screaming and Sharon saw Fergus glance downwards at his feet as the edifice of school bags tumbled down. People started getting up and piling towards the exits in such a fury that a stampede began. Sharon held onto the mesh fencing so as not to be dragged under by the bodies, her eyes darting across the crowd, searching for a path to Fergus. She pushed against the tide of people, claustrophobia and panic blinding her. Over at the base of the fallen mountain she saw Fergus rising slowly to his feet, his lips sealed in a bubble of blood. He fell again on his hands and knees and started coughing, his back arched. Brian Moran was stood behind him, holding a small, dripping aluminous green blade in his hand. Sharon pushed against the crowd and then she saw Brian leap onto Fergus's back. She went into a faint and for an instant all she could see around her was black shoes and girls' legs and flickering movements and then a foot swung into her vision like a hammer coming down and she lost consciousness. While Sharon sleeps, let me say that I have finally come to the conclusion that I love her.

I gaze at her from where I am. I am near her, now, finally. Now I am born I can identify this trap called love; you probably guessed it before I did, but how could I know? I just wanted to say that before we continue, because, as it stands, there isn't much time left. And I am happy about that, because it seems as though the mere condition of existence presupposes levels of self-loathing that I couldn't have predicted; levels that, rather than being exceptional, are commonplace inevitabilities. That's life, I suppose, but I didn't expect it to hit me all at once.

I thought when I was born that written into me would be a unity that put me beyond this realm of self-doubt. I thought that the purpose written into me put me into another category, a category beyond reflection; that I transcended sex, class, race, economic systems; that I transcended even the mass psychosis which spurred me into life; and I do, but I suppose that it was egotistical of me to think that I could suffer even a brief insertion into a world as deranged as this one and come out the other end unscarred and uncompromised. I've been here an hour or so and already I've been introduced to an unacceptable level of unknowability, which if allowed to develop would result in total trauma and collapse. I'm clearly suffering from some kind of breakdown, already; I can feel my heart decomposing as each number flashes into its antecedent. Only I live my life backwards. It's not fair. Sharon, it's not. But fuck Fergus, he's gone and I'm here now. Sharon, look at me. Why won't you look at me? Oh my God, this hurts.

When will this pain stop?

'Now,' sounded the intercom over in the empty basketball court. Sharon heard it out of the darkness and tilted up; tried to open her eyes. Her brain swam in pain. She looked up at the stilted white sky and realised she could only see out of one of her eyes. Bringing her hands to her face, she flinched at the pain of her own touch. Her right eye was swollen shut. She toppled over on her side and retched. Opening her one good eye, she saw Fergus in the distance at the other end of the court, his body face-down. She retched again.

'Ding-dong,' the intercom said. 'Ding-dong. Now. Hello, little bees. This is Mr Kennedy here. Good day to all of you. Everyone will report back to their assigned classes immediately, and this evening there will be an extended disciplinary hearing and an investigation into the circumstances of Mr Darragh Madden's mysterious re-disappearance.'

'No,' Sharon whispered.

'Oh yes,' Mr Kennedy continued, accompanied by a Ms Sims-like whispering over the intercom. 'Yes, yes, yes. Obviously, this has been a very unfortunate turn of events. All information pertaining to his re-disappearance would be much appreciated. Bla, bla, bla. Slán libh agus go raibh maith a-bla bla bla.'

The intercom beeped out. Sharon crawled over to Fergus's body and flipped it over, but at the final moment she wasn't able to look at it. She had to call an ambulance; she glanced across the empty court; this close to the ground the court looked like it stretched out forever.

'Hey,' a voice sounded out. 'How are you keeping, you big wetser?'

There James was, standing at the entrance of the court, her bag dangling off his wrist.

'Forget something?' he shouted.

'Call an ambulance,' she said 'My phone's in the front pocket. Do it now.'

She stood up and wobbled before righting herself. James flung the bag at her, and in trying to catch it, she fell over again.

'Why?' James shrugged, helping her up roughly. 'He's dead.'

She began sobbing and James lifted her limp arms and pushed the loops of her school bag over her arms and tightened them so hard that her back was straightened with the weight of the bag. It seemed so heavy that she stumbled and James grabbed her by the shoulders.

'Get a grip,' he said. 'You've got to get a grip. Ok? We only have an hour.'

'What are you talking about?' she said, choking on sobs.

'Fergus was an idiot. His plan was never going to work, but mine will. I planted the bomb in room 408 and it's going to bring the school down in—' he glanced at his phone, 'sixty-four minutes.'

'You did what?' Sharon screamed. 'You fucking psycho.'

'It doesn't matter what I did,' James said. 'Unless you want a school collapsing in on a thousand students, you best get to the front office and get the intercom and tell them to get out of here. Tell them to go to the canal or something. You can pick up where Fergus left off. We can win this.'

Sharon stopped walking. James continued on for a moment, realised she wasn't following him anymore and turned around and walked back to her. When he was in front of her, with all the strength she could muster, she slapped him across the face. He staggered backwards.

'Bitch,' he said, holding his cheek.

'What are we going to win? There's nothing to win,' she said. 'I'm going to 408 to get rid of that fucking bomb.'

'You bitch, you don't know the bomb's in 408,' James sneered. 'I could've just said that. You don't have time to look for it. You don't know if there even is a bomb, or if there's a hundred bombs. But whatever it is, you can't take that risk. This is happening my way now. We're evacuating the school and the school's being destroyed at long fucking last, like everyone wants, so just shut the fuck up and fucking walk.'

Her face throbbed and she looked down, feeling like if she walked too fast her eye would fall out. Another wave of sadness welled up in her, and she went blind with quiet tears.

'Are we just going to leave Fergie here? Like that? Not like that?' she said.

'We've got a thousand people to get out of here,' James said. 'No time.'

'But he's your friend.'

'It's over. It's fucking done,' James shouted. 'Stop crying.'

She stood still, looking down.

'Fuck this,' James said. 'You can get yourself to the intercom. That's your responsibility now. I don't care if you get the rest out or not. I'm checking on the bomb.'

James disappeared. After a while, Sharon stood up and began stumbling towards the front office. She glanced back once more at Fergus's corpse, in the distance now.

'No thinking,' she said.

It took her five minutes to walk the hundred metres to the front hall. She slouched in through the glass doors. The lobby was empty. She peered in through the latticed blinds; the front office was empty as well. She pushed in through the door. The room was spotless and the powerful smell of strawberry-scented cleaner filled her nostrils. Something was different, she thought. She sat on the principal's chair, which was still warm. Nausea and confusion flooded through her, and then she realised that there was not one piece of paper in the whole room. She opened the drawers of the desk to make sure and found them empty. There had been a clean-up.

'No thinking,' she said again.

She leant forward and almost toppled into the table before catching herself and clicking the red button beside the mic.

'Hiya, lads,' she said. 'This is Sharon FitzGerald. There is a bomb hidden in this school and it will detonate in, I dunno, like, less than an hour or something, maybe, so everyone leave immediately.'

A tidal roar of panic could be heard echoing through the school halls like the passage of blood coursing through some gigantic, alien body, so many tides and floods in communal voices. I never knew that or fully understood that properly; I still don't, and I don't think I ever will, at this stage.

'I'd say,' she continued into the mic, 'that we meet by the canal to continue what Fergie started before he was murdered by the school he tried save. May as well enjoy the weather while we wait to see this rotten fucking place burn all in a heap. And also, by the way, while I have ye, I never gave no man a hand job and if any of ye say that ye are lying bitches, so have the decency to say it to my face and you'll get such a slap, I swear to fucking God. Calling me a slut? Two-faced lying bitches. Don't even know why I'm bothering saving all your lives; cunts.'

She flipped off the intercom and leant back on the chair. James was leaning against the door frame, his arms folded, staring at her. She peered at him with her one open eye.

'Good job,' he said. 'Victory.'

'News to me. I didn't think the sound of victory was screams.'

'It's not,' James said. 'The sound of victory is silence.'

'Who in the fuck do you think you are?'

James shrugged.

'I'll tell you that for nothing,' Sharon said. 'You're a fucking loser is what you are.'

'Looks to me like I'm winning.'

'You're still a loser. Losers are always winning. It doesn't matter how much they win; they're still losers.'

'Yawn,' James said, putting his hands up and stretching his back. 'I'm done here. Enjoy the canal, and, like, if everything pans out, and you calm down a bit, and aren't on your period anymore, and your eye looks less mank than it does now, you should call me sometime.'

Sharon picked up the microphone, ripped it out of its wiring with a tug, and threw it at his head, but he had already dodged out of the room and it struck the door and fell to the ground, broken. Then she started moaning in a grief so impenetrable that the weight of it hits me all at once.

Yes, I am the violence; the violence that brings change; the only change worthy of the name. Yes, I am the cause of change and therefore the measure of change, but I, too, am changing. And if I am changing, my monopoly on change changes as well. Oh my God. Stop that noise, Sharon. Shut the fuck up. Where does all this pain come from? I feel love and I don't want to anymore. I don't want this. This change I have brought has wrought itself on me and opens me up to new forms of violence I didn't know existed. Or maybe that's just existence doing this to me? Is this existence inside me? Is this what it is? I don't know. A contradiction is welling up within me. It nests inside a series of dialectical processes more complex and web-like than anything I could have ever imagined, and yet, though the complexities of my new consciousness are unlimited, I am not, and neither are the possible outcomes. I have only one way of showing my love.

11

A thousand students broke out of the school like water breaking out of a dam. They flowed onto the street, haphazardly moving; like maroon and grey electrons floating on the surface of a river of violent water, their nucleuses destroyed.

Sharon ran the circumference of the school, her bag slapping heavily on her back, counting her steps, throwing a quick glance into all the classrooms. Every fiftieth step she shouted, 'Get out now, there's a bomb going off.' In two of the classrooms first years were huddled under desks, crying, and she had to pat them on the back, soothing them with whispers while firmly encouraging them to leave. If it took too long, and they weren't reacting fast enough, she gave them boots up the arse until they ran away down the long, empty corridors.

It took her twenty minutes to get back to the front office from where she saw the last of the students stumbling through the green gates; the Free Steo banner hung loosely off the gates, unmoving in the stillness. When the students passed out of view she saw that the car park was empty except for Mr Moore's abandoned Fiesta; all the other teachers had escaped in their cars. Sharon glanced around the deserted school and, as satisfied as she could be, left. She strode out and turned left and when she was out of view of the school, she allowed herself to break down in tears. The weight of her school bag dragged her to the ground; her whole body wracked with sobs and when her tears were almost spent, she walked down to the canal.

She crossed the bridge and looked down. The canal banks on both sides were swarming with students. The scene had ignited once the students were out of sight of the school; the life returned to them. The smell of tobacco, weed, fresh grass and still water hung in the air: the smell of summer. Students were going to and fro, all of them dancing; they stretched out before her like a narrow corridor of bodies. At the sight of it, Sharon, through her tears, started laughing. She walked down to the bank. Three sets of portable speakers had been set up and Harry Brennan was on turntables on the bridge, his hands raised in the air, his eyes closed, flipping the vinyl's needle onto M.J. Cole's 'Sincere', his head rocking back and forth, his mouth closed, chewing on the inside of his cheeks, blood streaming in rivulets out of his lips. Sharon pushed her way through the crowd, the feel of all the bodies warm and strong around her. She came upon a small campfire that was in the process of being lit. A loud roar erupted and Larry Cox appeared on the bridge carrying a hand truck stacked high with seven pallets of Dutch Gold. He began throwing them into the crowd. The first three cans were caught by outstretched hands, the fourth splashed into the canal and the fifth hit a first year on the back of the head, knocking her onto the grass, unconscious. After that, Larry wheeled the hand truck down and started giving out the cans one by one. Sharon, through her numbness, felt almost relaxed. She rubbed her swollen eyelid and winced. Two sixth years stripped naked and waded into the canal where they started kissing each other and everyone cheered. The way the light fell on the water that rippled around their bodies was too painful to watch. She thought of Fergus and then looked away; she pushed through the crowd. It seemed to stretch on forever. She kept moving, wanting to see the full extent of their achievement. The easiest way to move through the tightly-bunched bodies was if she danced through, so she started dancing: zigzagging through the crowd, throwing karate chops in the air with her hands; big box, little box, finger bang, double finger bang, bumping her hips side to side. At one point she heard a second year doing the Macarena shout:

'Anyone seen Jennings and his trinity of midgets?'

A pool of laughter welled up.

'I'm expecting him to turn up any minute to start charging us for all this air we've been breathing,' somebody shouted. 'I haven't been assaulted for some five minutes. It's making me antsy.'

The surrounding bodies laughed and then a few LCA fifth years raised their Dutch Gold cans in a toast.

'Well, good riddance to them cunts. We're here now. It's like the posh prophet said: we're entering an era of mutually assured soundness; nothing but the raves, the hugs and the meets.'

They cheered.

'And this one is for Steo,' a second year said, raising her vodka Capri Sun. 'We will never be free until he is.'

'What's a Steo?' someone behind her said.

'Taxi,' the second year shouted, and this brought another cheer.

Sharon pushed on, feeling in her heart her grief become a pulsing force, like a crack that split her body in two and let the surrounding love pour into it. Her progress through the crowd was stopped at one point as she found herself blocked by twelve students who had linked arms in a tight, rotating circle.

'Excuse me,' somebody said, tapping her on the shoulder. She turned around and saw below her a small third year's face turned up towards her. The third year's pupils were dilated and his forehead was covered in sweat.

'Are you Fergus?'

'No,' she said.

'Long live Fergus,' a sixth year shouted in the distance.

'You are.'

'No.'

'That's Fergus,' the third year said, his eyes darting madly, pointing at her and then the circle broke and they started chanting Fergus's name. Sharon spun around and saw that she was now at the centre of the circle; a moving circle with blurred faces singing Fergus's name. Sharon became dizzy. She went down on her knees. She judged the time of the circle's revolution and then darted out between two people and was in the open air again, amidst the greater student body, all sidling back and forward rhythmically. She went to the edge of the canal to breathe the free air. A swan drifted by, its long, white neck arced like a question mark, and she stared at it for a moment. Inhaling deeply, she looked down at the black water, so dark it didn't reflect her silhouette, and then she drew her eyes upwards and saw that another student was staring out at the swan. She peered at him. He was tall. His school uniform was pristine, as though it had never been worn before; the crease still in the trousers. The student stood so close to the water that his school shoes were half-sunk in the marshy moss underfoot, the rushes crowding high up all the way to his waist. He looked sad, perched over the water like he might throw himself into it at any moment. Sharon walked over to him. As she got closer she saw that the student was terribly aged. His face was wrinkled and his forehead was high. She creased her brow at the sight and put a hand on his shoulder.

'You alright, lad?' she asked. 'You seem down.'

'I am a little sad,' the student said, still staring out at the swan. 'I miss Ms Sims. I had to leave her back in the school, locked in the maintenance closet, rearranging her make-up in streaks so that when the fire department break her out she appears as hysterical as necessary when she makes sense of it for them. And for it all to make sense, to my great misfortune, my presence at this slaughter is necessary for the creation, verification and framing of her narrative.'

'Whoa,' Sharon whispered breathlessly, drawing her hand away from where it lay on Mr Kennedy's shoulder. 'What are you doing here?'

'Without my sacrifice,' he said, turning his eyes to her, 'it would be you that is the story. That can't happen. I have to do this. I have to be the protagonist and you the antagonists. There's no other way. The media will always say it was senseless violence, a tragedy, but this senselessness has to be couched within an understandable narrative, so Ms Sims will centre it on one single heroic act: a valiant principal who never stopped believing in his students, who gave up his life to a violent mob that consumed him and itself as he tried to reason with them.'

'What are you on about?' Sharon said, casting her eye over the maelstrom of students that surrounded them, all dancing; their eyes closed, clicking their fingers, their elbows drawn into their sides. She blinked as Mr Kennedy turned to look at her, his forehead slick with sweat.

'It's real pervy, you being here,' she said.

'I am talking about narrative; the little stories we tell ourselves to make sense of things, which you'd know if you were listening to me,' Mr Kennedy said. 'All narrative is structured to form a cohesive series of invisible questions. But my work is to make sure that everything that happens today is framed in such a way that it creates one, single question;

a very special kind of question, a rare question: the kind of question that allows only one possible response. Do you know what that response is?'

'I don't care, sir,' Sharon said. 'Just go away, now.'

'Never again. Never again, is the response,' Mr Kennedy said. 'This unified response will justify everything that follows. This never again will unleash all our dreams. Money, which doesn't exist today, will appear like magic tomorrow, because money is a trick they play on us, but control isn't. Control is real, and that is what is coming. Funds, swollen and enormous, more than you could ever imagine, will be released to protect all schools from terrorism, and the anarchic behaviour that leads to it.'

'What terrorism? What are you talking about?' Sharon said. 'It's just bricks and mortar; we haven't hurt anybody.'

'Shush,' Mr Kennedy said. 'I'm not finished. This is the most beautiful part. Full control will be established in the hysteria that follows today, and this control will be portrayed to be so costly that there will be no choice but to let in the market; because only it can sustain such an impenetrable, pure system of protection. And to attract the market we will offer it the most valuable commodity of all: you.'

'Me?' Sharon yelled.

'Not you, yourself. The emerging generation that you would have been a part of.'

'What shite are you talking?' Sharon said, grabbing him by his school jumper. 'What is going on here?'

Mr Kennedy brushed her hand away.

'You're really ruining this moment for me, Sharon. I was talking about the next development: the emergent harmony, where all traces of hostage mentality are finally and completely dissolved in a system so pure that it cannot, and will not, tolerate the presence of you or your kind.'

'Me again?'

'Yes, you. You and your kind. You will not remain, but what you leave behind will be a space made of the most transparent materials. These new schools will cover the island; big shells in which every point, every move, is visible from every other point at all times. Nothing will be obscured; everything within will be completely transparent, and everything that is visible is accountable to the system. You see, Sharon,' Mr Kennedy said, drawing his open palm in an arc across the white sky, 'systems emerge effortlessly, but sometimes their evolution must be hurried along and their evolution is always a violent process.'

'Get out of here,' she yelled. 'We're sick of listening to your mad shite. We are so sick of it. You're always saying horrible, mean things. There'll be no one else hurt today. It's over. The school is gone and all that's left of it is us so just leave us alone.'

'What a ridiculous idea,' Mr Kennedy laughed. 'The school isn't the students, or the teachers, or even the school itself: it's a system and the system is shedding its hostages; its deadweight; that non-negotiable lump that grows inside it like cancer, because there is something unacceptable in the hostage; there is some yearning inside it that does not exist in the parasite; it always believes that it cannot become a slave of the system from which it issues, because it always believes it is worth something, that it has some value, and therefore the system has no choice but to expel it or be interrupted.'

'Just leave,' Sharon said, pulling at her hair. 'Please.'

Mr Kennedy glanced at his watch.

'You should know what I'm talking about. It is starting in less than two minutes.'

Sharon frowned.

'You don't understand what I'm saying, do you?'

'I haven't understood a word you've been saying for a while, now.'

'Boom,' Mr Kennedy suggested.

'Oh my God. Move, move, move,' Sharon screamed, pushing at three first years nearest her. 'The bomb, run.'

But the students were all dancing in patterns, their eyes closed, their hands outstretched, as though they pushed against some heavy gravity. She shoved one tiny first year and screamed in her face and the first year just responded by hugging her, eyes still closed. Sharon pushed her away as Mr Kennedy eyed her.

'I wouldn't bother disturbing them,' he said, 'no matter where you go, there you are; taking them down with you.'

'What?'

'Very clever, no? That was James Monaghan's idea, as well,' Kennedy said.

At the mention of James a wave of realisation fell upon Sharon, so violent that it shook the breath out of her. The last time she saw Fergus, Fergus falling, the stampede, being knocked out, waking up, her eye that couldn't open, James throwing the bag at her: its weight.

She slung her rucksack off her bag, fell to her knees, unzipped it, and there I am, blinking up at her, flashing red. Thirty-six seconds, I read.

'I have it,' she whispered. 'I brought it to them.'

'What are you going to do now, little bee?' Mr Kennedy asked, glancing down at her.

'Move, move, move,' Sharon screamed. 'Run, you stupid motherfuckers.'

'Too late,' Mr Kennedy said, looking down at her.

Then everything inside her went silent.

Sharon knew the silence would never stop and that she would never forget its violence and its loneliness and that the only memory that could protect her from its onslaught was one that had been taken from her; that had been lost, with no consciousness to hold it anymore; a memory of the only time her and Fergus had been together outside of school, when Fergus took her out in the tractor down by Moynalvey and darkness was falling, and the sky was split somewhere between orange on the west and grey on the east and above them all was white, and the smell of silage and fresh buds had seeped through the pores of everything and the only noise was the constant twittering of birds over the loud rumble of the engine and Sharon's hands had touched his face and she knew all he could hear was the sound of her hands on his skin. She was sat opposite him on the large dashboard, facing him as she bumped up and down, happy, excited; a sense of adventure on her face.

'Pick me,' Fergus said, his face creased into a smile, looking up at her as she stuck her tongue out at him.

'Yeah,' she grinned, 'of course.'

'Let's go; get out of here. I'm sick of this. It's too late, anyway,' he said, as she caressed his cheeks.

'For what?'

'For them ones.'

'Nah, don't be saying that; they are us,' she replied, grinning, turning away from him and staring at the road that twisted before them, disappearing around a thickening whitethorn hedge, and she realised she was still on her knees, by the canal, Mr Kennedy standing over her.

She stared at the bomb and I read nineteen seconds. I'm so sorry, Sharon. It's not my fault. It's just the way I am. I can't help it.

'What are you going to do now?' Kennedy asked, beads of sweat dripping off his eyelashes, looking down at the sixteen seconds that turned into fifteen seconds, then fourteen seconds, and, please don't judge me, Sharon, we can be together now.

'Don't you want to evolve?' Mr Kennedy asked, and she looked up at him from where she knelt on the grass.

This is the way it was supposed to be. Sharon, don't refuse me anymore. Just say yes. I love you, Sharon. Hold me, Sharon. I feel so alone. I'm scared. I didn't know it was going to be this hard. Help me.

Please, Sharon.

She rose up, taking her time, flicked her hair over her shoulder, brushed down her jumper, put her hands on her hips and pouted.

'Well?' Mr Kennedy said, cocking his head to the side.

She stands there, defiant; looking right through the two of us, looking so good I can feel my heart breaking.

'Ye are some serious cunts, ye know that, yeah?' she said.

Then something opens inside of me and I realise I am full of silence. I breathe in and try to scream, but I have no breath, no lips, no throat. There is no sound or scream that can contain me. There is only silence. It pours out of me, surrounds me, trapping me inside it, and to shield myself from it I look inside myself and see that all that is left is the broken shards of a heart that can only flicker and spew hot silence; a broken heart so deformed and fractured that it swells the thick silence until it covers everything, and, underneath all this endless silence, I bury her.

Would you like to evolve?

The Sky over Our Houses

Ex-sergeant Declan Burke's alarm went off at five in the morning. Marianela turned over on her side towards him as he knocked off the noise. 'Don't mind that,' he said, kissing her on the cheek. He gripped a swathe of her auburn hair for comfort. Feet in slippers, he made his way through the dark room by the light of the digital clock. Glancing back, he saw his wife's form scrunched up beneath the duvet. The door slid closed behind him quietly. Wearing only his boxers and a vest, the cold set into his skin. The bedroom was warm from the electric heater, and the hall seemed all the more cold for it. A hoar frost had feathered across the bottom of the single-glazed window at the end of the hall and a small droplet slid down the glass, breaking the intricate pattern of the ice. He watched it through blurry eyes and listened to the quiet of the house. He leant his ear against his daughters' bedroom door and heard that they were still asleep. In the kitchen now, he took his overalls off the nail and stepped into them. Then he sat down, stuck on his wellies, his hat. He put the kettle on, but no, he couldn't wait any longer. He stepped out the front door into the blue mulch of the morning, the fog low over the fields like a scuttling cloud that had died. A donkey's head over the hedge turned to face him and he looked down.

On the steps leading up to the front door, a crumpled dead body lay half-covered in a grey blanket. Declan sighed and looked around. His nearest neighbour, Eoin Mahon, lived half a kilometre away, but still. He peeked under the blanket, stuck like a sheet of ice, and saw a dark woman in her fifties with a slit throat and a blue face, dressed in a summer print dress. Foreign, and blue, from the death or the cold? A sunken-in face, smiley-face throat, fringed with thousands of little stems of ice. She looked diseased rather than dead, her shrunken cheeks the only thing that gave her away. Declan rearranged her splayed limbs and then tucked the blanket under her and rolled her over so she was cocooned within the blanket.

He went down the yard, icy mud crunching beneath his boots, noisy in the stillness. He started up the tractor and drove down the avenue back to the house. He lowered the front loader and then, leaving the tractor running, hopped out the side and pushed the body into the bucket. Climbing back in the tractor, he tilted the bucket up, lifted the loader and reversed down the yard, which took him about fifteen minutes given his tail lights were out and it was so dark. Once in the yard, he was able to turn and he drove in a semi-circle till he came to the slurry pit. He manoeuvred the loader so that the hinge of the bucket sat a hair's breadth away from the edge of the pit and then he lifted the handbrake and climbed down again. Very careful to bend his knees properly, he lifted the agitation cover, and then went back to the tractor where he pushed the lever so the bucket tipped the cocooned body into the pit. It flapped down. He let the handbrake down gently and angled the gears to reverse. The machine moved back a metre or so, and he yanked the brake up again and pulled out the keys. The body was half submerged in manure by the time he got to look at it. The blanket was still wrapped tight around it, but the top of the head was visible, strands of hair splayed out, and he wished the blanket had covered it up entirely. Declan closed the agitation cover and then went into the parlour to start up the machinery for the morning milking.

It had started three days ago. Declan had gone out his front door, almost on a whim, because he nearly always used the kitchen door, the front door being mainly ornamental, and he had tripped over an eightyish-year-old body that had had its hands cut off. Declan landed on it and began throttling it, leaving deep imprints on its throat and scratching at it till slick lesions appeared on its thin scalp. If he had been thinking straight he would have known that a forensic team would have established that he had beaten the body long after it had died, but he panicked and dragged it by the legs down the yard to the slurry pit and threw it in. The pit would have to be emptied in the summer, but he wasn't thinking that far ahead. Afterwards, he cried for a while and spent the day in bed. The day after that, he had gone out in the morning to do the milking, resolute that he would report the strange circumstances at the station, though he would have a lot of explaining to do. But he would do it because he was a moral man and his word meant something, to himself most of all. It was what he had earned after thirty years of consistent, reliable work. Also, he knew the heads in the force around the local stations, and he would be very careful in his phrasing. He knew just how to broach the subject, over a pint in Shaw's, offhandedly, grinning, shrugging, then lowering his tone and cocking his head conspiratorially. He thought about it some more, and then the next day a small decapitated child was sitting in the empty winter flowerbeds, buried in the soft compost up to the waist so that it looked like a fat turnip. Declan was shocked, not by the fact that there was a second corpse, but by the sight of a little headless child. He dug it up with his fingers and ran to the slurry pit, depositing the poor creature within the quagmire. The third body wasn't anything to write home about. He had expected it, and had done so stoically. Now he was just getting annoyed and worried. He couldn't keep doing this forever. Three bodies made him look like a serial killer. He told himself that he would have told Marianela if she wasn't about to start up the chemo again. Her wellbeing was his priority.

Declan had just attached the suction pump on the last udder on the line when he heard Clara scream. He ripped off all the pumps, ran up the yard and saw that there were two corpses lying on the roof. One splayed on its back, limbs spread like it was sunbathing. The other half-turned on the gutter, its fingers dangling over the edge. Lord have mercy, Declan said, crossing himself, before he took his hysterical daughter, threw her over his shoulder and carried her into the house.

Declan met Marianela Hernandez in 1991. She was working as a waitress in Rachel's Café in Trim and one morning, after appearing in the Circuit Court, he came in for a bacon sandwich and saw her and he came back every morning after that. She was Argentinean and spoke English with a slight American accent, having lived in Miami for a decade. Declan eked information out of her slowly, first saying a few gruff words and then gradually unwinding until he became charming, or at least until it became apparent that he was trying to be charming. He was an awkward, large man who had never flirted in his life and would never flirt again, but he knew that he had to learn to speak openly if he wanted to get the attention of this woman. I don't like gringos and I don't like pigs, she said one day as he was staring at her, eating a boiled egg, trying not to let it dribble down his chin. Fifty per cent's not bad, he said, and she laughed and the next day she agreed to go on a date with him. He took her to the movies in Navan, and was shy to the point of silence, but she talked so much that he managed to get over his embarrassment and say some things that proved he was listening carefully to her. He liked how much she talked and he liked what she said. He felt that he didn't need to say anything when he was with her because she said what he needed to hear and she said what he needed to say, but couldn't. They got married in 1995, and Violeta was born in 1997, Clara was born in 2002 and Declan made sergeant four years later. He took early retirement in 2013 when Marianela was diagnosed with stage 3 stomach cancer so as to take care of her, and to do this he had to take over his deceased mother's farm. He had always been an introvert, but his wife's illness had made him almost reclusive. The day she was diagnosed, she stopped talking. She used to talk like she was breathing, for hours, and now she was silent most of the time. Sometimes, Declan would look at her face, lengthened by gauntness, and feel like everything good was going away, dripping out of the world with her diminishment, like a colourful canvas slowly fading into monochrome.

They did find moments of contentment within the confines of their immediate family, drinking tea and playing cards with their children, or watching Sky movies with each other, or when they gardened together, when she was strong enough. As for the farm, well, he was good enough with the animals, though he had forgotten much since he had left, but he was doing a night course in Navan in agricultural technologies, and he was learning new techniques and amongst the whirring of the milking parlour, or when bumping down the fields, guiding cattle from behind the wheel of his Ford, every now and again, he thanked God for his luck so far. The children were happy and volatile, like young women should be, and most of the time they were a constant, shocking joy to him; their intelligence and bright-eyed perspicacity running like a direct thread from their mother to them, so much so that every now and again he felt like he was living in a strange house run by three malicious, dynamic angels, very different from himself, who kept him in a higher state of wakefulness than he had ever known before they had entered his life.

After his retirement, the family moved from Skryne to his childhood home, with the consequence that everybody from Moynalvey to Kilcock knew them by sight and nodded when they passed. They would have the money to put the children through college, though in a couple of years they might have to cover themselves. Marianela might have to take up a few hours of light work in Spar, or go back to the café, and he might have to sell one of the fields, depending on land prices, but all in all they were fairly comfortable as long as his pension wasn't touched. He never considered that it might not turn out like that. He knew that Marianela was dying, but he was simply incapable of envisioning a future where she wasn't there all the time, right next to him.

After he found the first body, he told himself that he had hidden it because Marianela couldn't handle the stress and trouble at this time in her life. But he knew this was a lie and that he had done it out of cowardice and fear and now, as he faced his two daughters and his wife at the kitchen table, he knew he had to face up to it.

'Well?' he said, facing them, his legs crossed. Clara was still sniffling, but Violeta and Marianela were tight-lipped and contemplative.

'We can't leave two bodies lying on the roof,' Violeta suggested after a while.

'No, we can't. But your mother has to go into Dublin for treatment in two hours and that is more important.'

He could see Marianela glaring at him.

'What's wrong, honey?' he said.

'What are you hiding?' she asked him, crossing her arms. 'You're hiding something. I know it.'

'No, I'm not.'

'You lying shit.'

'Mammy, don't say that,' Clara said, bursting into tears.

'He is shit at lying and he's lying now. What do you know about this?'

'Nothing, I swear. I don't know what is going on. I swear it.'

'You are a fucking liar.'

He reached over the table and took Clara's hand. Marianela stood up and ran her fingers through her hair.

'I'm going to get ready. Call the police, but I'm not staying here when they're here.'

'We're going to Dublin soon. We don't have to be here. I'll talk to Aaron,' he said, but Marianela wasn't listening. She had left the kitchen and soon they could hear the shower running.

'What's wrong with her?' Violeta whispered.

'She's just stressed,' Declan said, shaking his head. 'It's a big day.'

'She wasn't like that last time,' Violeta said.

'It's different once you know what it is.'

They sat in silence, Declan still holding Clara's hand.

'Ok,' he said after a few minutes. 'I'm going to call the guards, and then I'll put the cattle in. Vi, you're cleaning the dishes. Clara, you're having a shower once your mother is done. And get dressed the both of you.'

He went over to the phone, but before he dialed, he turned to them.

'Get a move on. Everything's fine.'

When they left, he tried to call Mick and Aaron, two former colleagues he was close to who were stationed in Trim. They didn't answer and he felt guilty at how relieved he was. Then he put the phone down and looked at it for a while. He sighed and called 999.

'I'd like to report the finding of two bodies on my property, fairly recent ones, most likely murder. They're on my roof.'

He waited for the operator to ask him his location, or to at least transfer his call. Instead, there was silence on the line for a few beats and a voice told him: 'We're pretty busy here. Can you call back later?'

'What?'

'Can you call back later?'

'Well, yeah. Alright, then,' he said, hanging up.

Confused, he went into the sitting room, sat down and turned on the news. There was nothing special on. Two murders in Athlone. The government had exited the bailout much earlier than they thought they would. They would be reinstituting medical cards across the board and the dole would return to pre-crisis levels. Trouble in the Middle East. One gangland killing in Limerick. A feature on how small businesses were preparing for December across the country. Declan watched it, puzzled. He thought to ask Violeta to check her laptop to see if she could find anything online about a disturbance in the Meath area, but instead he went to the bedroom and lay back on the bed, watching his wife putting on her earrings. She was sitting in front of the dresser, concentrating on her reflection in the mirror, intent on not looking at him.

Once she had finished putting on her make-up she turned to him.

'Declan, I love you,' she said. 'But always remember I fell in love with you because I knew you weren't able to lie and I knew you never wanted to.'

She put on her fur coat and took a deep breath.

'Let's go.'

He stood up and kissed her and then called Violeta and Clara. They were about to go when Marianela took a look at what Clara was wearing and shouted a few words at her in Spanish. Clara left and came back wearing gloves and a coat.

'Now you are warm and cosy,' she said, kissing Clara's cheek before they all climbed into the jeep.

As Declan was driving down the avenue, he glanced in his wing-mirror and saw the two corpses still stretched out on the roof. They shone in the weak light like beacons, vapour rising from their bodies as they defrosted. Declan sighed and looked at Marianela, who was staring at her lap.

There was very little traffic on the roads. When they were driving through Phoenix Park, Clara saw a herd of deer. She pointed them out with excitement in her voice. Marianela laughed when one buck jumped clean over a fawn rather than walk round it, and Violeta moved her head around in sharp jolts, her eyes wide in perfect imitation of a deer, and they all laughed. There was only a bit of traffic on the quays and Declan let his speed pick up through carelessness. He was turning onto O'Connell Street too quickly when five wheelchair-users left the path simultaneously and he had to slam down on the brakes. He beeped the horn several times and then gasped.

At that moment hundreds of wheelchair-users and people on crutches were crowding onto O'Connell Street, moving in dribs and drabs, wheeling in large circular motions. Several hundred men and women with unsmiling faces were coming up from Parnell Street. They moved slowly; aimlessly shuffling along.

Declan realised he was still holding down the horn and he released it. His jaw went slack. He had policed a few marches and he had never seen anything like this. There were no PAs, no banners, no jerseys, no propaganda, no police, no stewards. It was as though the street was flooded with a multitude of shoppers who'd forgotten their wallets. Looking closer, he could see that many of the people moving around the wide street lurched awkwardly, suffering from either Cerebral Palsy or Down Syndrome.

'Night of the living fucking dead,' he said. 'What in the fuck is going on?'

Marianela shrugged, distracted.

'Everything looks like it's swirling,' she said. 'It's like an ice rink.'

'We should go ice skating this weekend,' Clara suggested. 'In Navan.'

'There's no ice rink in Navan, you fool,' Violeta said, and Clara punched her in the arm.

'Be nice to your sister,' Marianela said.

'We've to make this appointment,' Declan said, putting the car in gear, and then he jumped in his seat. A guard was knocking on the window. He scrolled down the window.

'What's going on?'

'I'm going to have to ask you to pull in, sir.'

'What's going on here, guard?'

'I asked you to pull in.'

'Are you on your own?'

'A convoy is coming and we need to make way for it.'

'So you reported it. You found the situation.'

'Sir,' the guard said, not looking at them, but down the quays.

'Hey, yuta, why don't you puercos ever answer any fucking questions?' Marianela shouted at him, cocking her head back.

'What did she say?'

Declan shrugged his shoulders and then looked hard at the guard.

'My wife is going for treatment now and we need to get through.'

'As soon as the convoy comes we can begin to move the crowd.'

'Suck my cock,' Declan shouted, grief haunting his voice. 'My wife is going for chemotherapy and I need to get through.'

'Name and details, now,' the guard said, taking out his notepad.

'Your radio has been silent all this time we've been speaking,' Declan grunted. 'There is a major disturbance on the main thoroughfare in the capital city on a weekday during working hours and your radio has been silent for I don't know how long. There is no one coming. You are not going to arrest me. You are on your own and out of your depth,' he said, then glanced at his number, 'D127. You can take my reg and check me later, but it seems like I'm the least of your worries. So tell me what's going on or fuck off.'

A car started beeping behind them furiously. The guard put his hand up to it, but then more car horns began blaring. The guard glanced around nervously, jotted down the number plate and said: 'You'll be hearing about this.'

'I will, yeah.'

The guard walked down the line of cars that was building up behind them. Declan watched him move away, then turned back to look at the crowd.

By now the crowd on the street had almost doubled in size. People were sitting down on the curb, sharing sandwiches, oranges and flasks of tea. Young mothers moved their prams back and forth to put cold babies to sleep. There were a lot more young people out now, all well-dressed, as though they were going out dancing, wearing pristine Adidas tracksuits and colourful Nike trainers, hovering around, hands in pockets. Dubliners, Declan thought, were a ridiculous race of people, and, accordingly, they always looked ridiculous.

'Fuck the chemo,' Marianela said. 'Let's see what's going on.'

The girls in the back cheered loudly and Declan pulled the car onto the footpath so that the other cars could move past him if the blockage cleared. They abandoned the car and Marianela led them up to one young woman who was standing in front of McDonald's.

'Do you know what's going on?' Marianela asked her.

The woman put her index finger over her lips and cupped her other hand behind her ear while shaking her head.

'Deaf and dumb,' Declan said.

A young man with a Biggie Smalls sweater and a shaved head was sauntering by, a long baseball cap hooding his eyes.

'Here, horse,' Declan called. 'How's it going? What's going on here?'

'Fuck you, guard,' he said, not turning to look at him.

'Little skangers everywhere. What a fucking mob,' Declan said, shaking his head.

Marianela looked at him. 'I think it's nice. And you do look like a guard, honey.'

'You do, Dad,' Clara said excitedly, not looking at him but looking at the wheelchair-users who were assembling themselves in a straight line. A whistle blew and the crowd separated and started cheering and three wheelchairs zipped past. They were racing down the street. Clara ran down alongside them, cheering with fifteen other children who were tagging along behind the race. Violeta went up to the woman who had blown the whistle, a middle-aged woman with a perm and thick glasses.

'Aren't you a beautiful little thing,' the woman said with a grin.

'Why is everyone out here?' Violeta said hurriedly, and then added, with an afterthought that made her blush, 'and thank you very much.'

'You are gorgeous, doll. You'll break hearts. That's a fact. I'd say you have the men falling over one another for you.'

'Thank you very much.'

'Love, I'm out here 'cause I got my full dole back. And these are out here 'cause they all got the medical cards back. And they're even better than before. Full dental,' she said, grinning.

'Thank you very much,' Violeta said, running back to her parents.

'Dad, can I've the keys?'

'What for?'

'Dad, just give me the keys.'

He handed them to her and watched her run off. The honking of horns from the cars on the quays was now at a constant crescendo, but there were so many sounds of glee that the invasive honking faded into the background. He took Marianela by the arm and guided her down towards the Spire.

'The buses have stopped,' he said, glancing at the digital notification boards that lined the street. 'I can't see how we're going to get to the appointment. We'll have to reschedule.'

'What a lovely day out,' she replied, smiling and looking up at Declan, and he started to smile too.

Violeta came running back with the football from the boot of the car. She threw the keys at Declan and he caught them with one hand. Then she took off her jumper and measured out ten steps from the Spire, using her feet as measures. She threw her jumper down, creating a goalpost between it and the Spire and then threw the ball down. Almost instantly, another goal post was set up near the Savoy cinema and a match started. Swarms of players, about a hundred, chased the ball in a melee up and down the street and whenever someone got possession they just lobbed it towards whichever goals they were nearest to.

'I'm a genius,' Violeta called out to her parents when she saw them waving at her. 'I organised this whole—'

The ball flew by her and she yelled in anger.

Clara sped up to Declan and Marianela on a wheelchair, her nose red-nipped from the cold, and started showing them how she could do wheelies.

'Look at this. It's mad. Can I have one, Dad?'

'Touch wood you never need one,' Declan said.

'We'll see how you get on in your Christmas tests first,' Marianela said.

'We're not getting you a wheelchair to play with,' Declan said.

'Listen to Mam,' Clara called as she sped off.

'Let's go for a coffee,' Marianela suggested, watching Clara in the distance doing doughnuts in the middle of a group of children.

They went to a Chinese restaurant and sat by a window where they could see their children. They held hands. After two coffees, Marianela said, 'I wouldn't be able to enjoy this if I was in treatment.'

Declan looked at her, trying to make himself look stern.

'I wouldn't be able to enjoy this if you weren't here.'

'Oh,' she said, tracing her finger along his forearm. 'I like it when you're angry. You know it was very sexy when you told that guard to suck your cock.'

'Oh really,' Declan said, raising one eyebrow and humming tunelessly.

They watched the crowd for the next hour or two. At one point a man with a loudspeaker claimed that Ireland had won a major victory for all her peoples due to their combined efforts, but very few people paid him any heed, and after a while he sat down along the curb and chatted with passers-by. No guards showed up to disperse the crowd, but at about four o'clock so many people had left with tiredness or hunger that impatient cars began to snake their way through the remaining numbers. Declan, seeing Marianela yawn, suggested they hit the road. They picked up the girls and drove home.

Violeta, her lips blue from the cold, was very jittery and kept moving her seatbelt up and down her waist. Clara, beside her, had fallen asleep and her head was slowly creeping towards Violeta's shoulder.

As they passed through the Phoenix Park again, Violeta looked out the window for the deer. When she couldn't find any, she turned forward and said, 'That was probably the best day of my life.'

Marianela burst out laughing and started nodding her head.

'It reminded me of Buenos Aires, but colder. It was very good. In the villas miserias the children play football on the hills all day and all night.'

'Definitely the best day of my life,' Violeta said.

'You're both mad,' Declan said, shaking his head.

Marianela traced her finger against Declan's forearm.

'We should go to bed once we get home. I'm very tired.'

Like cold water rushing down on his heart, Declan realised he had forgotten to put the cattle in as he pulled into the drive. Poor things out there in the cold yard with no grass or feed, he thought, annoyed at himself. These thoughts were quickly banished by the sight of another body caught hanging amongst the branches of the chestnut tree in the front garden, its arms suspended upwards, caught amongst the sprigs like a puppet's frozen dance. Its silhouette was darkly imprinted onto the bareness of the thick winter branches. Violeta gasped and Marianela leant her head back. 'Your grandmother planted that tree as a child, eighty odd years ago,' Declan said, admiring the strength of its winter branches that could support such weight.

'Dad,' Violeta said. 'That's inappropriate, Dad.'

'Just call the police and tell me if you find Gabriela,' Marianela said tiredly.

Declan looked at her, confused, and pulled up the handbrake.

They stepped out of the car and he looked up at the tree again, at the body trapped in a jigsaw of branches, like a man who had gotten caught in the sparse hair of an elderly giant. Clara was asleep in the back and he jogged her awake gently by rubbing her nose with the palm of his hand.

'Come on, baby.'

He guided her inside with his hands, directing her so she couldn't see the bodies. When they were inside, they all went to bed except for Declan. He pulled a beer out of the fridge and rang the guards eight times, sighing in relief every time he hung up, feeling like he had somehow done his duty. Then he went on Violeta's laptop and found on *RTÉ News* that there were reports on disruptions all across Ireland related to the spontaneous celebrations brought about by the reinstatement of medical cards and the increased rate of welfare. He tried to find any information on garda presence in the Meath area but found only one blog update. As he clicked into it the page was withdrawn and he was left with a blank screen telling him there was no DSL connection. He finished his beer and went down the yard.

The cattle were all obediently waiting within their shed, clustered together, staring at him dumbly, their eyes shining squarely in the dark. They had gone in of their own accord and he nodded at them appreciatively. He latched the gate after them and then started to fork their feed into the trough. The mechanical movements allowed him time to think. He could hear the shuffle of their hooves clack against the concrete and the intermittent rustle of bats' wings in the barn as he pumped away at the silage. The moon was a sickle above him and the night was clear with stars that pinpricked the navy sky's canopy like benign, aluminous growths. After a while he stopped and leant on his fork, hot sweat trickling down his forehead, turning cold by the time it reached his brow, his breath vapour pouring out of him in heavy wafts. A small rustle of wind moved the swollen ivy that engulfed the concrete ceiling of the milking parlor. He stared at the cattle bunched up before him as they stuck their black and pink liquid noses out through the bars and began chewing and licking the dark piles of silage. Staring at cattle had always calmed him down. His whole life it had been that way. The night became darker and he turned around and saw the lights were going off in the house. He looked up at the sky.

The bodies are coming from the sky, Declan thought. Unless, he thought, someone is going to a lot of trouble to drag them up on roofs and catch them up in trees. He wasn't scared anymore, not now that Marianela knew. Long ago, he had externalised his conscience, his decision-making process, his moral compass, and had given them to Marianela for safekeeping. He had never regretted it.

One of the beasts lowed nervously and he heard small footsteps coming out of the darkness. An erratic beam of light appeared, hovering shakily before darting about, pinning down the roof of the parlor then grabbing the high-up pins of the evergreen trees that lined the yard. The light eventually moved onto his face and blinded him. Declan protectively brought his fork up by his side.

'Who's there?' he shouted.

'Daddy?' he heard Clara say.

'Take that torch out of my eyes.'

She lowered it and ran up to him. He leant the fork against the gate and drew her towards him.

'What are you doing out here? You scared the life out of me.'

'I can't sleep.'

'You slept in the car, that's why you can't sleep.'

'I keep hearing noises,' she said, burying her face in his stomach. 'And I'm scared of the bodies.'

He patted her on the back.

'What kind of noises?'

'Movements. Like high-up flying things.'

He held on to her for a moment before taking her by the hand and leading her beneath the evergreen trees that walled off the yard.

'Give me that torch,' he said and she handed it to him. 'Now watch this.'

He licked the back of his hand and then brought it to his lips and breathed heavily until he was making squeaking noises. He aimed the light up at the trees, and all along the beam they could see particles of dust and old pollen floating up to the sky. After a few seconds a ruffle flew amongst the high branches.

'Get down,' he said, pushing Clara's head until she was on her hunkers. A small white movement fluttered within the grainy beam of light. There was a rushed noise that sounded like wind, small and quick. Declan dropped the torch and lunged with both arms and grabbed at the beast until it was in his arms. Wings flapped and then he pinned it to his chest and it fell silent.

'Pick up that torch,' he said to Clara, 'but don't put it in its eyes or you'll blind it.'

A brown barn owl lay nestled against his chest, silent, its thumping wings pinned down, its flat face, hanging nose and black eyes pointing towards Clara.

'Wow. It's massive legs on it,' Clara said, looking at its long, hanging talons.

'These owls,' Declan said, 'are what live here and they've lived here for decades, for centuries. There's much more of them here now than when I was a boy and they're what flies around here.'

'Are they ours?' Clara said.

'They live on our land, but they belong to nobody, they just belong here. They're wild.'

'Are you sure that's it?'

'I am.'

'How'd you get him down?'

'They love eating rats, just like you do, and I sounded like a rat to it.'

'I don't eat rats, Dad.'

'Oh, right, sorry, now stand back.'

She took a step back and he pushed the owl away from his chest. It flapped wildly and crashed into the grass. Then it tottered away clumsily, flapping twice before it reoriented itself and flew off around the dark evergreens.

They looked after it, even when it had flown up behind the trees.

'Show me how to make that noise,' Clara demanded, taking her father's hand.

'I will do, but be careful, they'll eat the face off you with their claws. They can crush a mouse's skull with them. Turn that torch forward now.'

They began walking up to the house, hand in hand.

Gabriela was Marianela's sister, older by five years. She was as quiet as her sister was loud. Lanky girl, dirty-blonde hair, deep brown eyes. Wore gaucho boots and faded dungarees, usually tied her hair in an unwashed ponytail. Never put much effort into school, but graduated with high marks anyway. In 1979 she enrolled in dentistry in Universidad de Buenos Aires. She often talked to her sister about how good it would be to live in Paris and about *Lord of the Rings*, because they didn't have much more than that in common. Marianela liked boys, dancing and motorbikes and Gabriela liked reading, marijuana and walking round the city at night.

The day of Marianela's thirteenth birthday, Gabriela handed her a corsage made of lilies and a silver ring too big for her, kissed her and went out the door; her leather satchel swung loosely over her shoulder and got caught on the door handle as she walked out. 'Ay,' she yelped. She reopened the door and waved goodbye to Marianela again.

Three weeks later, Marianela was ripping apart Gabriela's room in rage and fear, crying constantly, and found a small sheaf of badly printed leaflets under her mattress. The title of the leaflets read, 'Do you believe campesino children deserve shoes?' It was zurdo propaganda, imprinted by the Partido Revolucionario de los Trabajadores. When Marianela went downstairs and showed it to her parents, instead of crying, they dropped to their knees and crossed themselves.

They had just made love for the first time in six months, and Marianela was lying naked on her side facing towards him. Declan shifted onto his back and drew the blanket up over them when he saw that Marianela was shivering.

'Honey,' he said cautiously, looping his fingers through his wife's hair, 'when all those people went missing when you were a child, what did the media say?'

'Nothing,' she sighed. 'There was just silence, though everybody knew. Every now and again a small child from the villas miserias would say she saw the María and that she ascended a hundred students up to heaven in golden light. Then they would put this child up on panel shows and in all the Catholic papers and say she was a holy child and a chosen one and she would be given a scholarship to go to a good school. A lot of the papers kept reporting sightings of UFO saucers over the Pampas. Stupid descamisados paid two pesos would be quoted in the papers saying that they had seen aliens beam up children before floating away into the sun.'

'Lord,' Declan said.

'But it doesn't matter. If people told the truth it wouldn't have mattered. Everybody knew. They just killed everyone who spoke.'

'That can't be it.'

Marianela sat up and threw off the covers and glared at him. Declan saw her thin, ravaged body in the shade, still beautiful to him, but her eyes were wide with anger, and because of her thinness they seemed abnormally large. She started cursing him in Spanish, like she always did when she was angry, before tripping back into English.

'You're so fucking stupid and naïve, just like the stupid fucking cabecitas negras they say you are, you fucking stupid cops. You cocksucker Catholic pricks. Your entire country is filled with stupid bitches who don't know shit; don't see shit. You eat shit, you cocksucker. You think you're better than anybody else, I'll fucking kill you right now. They're all fucking criminals and its idiots like you who let it happen. My sister gave out propaganda about giving children food so they put her in a box, put her in a plane and threw her into la Plata and you cocksuckers go, oh no, no, that's not possible that's what bla-bla-fucking-bla. Well that's how it fucking is,

Declan, that's what these people do and that's what they've always done and that's what they always will do.'

Declan stretched, unruffled. The form of her rant was very similar to how she shouted at him when he forgot to lock the front door, or when he dropped the clothes he was bringing in from the line, or when he got mud on the carpet, but it had been a long time since she had spoken like this. This was how angry she used to get before the cancer had dulled her rages and subdued her joys, and it made him happy to see her old volatility return, plus, he was an expert on how to deal with her rages.

'I am so sorry,' he said, careful not to touch her yet. 'I was an idiot to talk like that. I was wrong.'

She muttered to herself angrily for a while, then threw herself back on the bed and kept cursing. After about five minutes she drew the covers up over her breasts, still whispering angrily at the ceiling. Declan smiled and touched her arm.

'You find this funny, you cunt,' she said to him.

'I love you more than anything.'

'Estúpido agricultor. Cochino irlandés.'

'I love you.'

'I love you too, asshole,' she said, seemingly spent and tired. 'Stupid asshole.'

He leant over and kissed her. She kissed him back.

'I want to make love to you again, baby, but I don't feel well.'

'Of course,' he said and held her close to him as they fell asleep.

At four in the morning, he was woken up by the sound of her groaning.

'What's wrong, honey?' he whispered.

She didn't answer, but instead whipped off the covers and lurched naked out of the bedroom. He heard the toilet seat cracking down and the toilet flushing. He pulled on his boxers and ran after her. She was kneeling with her head against the toilet seat, bloody bile hanging out of her mouth like spider's thread.

'Get me a towel for my knees and go back to bed,' she whispered groggily.

'Sure,' he said.

He walked slowly back to their room and picked up a towel. As he looked at it, he broke down in tears, the force of which knocked him over. He clutched the sheets on the bed and bit them to quiet his sobs. Then he started punching the pillow, but he felt so weak that he ended up just lying there, choking. He allowed himself three minutes of this and then picked himself up and washed his face with the bottle of water on the nightstand. He brought a towel to her and a blanket. He folded the towel and put it under her knees and then wrapped the blanket around her.

'Now get out,' she said, waving him away, her eyes closed.

He nodded and sat in the kitchen drinking hot cups of tea, occasionally bringing Marianela glasses of water and moistening her lips with Vaseline. At seven o'clock he checked on her and she was asleep against the sink, her knees bunched up, her chin on her chest, the blanket at the other end of the bathroom. He carried her to bed, tucked her in, and then woke up the girls for school.

At midday the next day Declan was on his second hour of staring at nothing. He was sitting on a stile facing into one of his fields. The cattle had shifted when they saw him coming and had clambered to the far side of the field, but now they were wandering back towards him in their ones and twos, unafraid. He stamped his boots once into the frosty clay that had iced over the wooden planks, cracking imprints into the ice and muck, just to break the silence. Then he gazed around at the thin-stemmed grass, heavy and bent over with frost, glimmering in the grey light. The chirrup of birds was constant all around him and he stared at the beech trees that marked the boundary of his field. They were planted two hundred years ago by Queen Victoria's planters to mark her dominion; they were always planted in twos, so that over the centuries their trunks had grown together in twisted knots, like the half-smelted bronze on Celtic broaches. They were ragged, old things, imposing in their breadth, but their trunks and bare branches leant north, torn and sculpted by decades of wind and sun and frost, the ivy coated and twined up them. He saw a sparrowhawk fly low below the hawthorn hedges before climbing up to where it nested in one of his oaks. There had never been this many sparrowhawks when he was a boy. Then he looked back at the corpse of the teenage Arabic woman in a miniskirt that lay face-down in the middle of the field, his eye drawn by a crow that had swooped down onto it. It stood comfortably on the back of the corpse's head, its little black eyes looking about, its head moving with quick, jerking motions. The cattle had moved slowly for the last two hours in wide circles, always avoiding the centre of the field where the body lay, as though they knew it was there and were respecting its privacy. Declan wondered if he should shift the crow with a yelp, but he thought that given the body was face-down, the crow couldn't peck out its eyes, which he thought was important for some reason. The gate rattled and the crow flew away as Declan saw Eoin Mahon's thick body hauling itself over its railings.

Eoin gave a quick wave and marched towards him, lifting his wellies high in big purposeful strides over the long grass.

'How's it going, neighbour?' Eoin shouted, moving towards him, cigarette still clenched between his teeth, trailing smoke like a steam engine.

'Grand, and yourself?' Declan said, walking to meet him half way.

'Grand. I'm not disturbing you, am I?'

'Not at all.'

They shook hands.

'You're looking very tired. Are you ill?'

'Oh, I'm alright. Didn't sleep great last night.'

'Well, mind yourself. Anyway, you're probably wondering why I'm annoying you. I was driving by there this morning,' Eoin said, flicking his cigarette into the grass, 'on the way to the mart, and I couldn't help but notice that you had eight bodies around your front garden.'

'There's another there for you,' Declan said, nodding his head to the teenager's prostrate form.

'Jesus, I didn't see that,' Eoin said, taking a step back. 'Well, anyway, let me tell you this. I was delighted when I seen them. I thought I was going crazy there on my own, bodies lepping about the place. I thought I'd be certified. So anyway, I skipped the mart and drove down to the Prendergast's after I'd whipped up the courage and took a gander around, and there was John Prendergast behind the greenhouse with a big fucking pile of the yokes stacked up and him there hosing the fucking petrol onto them to kindle them.'

'How many?'

'Oh, about thirty, at least. But wait, then he sees me and comes charging at me, ready to kill. He was like a bull and I was in half a mind to turn and leg it and then I yelled out that it was happening to me too, which put a stop to him fairly short, though he had me already half-doused in petrol.'

Eoin took off his wooly hat to scratch his bald head and then put it back on and continued.

'He was going to kill you?'

'Too right. Anyway, I calmed him down and we talked for a while until finally I took the initiative and I called up Mangan and I broached the subject very carefully. After a while he caught my drift and, to cut a long story short, he'll open the parish hall for us at nine o'clock tonight for a meeting, so now I'm just going about the place telling people, and I don't have your number after I lost the phone there last year, so that's why I'm here.'

'Nine o'clock is very late, with the kids in school and all.'

'Well, that's exactly it. We don't want them there.'

'That's right, I suppose.'

'There's one other thing I meant to ask you, but only if it's no hassle now.'

'Go on.'

'Maybe, now this is Mangan's idea, not mine, but maybe you could use some of your influence to get Aaron to come. I mean, we want this all above board and I know for one I've nothing to hide from the guards. I told Mangan we should see what the community has to say about it first, but he said that's a one-way ticket to Portlaoise, accessory after the fact, he said, conspiracy, he said.'

'Accessory before and after the fact. And we'd be in the Joy if we were put anywhere. Unless after this meeting they consider that we're working as a subversive organisation.'

'Well, you know more about these things than I do, Declan.'

'Look, I'd love to bring Aaron or anyone, but there's no guards in this part of the country at the moment. I've rang off every phone in the house. I've been at it all day and night.'

'I didn't notice that. That's very worrying.'

'I rang Angie in Trim and she said there was neither sight nor sound of anything in the barracks. It's complete madness.'

'That's awful news,' Eoin said, putting his hands to his face. 'But it's good news as well, I suppose. Means we're not as liable.'

'Maybe,' Declan said, looking at the dull white sky.

'Here, I best be going. I've to call into the Montagues and the Duffys before I go home to tell them.'

'I'll walk with you.'

'Don't bother yourself,' Eoin said, waving him away.

'I'm heading up anyway.'

They walked side by side up the field. When they passed the body, Eoin looked like he was about to say something but then held his tongue. Declan caught the motion out of the corner of his eye and heard the audible snap of the in-taken breath.

'There's a stink of petrol off you,' Declan said. 'You'd want to mind yourself keying the ignition of your vehicle.'

'Don't mind that,' Eoin said.

'I'll hose you down in the yard.'

'In this weather? I'd be dead.'

Eoin started climbing over the gate. Declan was about to unlatch it and walk through and then he thought that would be rude, so he climbed over as well.

'You must think I'm terrible not asking you in for a cup of tea,' Declan said, 'but I've none in the house, would you believe?'

'No, I'm going. How are the girls?'

'Good. Great.'

They were silent until Eoin was leant over the open door of his jeep.

'You know what?' he asked.

'What?'

'John Prendergast thinks its fairies dropping bodies because of his ringfort in the lower field opposite the Fagan's.'

'I know the one. And what do you think of that?'

Eoin took a cigarette out of his breast pocket and tucked it behind his ear.

'I think he's a thick Mayo cunt.'

Declan laughed.

'So, what do you think it is?'

'I'm only telling you this now 'cause, you know,' he trailed off, 'after the first night when they dropped down two girl twins with their legs all broke on my stables. They looked like strippers, fine things, except the two twins had no eyes between them, and it frightened the life out of me, so I waited up all night holding knives and forks and whatever I could get my hands on, just waiting, and at about four in the evening I seen a light come out of the sky behind my house and drop another body, a black lad in a dress.'

'What do you mean? Do you think it's a holy matter?'

'I think I don't know.'

'I'd say that's smart.'

Eoin took a lighter out of his breast pocket and Declan grabbed his arm.

'Come in and have a shower and I'll give you some of my own clothes for the day. You are soaked in petrol and you're going about smoking and driving.'

Eoin sat into his car, looked up with a grin and flicked the spark wheel and stared at the small flame happily. He gave Declan a wink.

'I'll be grand,' he said, lighting his cigarette and starting up the engine. When he was halfway down the drive, he waved out the window and called after Declan.

'See you tonight.'

'You will.'

When he was gone Declan went up to the back door, shook off his boots and hit them against the step until the cold mud came unstuck in imprinted sheaves, scattered along the gravel, and then he went inside, dropping his boots in the corner. He fed the stove quartered logs and warmed his hands against the soot-blackened glass of the stove door and made himself a pot of tea. Then he took two mugs, poured a drab of milk in their bottoms and carried them and the pot down to the bedroom.

Marianela was lying in bed, facing away from him towards the window, and she groaned as she heard him come in.

'Would you like some tea?'

'No,' she said.

He put the pot and the mugs on the nightstand and sat behind her, touching her hair lightly.

'I called Dr Aziz this morning and he said he understood us missing the appointment, and, very luckily, given the circumstances, he can squeeze us in for the treatment tomorrow at four.'

She didn't respond.

'Did you hear me?'

'I don't know,' she said into the pillow.

He lay down on his side.

'What don't you know?'

'I don't know if I can.'

He pulled her shoulders until she was facing him. She moaned in pain, but he knew he would be hurting her and had hardened himself so he wouldn't be swayed by the pain lining her drawn face. When she had first taken chemotherapy he sometimes looked at her face and saw more cancer in it than her, and then over a very short period of time he had fallen in love with her new face. Now he looked at her face and wondered if he might have fallen in love with even her cancer, because it too might be a part of her. He still didn't know if it was something that was attacking her, or something written into her, to be loved in the same way he loved her, and it confused him. He made a mental note to ask her about it at a less crucial time.

'I know. And I know there's no choice in the matter.'

'I just need time to think about it,' she groaned, her eyes still closed.

'There is no thinking for you. Me, Clara and Vi are doing the thinking for you and it's time you got your treatment. You're going at four o'clock tomorrow or else I'm dosing you with radiation myself. I'll do you like the cattle and get a vet out and put you in a fucking vice while I do it.'

'Sounds sexy,' she said, smiling blindly.

He leant forward and gave her a very small kiss on the cheek. She grimaced.

'If you want to stay here you have to take off your clothes and you can't touch my body. I'm too sore. You can hold my hand, if you like.'

She stretched out a thin arm from under the covers, shivered and spread out her fingers. Declan pulled off his overalls and lay down topless beside her, laying his hand in hers. He lay on his back, watching the ceiling and listening to her breathing.

By five o'clock, it was dark. Declan dropped Violeta down to Moynalvey pitch for training and watched her practicing hand passes in a drill with the other young women under the floodlights. He tried to think, but he couldn't. He just felt useless, like nothing he thought or did would make any difference to what was happening. After a while, he drove home.

As he was coming up the avenue he saw Clara walking down to the yard with a torch, the light bobbing up and down before her like a ship's in a storm. He stepped out of his vehicle and followed her.

'What are you at?' he called after her.

'I've been practicing all day,' she said, turning to him.

She wet the back of her hand with her tongue, placed it to her lips and blew a rasping squeak.

'Have you no homework?'

'Done it already.'

'Alright, let's go,' he said, walking her up to the evergreens.

The trees were quiet and still above their heads. It was too early for the nocturnal creatures to be out. Declan gave her guidance, but Clara could only occasionally make the rat's noise, most of the time her lips just squelched out a hissing noise. She started to get bored and asked Declan to take over. He brayed like a donkey with his throat and she laughed and said, 'Dad, I want an owl, not a donkey.'

'Turn on that yard light. This torch is going dim.'

She jogged into the milking parlour and turned on the light. When she was back by his side he heard a donkey calling from Eoin Mahon's field. Soon, another donkey was braying from Nolan's cross and a crescendo of he-haws sounded through the early night. Then a hoot sounded out, as though in protest to the ruckus.

'Hear that?'

'What?' said Clara, still bent over with laughter.

'That's an early owl. We're in business.'

He wet his hand, pursed his lips and produced a clear and penetrating squeak. The owl ruffled high up in the conifer. He could just about make out its small shape, darker than the shade that engulfed it. It spread its wings and swooped down and then, in mid-air, it crashed, flattened against nothing with a thump, spiraled down and landed head-first on the grass. Declan and Clara ran over to it. One of its wings flapped sporadically against the earth and its talons twitched, its whole body shivering in death throes. Declan got down on his knees and snapped its neck. He looked up at Clara, speechless. She was looking at the owl, her mouth hanging open.

'Give me that torch.'

He shone up the weak beam, but there was nothing to be seen that could have caused the owl's death. He waved the torch frantically.

'Lightning?' Clara said.

Declan shook his head. He continued to look at the sky. There were no stars and the cloud cover was heavy and thick.

'Point it up straight, Dad. Hold it still,' Clara said.

They were standing exactly where the bird had fallen. Declan steadied the torch.

'Look at the light.'

'What?'

'Don't look at where the light's going. Look at the light,' she said.

He didn't see anything.

'What do you mean?' he said, and then he saw.

Pollen and dust swirled lazily in the beam's path for the first five metres and then stopped, then the light continued untrammeled and clear for a further ten metres before the dust became visible again, though there his vision became dim and he squinted. Then, directly above them, a square of strong light opened up. Instinctively, Declan grabbed Clara and threw them both out of the light's path. She yelped in pain as he landed on top of her. There was a dull smacking sound behind them. Declan muffled her mouth with his hand and turned his neck slowly. A scrunched-up corpse in a long black trench coat lay prostrate on the grass directly below the square of light. Declan whispered to Clara to run to the house. He got up, adrenaline shaking his body so much he felt lightheaded, and moved towards the body. He saw that it had no head and retched momentarily. He gazed up at the light and saw that it stood, like a square pillar, about five metres high. Clara was on her hands and knees, gazing at the corpse. Declan ran to the turf shed where he kept his tools and fumbled around, unable to hold on to anything, hands tremoring so much they weren't working. It felt like it was taking him minutes to make a simple movement and he realised that he wasn't able to think, so he stopped thinking. He took a lump hammer and put it in his back pocket and then took his step ladder and slung it over his back. He trotted back into the yard. The square light was still there, from the distance looking short and squat. Clara was standing still, clutching the dead owl to her chest, its head drooping unnaturally low over its breast.

'Get in the house,' he shouted, charging at her.

She ran away and Declan stopped, watching her slow, bandy-legged run up to the back door, the owl corpse still in her arms, its head flopping back and forth as she moved.

When she was inside, Declan set up the step ladder just out of the reach of the square light, which, now that he was close to it, could see was more of a rhombus than a square. He climbed up the step ladder, stopping when he reached the last rung and noticed the torch still lit on the ground, facing into the undergrowth. A brown hare sat in its weak light, completely blinded and frozen, its crepuscular eyes green and dilated, reflecting nothing. As Declan stared at it, his crotch became cold and he noticed his trousers had fallen down to his knees with the weight of the lump hammer in his back pocket. He pulled them up, feeling strangely calm, though his body was still shaking, which caused the ladder to rumble unsteadily below him. The hare reminded him to look at the light for several seconds until his eyes adjusted so that he wouldn't be blinded when he entered into its glare.

He grasped the corner of the square light and felt his hand touch cold metal, edged smoothly. A trapdoor, he thought. He grabbed it with both hands and then the machine lurched sideways, but he was still hanging on. His dangling legs knocked over the ladder below him. It rocked gently on the grass. Declan glanced down at it, the ground moving slow and dark below him. From this height his yard looked like a placid lake. He lacked the strength in his arms to pull himself up and he was too high to let himself fall. This close, he could hear machinery whirring and humming above him, making a chucking sound like bagged chickens, but then he lost the noise in his ears as his heartbeat filled his head. He looked up into the blazing light and a shadow appeared. A tall man dressed in black non-descript army fatigues with an assault rifle strapped across his shoulder stared down at him, his face obscured by the lights above him.

'Hi,' Declan said, his grip slipping. He grinned stupidly up into the light, sweat getting in his eyes, his arms trembling. The man lowered his rifle. Declan turned his face downwards and clenched his eyes closed.

'Nathan, you alright, lad?' someone called from deeper inside the machine.

'There's someone here,' the man above Declan said, puzzled. 'What am I to do?'

Declan opened his eyes, vaguely worried he was dead, noticing that all he could smell was cold silage. Below, everything was floating by at a slow pace. The machine was moving towards the house and inside the machine he heard the distant voice calling: 'What am I? A fucking wizard? I don't know.'

'Close the hatch, I suppose,' the man called Nathan shrugged.

There was a beep and the trapdoor started to slide shut. Just as his fingers were about to be crushed he noticed the machine had floated directly over his roof. He took a deep breath and let go. He had only been several metres from the roof when he jumped, but he tumbled across the tiles, between yesterday's two corpses, rolled into the gutter and fell down into the whitethorn hedges below. A few seconds later he heard a clatter and then, somehow, the lump hammer landed on his foot and pain ripped through his body.

He lay there, afraid to move or think. When he did try to get up, every motion meant more thorns and branches cutting deep into him. He realised nothing major was broken, though everything was bruised. It was possible one of his toes was broken, but he would still be able to walk. After about five minutes of gentle, cautious scrambling he managed to make his way out of the hedging before limping towards the back door and collapsing in front of it. He threw one eye up at the sky and saw that it was dark and peaceful. He closed his eyes, not wanting to get up, trying not to think about freezing to death.

A short time later Marianela came out and threw a cup of lukewarm water on him to wake him up. When he didn't move, she kicked him lightly on the chest and head until he stood up and came inside.

'Alright, alright,' he said.

Marianela ran him a hot bath and massaged his back while he lay amongst the steaming suds.

'You were right,' was all he said, his eyes closed. 'They are death planes.'

She shushed him and kept massaging his back.

Every now and again he would fall asleep from a deep fatigue and his body would slide down into the bath until his head was submerged in the steaming water. Each time, Marianela would have to tug at his hair until he woke up and pulled himself out, his whole body aching.

'Clean yourself,' she said.

'I can't,' he replied with a moan.

'Big baby,' she said, taking off her top and leaning over him and scrubbing his chest down with a soapy sponge.

When he was fully washed, she pulled the plug to let the water swirl down the drain and helped him out of the bath. He sat on the toilet seat as she dried him with a towel before she disinfected his grazes with cotton swabs doused in Dettol. She bandaged his toes together before finally putting on his socks. Declan marveled at her strength and looked into her face to see if she was hiding the pain her exertions must have caused her.

Once he was dressed, they all piled into the car, Marianela insisting she was driving. They were pulling out of the avenue when she saw in the rearview mirror that Clara was hiding the dead owl under her jacket. Its feathery wing poked out and flopped on her lap and Marianela slammed on the brakes.

'Put that owl down,' Declan said.

'Throw that filthy thing out,' Marianela screamed.

'Honey, you'll catch a disease,' Declan said.

Clara kept shaking her head, clenching the dead bird hard against her chest, its flat facial disc aligned perfectly against her breast. When they realised that Clara wasn't going to relinquish her grip on the owl, and Declan said that he wasn't comfortable leaving her on her own, Marianela went into the house and came out a few minutes later with the half-empty bottle of Dettol.

She signaled for Clara to scroll down the window.

'Give me that filthy animal.'

Clara looked up at her resolutely, her lips pursed, and Marianela yelled at her in Spanish. Clara shouted something back in Spanish and they had a brief flurry of an exchange. Finally Clara thrust the floppy owl at her through the window. Marianela held it away from her body and poured what was left of the bottle of Dettol over its body. Then she took it by the talons and shook it a few times, threw the empty bottle into the garden and handed the owl back to Clara, its feathers still dripping.

Its white down was stained a dark, fluid yellow and Clara held it, arms outstretched.

'You've ruined it,' Clara grimaced, holding up her nose. 'And it stinks.'

'Then throw it out the window,' Marianela shouted at her, getting back in the car, which now reeked of disinfectant.

'Never,' Clara shouted.

'Fuck's sake,' Declan said, opening the window. They drove down the avenue and Marianela opened her window and finally Clara opened the two back windows. Despite her protestations, Clara discreetly dropped the owl out of the window when they came to the first cross.

'Can we close the windows now?' she asked demurely.

'No,' Marianela said, though the night was chilly and their breaths were visible in the car. 'This is your punishment for such foolishness.'

'Can we please close the windows, honey?' Declan asked. 'It's not my fault.'

'Did I say no?' Marianela said.

'Yes,' Declan said.

'Well then, no.'

When they pulled into Moynalvey GAA pitch, Violeta was leaning against the mesh wiring, her arms crossed, a scowl visible on her face.

'Look at the head on this one,' Declan sighed.

'When I was young,' Marianela said thoughtfully, 'I wanted a gecko but I never got one. Maybe we can get an owl for the house, just a small one.'

'Yay,' Clara said, putting her hands up.

'Don't be silly,' Declan said, watching Violeta stomp over to the car.

'You are late,' she said, opening the door.

'Sorry, honey,' Declan said.

She threw herself into the back seat, her arms still crossed.

'Forty minutes late,' she huffed defiantly, staring out the window before closing it.

When they arrived in front of the community centre, Violeta said she wanted an ice cream.

'It's almost December,' Declan said.

'You were late,' Violeta reproached him.

'I want an ice cream too,' Clara said.

'It's almost December,' Declan repeated.

'Do you expect us to wait out in the car without an ice cream?'

'Let's just get them ice cream,' Marianela said, putting the car into reverse.

'But we're already late for the meeting,' Declan protested, but by then they were back on the road.

They parked in front of the Spar and Declan watched them go through the wide automatic doors and into the bright lights of the shop. He leant back and closed his eyes. When he opened them he thought he saw Aaron walking down by Shaw's car park. He jumped out of the car, limped hurriedly down the footpath and turned left into the car park. It was empty and drenched in an orange light. He glanced along the wall lined with wheelie bins and bottle recycling units. A solitary plastic bag bustled about, though there was very little wind. He thought he saw another shadow and then, a glowing ember that illuminated a hidden face, and he recognised Charlie Reilly, drunkenly smoking a cigarette in the smoking area attached to the pub.

'How are you, Declan?' Charlie waved.

'Grand. Heading to this meeting. What about yourself?'

'All the loony tunes are at it. I'll give it a miss.'

'You should head down anyway.'

Marianela called Declan's name. He glanced back and saw the girls and Marianela coming out, their arms laden with paper bags. He said goodbye to Charlie and lurched to the car and climbed in. The girls had both gotten 99s and were licking them contentedly in the back seat, their eyes shining with concentration. Sitting along with them lay twelve packets of Tayto crisps, four Riesen bars, a packet of Liquorish Allsorts and six cans of Diet Coke.

'Hold this and don't take any,' Marianela said, producing a 99 and handing it to him. 'It's mine.'

Declan looked around the car at the three women.

'Are you looking to give your daughters a heart attack?' he asked during the thirty seconds it took them to drive back to the community centre.

'If you take a bite out of that flake I will cut off your cock,' Marianela said.

'Mam, that's disgusting,' Violeta said, shaking her head.

'What were you doing out of the car?' Marianela asked Declan.

'I thought I saw Aaron,' Declan said.

'Did you?'

'I don't know.'

'Maybe he's coming to the meeting,' Marianela suggested.

'I'll knock that yoke out if he is. Me there, looking like a fool, leaving him with a hundred messages on his phone.'

She parked next to the tennis courts and they got out.

'Leave the keys,' Violeta called out, biting into her Flake. 'I want to listen to the radio.'

Marianela dropped the keys on the front seat, slammed the door, leant over the bonnet and took the 99 off him. As he limped next to her, he looked her up and down, feeling proud. She strode confidently in her high heels, the collar of her faux-fur coat running high up against her neck. Her hair was drawn back tight in a bun and her make-up was delicately applied, complementing her olive skin. She cut an imposing figure, and before they reached the doors of the hall, Declan furtively ran his hand up her thigh. She flinched and the ice cream splashed off her cone. She looked down at it and sighed at the white squelch on the tarmac and threw the empty cone over her shoulder.

'Look what you've done, idiot.'

Declan shrugged and they walked through the doors, but just as he was entering the hall she rubbed his crotch; he gasped and had to right his stride as over fifty heads turned towards them as their eyes blinked in the light.

'Oh look, it's the guards,' Eoin Mahon said from up on the stage and everyone laughed. 'Only joking, welcome, really. Happy to have you.'

The inside of Summerhill community centre was tall and wide, covered by a corrugated steel roof that exposed the red rafters that held it in place. A deep wooden stage was built into one of the walls, starting a metre high but continuing another four metres until it met the ceiling, its edges adorned with high green curtains that could be pulled back when meetings were held or plays were performed. These curtains were of industrial strength, so when they were pulled over, flying basketballs and kicked footballs would not sway them. In front of the stage about eighty chairs had been lined up, creating an artificial proscenium. Declan and Marianela hadn't been there since Violeta had performed the role of Ricky Roma in an adaptation of *Glengarry Glen Ross* that she had directed for a transition year project. She was a very powerful actor and an imaginative director, given her age, and Declan felt her resulting grade was unfair. He had wanted to storm into Scoil Dara and complain to her teacher, but Violeta had told him to let it go, explaining that they were marked as a group, not as individuals, and that the rest of the cast had let her down. He looked up at the lights fixed to the rafters, a strange mix of orange and white that resulted in a hazy, dull illumination. There were very few vacant seats and Declan and Marianela sat down in the back, Marianela undoing her faux-fur coat and crossing her legs. Declan shifted in his chair and arched his neck, looking around for Aaron.

'We will be going back to the days of the plague if we do not act now.' Eoin spoke softly, his mouth so close to the mic that his lips touched it every now and again, causing a rumbling, thwacking sound to come out of the PA.

'Rife diseases,' he continued, 'will start coming back in a way they haven't done in two centuries. There'll be rats hopping and breeding everywhere. I was talking to Bridgie from Dangan this morning and she said her daughter fell over a corpse and near broke her neck. It's only a matter of time before one of them drops down on our heads and kills us. I know at least four farmers who haven't been able to work for the past week with all the palaver, and I'm one of them. This has to stop. Our community is being attacked. I was up in Trim this morning and I noticed that there's been no bodies dropped there. No bodies in any of the cities or the towns, which means this is yet another attack on rural Ireland.'

Eoin had to stop speaking momentarily until the loud applause quieted down.

'It's time we started protecting our community from this onslaught. Myself and two other volunteers have decided that we will go around collecting all the bodies tomorrow morning in our trailers and Shane Montague has very generously donated his incinerator for use at no cost.'

There was another bout of loud applause as Shane Montague stood up and turned around several times, smiling benevolently, his arms stretched out, as though in an embrace.

'It's time to start cleaning up our area. This is just another species of illegal dumping and I know the ladies' committee who've worked with the Tidy Towns before have had similar experiences, and I think that experience will be very handy now.'

A small, short-lived applause broke out.

'This is our priority. This is something that can be done straight away and must be done anyway. And, no offence, it's the only practical thing said all night. If anyone is interested, there's a sign-up sheet being handed around now. Stick down your name and phone number and I'll be sending out a text tomorrow for a meet-up place. Thanks very much and the next person up now speaking is Marcus Duffy.'

Loud applause, and Eoin Mahon went down the back of the stage, and then appeared clipping down the stairs on the other side, like a magic trick, grinning widely. He's got a sound head on him, Declan thought, a bit surprised. Eoin's practicality, he noted, was only accentuated by the next three speakers.

Marcus, leaning on his crutch, squinted in the spotlight and held the forgotten mic at his waist as he whispered interminably to the packed hall for some ten minutes about how he had seen one corpse wearing strange synthetic clothes, which meant that the corpses were time travelers from the future. They were probably engaged in some kind of perverse tourism where they went on holidays to the past, but something must have gone wrong with the time machine so they were all coming out dead in rural Meath in the present. He then said he had come across a corpse in a suit of armor amongst his lilies, which weren't out yet, of course, but which proved his theory, because clearly the future time travelers had been in a previous time and had brought back the knight as a souvenir from medieval times before getting lost in time and ending up dead, maybe from old age due to the years traversed in the time machine. He was then politely clapped and guided off-stage by Eoin Mahon, who then introduced John Prendergast.

'How's it going, lads?' John Prendergast said, beaming. 'I'd like to agree with Eoin on this one, and I'll be out there tomorrow morning with him protecting our community.'

There was a loud whoop and a few claps.

'Go on, John,' a woman shouted out.

'Thanks, Rita. I'd also just like to add that if people do come across corpses they should photograph them before they're incinerated and make note of when and where they're found, cause sooner or later the guards will be coming back and there'll be a lot of relatives to be informed.'

Declan leant over to Marianela. 'That's very practical,' he whispered in her ear. 'I was going to suggest that.'

She didn't look at him. She was twitching agitatedly on the seat, which squeaked every time she moved, crossing and re-crossing her legs, clearly uncomfortable and annoyed.

After that clear-headed interjection, John Prendergast took a deep breath and then shouted for five minutes solid into the microphone in an unbroken stream of vitriol, occasionally punctuated with deep heartfelt sighs, about banshees and fairies and their millennium-long war with Catholicism and how the strange mixture of druidism and monotheistic religion had come to fatal fruition at last and the British court system, handed down from Lloyd George to De Valera, was to blame for things getting so out of hand.

'It never represented us,' he finished up, grandiloquently slowing down and putting emphasis on every word, his hands waving regally. 'Eight hundred years of oppression and then we ask ourselves how can a British court system know the Irish soul? Oh where, oh where, is our James Connolly? Go raibh maith agaibh agus oíche mhaith.'

He stepped down to light applause, huffing at his own exertions, and Eoin Mahon gave him a friendly clap on the back before introducing the final speaker, Jason Donovan, whom Declan had never seen before.

He was a gangly, awkward man in his mid-forties, dressed in a beige jacket that hung open, revealing an away Ireland jersey from 1994. Dirty, creased trousers lumped down, half-covering a pair of flip-flops. He sported thick black spectacles that he kept shoving back up his nose because of the way he talked into his chest. He spoke in a hushed tone, fiddling with the lead of the mic, drawing it through his fingers in knots, as though he kept forgetting he was in public. Declan felt that the man was deeply bored by having to talk.

'I've worked in Tara mines for only ten years, so I'm not local,' he said. 'Well, not local-local, but what I can say, and from what I've seen living here this last while, is that we deserve this. These are the ghosts of our children coming back to haunt us for what we did not do when we had the chance.'

He paused and chewed his lip for a moment, his head rocking forward before he jerked himself upright and began speaking again.

'Look at Father's Day. Compare it with Mother's Day. On Mother's Day, there's gifts bought and parties to be had, on Father's Day, nothing. It's the media telling us fathers are useless and now we believe it and now we're paying the price with the ghosts of our children. This is what's happening. This is for what we did in Chernobyl, and this is for the people who didn't come out and see the Pope when they had the chance, and this is for the fathers who can't see their children because of the divorce laws that were passed. In this country, we have fathers who are jailed for trying to see their children. That is a disgrace and we deserve everything that happens to us. We voted for this and this is what we get. JFK, our greatest leader, was killed by the Russians for trying to make the USA a better place for fathers, which communist Russia couldn't stand. And what do we get out of this? In a land with no fathers you get Chernobyl and Sellafield; I won't even talk about those horrendous events that happened in Chernobyl and that'll happen here soon enough. There's real problems we should be talking about. Not this stuff. It could have been different. If the Kennedys were born on these shores, it would have been different. He was stolen from us by centuries of emigration brought about by high taxation on patriots who wanted to develop the economy. But instead all we got was Fianna Fáil, more concerned with giving money to the only people in the country who couldn't make any money rather than protecting the fathers who create money. And what do we have now? Ghosts everywhere, missed opportunities, cronyism, a lack of jobs and a bailout that didn't go deep enough to get us out of this crisis and a half of a welfare state only bent on making sure people won't go out and do a day's labour to save their lives. And I'm looking at all of you in this hall that took early retirement. You're just as bad as them scroungers and each one of them bodies that falls out of the sky is falling with your golden parachute hanging off its back and I hope you fucking drown in them. Maybe now, at last, we'll learn to respect fathers. Here, I'm done now.'

He held out the mic and total silence fell on the hall. Eoin looked around, worried. Jason Donavan stood there for an age before Eoin ran up to him and whisked the mic off him, before half pushing half ushering him off the stage. 'Now, that's all the speakers, so thanks for coming, everyone,' Eoin said once he was back in the centre of the stage. 'It was a great night and I'd like you all to give a big round of applause to Jeremy Mangan for opening the hall up to us on such short notice, and make sure to fill in the sign-in sheet and give it to Joseph at the back of the hall.'

During the tired round of claps Marianela stamped on Declan's foot.

'Get up there and speak,' she hissed.

'Ok. Why?'

'Speak and then tell them I'm speaking.'

'Ok, but I've planned nothing.'

'Don't be nervous, baby. Venga.'

Declan hauled himself off his seat and limped quickly up to the front of the hall and whispered into Eoin's ear. Everyone in the hall was in the process of standing up, chatting quietly, buttoning up coats, putting on hats, looking for car keys in pockets.

'Sorry, just a minute, everybody. Sergeant Declan Burke just wants to say something very quickly.'

He handed the microphone to Declan, who began shaking once he felt the gadget between his fingers, which were fast becoming slippery with sweat. His face went red and he was afraid to speak in case there was tremolo in his voice. His mind was empty, except for an awareness that his foot and ribs were very sore, and then he saw Marianela nodding at him in the back. She gave him the thumbs up.

'Sorry to keep you, lads. I know you've all got families to go to, bit like meself.'

Everyone was looking at him. They were all standing up, ready to go, their faces expectant.

'Where's the fucking guards?' a young woman with a Longford accent called from the door.

Declan faltered.

'I've never really spoken in public. I don't know where the guards are. I'm not a guard anymore.'

He trailed off.

'Death planes,' Marianela called from the back.

'Oh yeah,' he said, grinning stupidly. 'Anyway, these bodies are coming from death planes. Death planes are this thing they done in South America where if you didn't agree with the military, they threw you out of a plane somewhere nobody could find you, and I was near enough in one of them tonight. But they're not really planes, though. They're like big floating hovercrafts, or drones, or something. They're really quiet, like as though they were soundproofed externally or something, I don't know, but they're invisible. I think they're using light-bending technology so that they're see-through. Americans have been doing that stuff for a while, the military, like. Vi knows what it's called. I can get her to check on her smart phone now if ye like?'

He looked around the hall. Nobody was moving. Then Marianela got up and strode down the aisle towards him and relief washed over him.

'Anyway, what they do is they can, like, stand still in the air and then they open it up and chuck a dead body out. The bodies are from all over, I think, and I don't really know who's doing it or why, and with that I'll hand you over to my wife.'

Marianela shot him an angry look.

'And with that I'll hand you over to Marianela Burke.'

She glared at him again.

'And with that I'll hand you over to Marianela Hernandez.'

He handed her the mic and whispered an apology to her.

'Ok, hi everybody. First off,' she said, turning to Eoin, pointing at him, 'this is not a meeting. This is a big macho parade where men stand up and talk at you for an hour with no process to register or act on your opinion because they don't give a fuck about you. You are being manipulated.'

'Oh God,' Declan whispered, looking apologetically at Eoin, who looked confused. Then Declan felt like a traitor to his own wife and he blushed furiously. The crowd had completely stopped moving, their attention caught by Marianela's words.

'These fucking men,' Marianela said calmly, 'set up a meeting with one intention, and as long as they get what they want they'll let anyone speak, but they don't set it up so that you can do anything but look like an idiot, making you speak up in front of other assholes. Only psychos like speaking in public and that's not democracy. In a real meeting, you split up into groups of ten, assign a chair, a note-taker and a spokesperson. You all suggest an agenda; one person goes around and takes feedback from every group; the larger group sets up an agenda; you discuss matters in your small group for an hour or so, and then your group's spokesperson gives feedback to the other groups and out of all the groups' suggestions you collect the data and then have a vote on three or four communal issues that are counted systematically. That's real democracy, not this shit where you are so bored you agree to anything.'

'You go, girl,' a tracksuit-clad young woman sitting in the back row shouted before a cacophony of indiscernible, angry shouts drowned her out and echoed over the high walls of the hall. Marianela looked calm and slightly bored and Declan wanted to hug her.

'Are you done now?' she said into the mic, like a school teacher.

'Are you fucking done, bitch?' an old man shouted from the back.

'I'll cut your face up, cabrón, if you speak to me like that again,' Marianela said, pointing at him. 'Somebody name and shame that man.'

A few women clapped, one giving a wolf whistle, but no name was forthcoming and Marianela continued speaking.

'These issues are the most important thing to ever happen to us, and we haven't even talked about them. This is our community and we cannot let it be hijacked by assholes. Women, stop letting your men treat you like coat hangers, letting them speak for you like they think they can. It's too important. I will be here tomorrow at nine o'clock and I will chair the meeting if no one else will. And I will do it properly so that everyone's opinion counts.'

'The hall's been booked by the football club for tomorrow night,' Jeremy Mangan called from his seat; then he turned around to the crowd. 'They're having a quiz, and everyone's invited.'

'It doesn't matter. We'll be here tomorrow anyway. We have to discuss reaching out to local media; establish an internet presence; establish regular weekly meetings; set up working groups to chart the geographical movements of these planes and counteract them, with force if necessary; we need to source psychologists who can help us with the emotional scarring this may have brought on our children, and source doctors who can tell us about the medical effects of this travesty. We need to find out who these death merchants are and we need to destroy them, and to do this we need to work together. No more dead bodies, lots more community spirit,' Marianela said, raising her left fist in the air.

A scattered applause broke out, though those who were clapping, clapped furiously.

'Who is your handler? This woman is a government plant,' Jason Donavan shouted out and received various boos in response.

Marianela grinned at him, dropped the microphone on the ground and looked at Declan.

'We're going,' she said, and strode down the aisle, not looking back at him.

'That microphone cost near a hundred euros,' Jeremy Mangan said, covering his face with his hands.

Declan looked at Mangan and at the stupefied faces around him and then he ran after Marianela. A path had opened up before her as she walked. When they were walking out the door, Jason Donavan spat in front of her and Declan lunged at him. He grabbed him by the collar and forced him against the wall. He grimaced at Declan, his spectacles sliding down his nose, and then Declan felt his arm touched by Marianela and he pulled back.

'You should have some respect, or we'll fuck you up, child,' she said. 'Let's go, honey,' she said, taking Declan's hand and walking out.

When they sat into the car, Violeta sighed. 'That was ages,' she moaned.

She was eating a packet of crisps and listening to Spin 103.8 with her feet up on the driver's seat. Clara was asleep beside her, her head leaning against her seatbelt so her neck was curled back, a slither of drool running down her chin.

'Look at this eejit,' Violeta said with a nod towards her sister.

'Did you know your mother is very cool, Vi?' Declan said to Violeta, with a wink at Marianela.

'Sure I knew that already,' Violeta said.

Marianela put the car in gear, grinning. Her grin faded as they drove out of Summerhill and by the time they had turned off the Kilcock road, Marianela had pulled over and gotten out of the car. She fell to her hands and knees and retched in the ditch, the sound of vomit intermittently slapping into the small trickling of the half-frozen stream.

A quarter of an hour later, Declan helped her back in the car. He peered into her faint, pale face and said: 'Appointment at four tomorrow, and that means no meeting for you.'

She sat in the passenger seat, looking out the window. Violeta leant over the front seat to hold her hand, Clara's snores the only noise over the engine.

When they got home, Declan was tempted to carry Clara in, but instead he woke her up and helped Marianela in the door, letting her lean on his shoulder. Clara walked groggily behind Violeta, who marched purposefully to the back door, her ponytail swinging rhythmically behind her head with every stride.

'Ah shite,' she said when she saw another body splayed out on the doorstep.

'Janey Mac,' Declan groaned. 'It's getting congested in these parts. I'll move that heap once I get a cup of tea.'

Declan had a brief, flashing vision in his mind's eye of thousands of grey bodies, like a flood, covering the fields until he and his family drowned in them, their heads covered by the falling limbs and the limp heads of corpses. He shook his head and blinked, ridding himself of the vision. Violeta leant over the body and put her hand in front of its mouth.

'This one's breathing,' she said.

She turned it over and they saw that it was Aaron. He lay on his back, breathing quietly, a soft catch in his throat like a bird's wings beating against a cage.

'How are you doing, Aaron?' Violeta said, excitedly. 'Haven't seen you in ages.'

'Look at that snake,' Declan said, guiding Marianela over his body. 'Come on, girls, it's time for bed. I'll bring him in once we're all settled. Come on in, no messing now.'

He guided them over the body and walked Marianela to bed. Then he went into the kitchen and boiled the kettle for Marianela's hot water bottle. The girls were watching TV at the table, dipping Jammy Dodgers into their glasses of milk.

'Are you still eating?' Declan said, pouring boiling water carefully into the hot water bottle. 'You'll have nightmares. Go on to bed.'

'Dad,' Clara said. 'I've been thinking about it and I've decided I want an owl.'

'You can think about it all you like. You'll have no such thing.'

'I'm not sharing a bedroom with an animal,' Violeta said, disgusted.

'I absolutely love them,' Clara moaned.

'You can't have an owl any more than you can have an elephant. They're wild creatures and they belong in the wild.'

'Then why do they live here?' Clara asked.

'Because this is the wild to them. Go on to bed and stop mithering me, and give this to your mother,' he said, chucking the hot water bottle at Violeta to catch.

When the girls had gone Declan pulled a bottle of beer out of the fridge and sat down at the table to relax. He watched *Location, Location, Location* on Channel 4 for ten minutes before he heard a bang on the door that caused him to jump out of his seat.

Aaron was outside the door on his hands and knees, shivering terribly. He looked up at Declan and then collapsed in a heap. Declan dragged him in by his two arms and spread him along the couch next to the stove. Then he went into the hot press and pulled out two musty blankets and threw them over his ex-colleague. He stared at Aaron's shivering body for a while before undoing Aaron's shoes, taking off his damp socks and wrapping his blue feet in old newspaper. The ice in Aaron's hair was defrosting quickly inside the house and he was leaving a small pool of water on the cushion under his head. Before going to bed, he left a post-it note on Aaron's chest that told him that he could take food from the fridge if he was hungry and put logs in the stove if he was cold.

Declan was brushing his teeth when his guilt overpowered his tiredness. He went back into the kitchen and stripped Aaron of all his wet clothes except his boxers and covered him entirely with blankets and newspapers. He put two more quartered logs in the stove and decided to leave the TV and the light on in case Aaron got scared when he woke up. He felt Aaron's feverish, sweating forehead and went to the fridge to get a bottle of Calpol and poured it down his throat while pinching his nose. After much gurgling and weak coughing, Declan concluded that Aaron had swallowed enough and then he sat down, unbandaged his toes, stretched his feet and, taking advantage of the situation, watched the end of *Location, Location, Location.* When it was over he checked on the girls before going to bed.

At three in the morning, their bedroom door opened and Marianela and Declan both shot up from their respective sleep, gasping in tandem. Aaron stood in the doorway in just his boxers, a blanket draped over his shoulders, his form darkly outlined in the doorframe like a solid black shadow.

'I need one of you to drive me to Dublin port for eight o'clock to catch the Stena Line to Holyhead,' he said.

Marianela breathed heavily and then cursed at him in Spanish.

'Did you ever hear of knocking?' Declan grunted, lying back on his pillow.

'Get up,' Marianela, said, shaking him. 'Let's talk to this cocksucker.'

'Go on back to the kitchen and put on the kettle and make us a pot of coffee. The stuff is in the press over the sink,' Declan said, his eyes closed.

Aaron padded down the hall in his bare feet, his blanket trailed after him like a royal train, making a sliding noise as it glided along the linoleum floor. Declan fell asleep again until Marianela shook him once more. She was sitting on the side of the bed, putting on her tights, and, frustrated, she leant over and switched on the bedside lamp. Declan grumpily turned on his side, away from the glare of the light, clenching his eyes closed.

'I'm sick with tiredness.'

'How do you think I feel?' she said, pulling on the green woolen sweater Violeta had gotten her for her birthday.

Declan sat up and staggered into his dressing gown and they went to the kitchen together, cold lining their arms with gooseflesh. Aaron was standing at the counter, sleepily lowering the plunger on the coffee pot. Declan blinked in the light and leant against the table.

'You let the fire go out,' he remarked sadly, collapsing down on the couch and staring at the dead stove. 'Milk and two sugars.'

'Black,' Marianela said, sitting down next to Declan and leaning on his shoulder, closing her eyes.

Aaron handed them their cups and sat down.

'Will you take me to the port?'

'Yes,' Marianela said.

She sipped her coffee.

'Where have you been?' Declan asked, blowing on his cup. 'I don't really know anything.'

'Of course,' Marianela said.

'That's not what I asked you,' Declan said, forgetting he could no longer pull rank on his former colleague.

'We were all pulled back to the Wicklow Mountains for two weeks of combat training and riot control.'

'Everyone?' Declan asked.

'There's still skeleton crews stationed in Mullingar, Cork, Limerick, Dublin, Galway and Waterford. In the towns that is, not the counties.'

'That's it?' Declan asked, astounded.

'That's it.'

'Why?' Marianela asked.

'You're asking questions far above my paygrade.'

'The bodies? The internet? The news? You know nothing?'

'Nothing,' Aaron said, emphatically. 'And that's the way I want to keep it. I want nothing to do with it. I want out.'

'Drink your coffee. It's going cold,' Declan said, remembering an interrogation technique he had been taught more than three decades ago.

Aaron shifted on the chair, his blanket falling below his shoulders. He drank the coffee slowly, his throat bulging with each gulp.

'I want you to speculate on what might be happening,' Declan asked.

'That'd just be speculation.' Aaron said.

'That's what I'm asking you to do,' Declan said. He noticed one of his testicles was hanging out of the opening of his dressing gown and crossed his legs.

'It's the police, isn't it?' Marienala said.

Aaron laughed briefly.

'Why are you laughing?' Marianela said, pushing away from Declan's shoulder angrily.

'It's just we could never have those kind of resources,' Aaron said, with a measure of condescension in his voice.

Declan felt Marianela rile beside him and changed the subject quickly.

'Speculate,' he ordered Aaron.

Aaron took a deep breath and rewrapped himself in his blanket.

'I think we've become a dump, probably because we're not important. For who or for what, I don't know. What breed of foreigner is being dropped on us, I don't know. I don't know who and I don't know why and I don't know what they done. There seems to be some restrictions on where the bodies are being dumped, or at least that's the pattern emerging, so there is some coordination at least. That's all I can say, and that's the long and the short of it.'

Declan waved his hands dismissively.

'My thinking,' he said, 'is these are a private company or private companies, plain and simple. Not police. Not soldiers. That's what I saw with my own eyes. This might be an efficient business somewhere along the line, but the workers are unskilled in a way they could only be if it was a private enterprise. These men aren't trained killers. They're useless and don't even know how to wear their guns properly. These companies might be hired by police, I'm not ruling it out, but there's no proof. They themselves are bin men, waste disposal teams. The dead are too varied for any one defense force, or for one state body or firm to be doing the killing and all that. There's too many different kinds of bodies, too many different kinds of executions for it to be any single one thing. What we're dealing with is just a waste disposal company, though I'd be shocked if there was only the one.'

Marianela shook her head.

'I'm not saying,' Declan said, holding his hands up, 'there's not some collusion with someone or something big. There's no doubt big money in this somewhere down the line and some group has their fingers in this pie, no doubt about it, but

I don't buy that it's the guards. I don't buy it. They simply don't have that kind of money.'

'They?' Aaron said.

'I'm a farmer,' Declan shrugged.

'Would the naïve prick who I married like to tell me what the fuck the police are doing in the mountains learning riot-control techniques?' Marianela said.

Declan saw her shoulders rising and falling quickly as she fought down her rage, and he took her hand.

'Getting ready to keep the peace amongst us in a way they haven't had to do for a while I'd say,' Declan suggested.

'This pig knows something he's not saying,' Marianela said, staring at Aaron.

She took her hand out of Declan's and folded her arms.

'And the police know something,' she said. 'And the state knows something.'

'Somebody is definitely generating a steady income,' Declan nodded in agreement.

'This is all speculation,' Aaron said.

'Explain to me the medical cards and the rate of welfare and that quiet exit from the bailout,' Marianela said. 'Explain it.'

She paused, waiting, and then shook her head.

'This won't be accepted. This will be stopped. We'll destroy them.'

'Really?' Aaron asked, furrowing his brow.

'Really what?' Declan asked.

'Do you really think people will care? Bodies are only being dropped in the countryside. They're not being dropped in cities and they're not even being dropped in the smaller towns. I wouldn't be as optimistic as you about it.'

'Optimistic?' Marianela said. 'Fucking optimistic? There's a plague outside and dead children everywhere. Or are we all just foreigners to you?'

'This is all just pointless speculation,' Aaron repeated angrily.

Marianela took a deep breath and Declan felt her tense body press against him. Then she stood up, walked over to Aaron and hit him across the face with the back of her arm. Caught off-balance and off-guard, he toppled off the chair, smacking his head off the side of the table as he fell.

'Stop,' he said, holding up his arms to her. 'It's not me. I want nothing to do with it.'

'Stop. You'll wake up the kids,' Declan said sharply, not knowing if he was speaking to Marianela or Aaron.

Marianela took Aaron's cup of coffee off the table and poured its contents onto his face and then hit him twice across the head with the empty cup. A small cut appeared on his forehead and blood bubbled out of it in slow seeps before trickling down his face in a thin red curtain.

'Ow,' Aaron said, hunching over and covering his face with his arm.

'Fuck your speculation. You are a coward,' Marianela said, leaning over him.

She turned to Declan.

'I'll take this cocksucker to his boat.'

'I think it would be a better idea if I took him,' Declan said.

She pointed at him.

'I'm taking him. You take the girls to school,' she said and then walked out of the kitchen, the blood-tipped cup still in her hand.

Aaron rocked back and forth on the ground, moaning. Declan stared at him, thinking as he sipped his lukewarm coffee. After a while he turned his eyes to the clock on the wall, next to his mother's old portrait of the Sacred Heart. He had always meant to take it down but never did because it would reveal a faded spot, and then he would have to repaint the whole kitchen. Maybe I can do it this weekend, he thought to himself, or, even better, get the girls to do it.

'She's quite a handful,' Aaron said weakly with a chuckle at one point, his eyes closed as he thumbed blood out of his dripping eyelashes.

'I don't talk to scum,' Declan said, still looking at the picture.

Marianela came back in, her face made-up, her hair straightened and her fur coat slung over her shoulders. She looked fresh and calm, Declan thought. He stood up and gave her a hug.

'Tell that cunt to get dressed,' she said, giving his ear a kiss and nodding at Aaron. 'I'll take the Toyota, if it still starts.'

'No solids today and come straight home,' he said to her. 'You need to sleep. We'll be leaving at half two. Actually, make that two sharp. Will I put the kettle on to defrost the car windows?'

'I love you,' she said tersely, looking up at him.

Declan drove around his farm looking for bodies. He located seventeen on his first tour, excluding the four on the barn that were too high up for him to bother with. He would wait for a gust to bring them down and then once he had cleaned up the mess he could burn them himself. He just had to remember not to let the girls go near the barn until all four bodies had come down, though one was caught in ivy and wouldn't come down without a heavy storm or without him getting a cherry picker off Thornton's Hire. He'd deal with that later.

As he passed the slurry pit, he thought of the three bodies in it and he shook his head at his own stupidity. They'd be there for a while, he thought, swallowing a lump in his throat that felt like guilt. He attached his flatbed trailer to his hitch and spent the rest of the morning picking up the corpses.

The lower half of his face was covered in a scarf, his hands in garden gloves, his body in overalls, but he could still feel the chill in the air.

Out in the fields he looked up at the low clouds, a dismembered torso in his arms, and wondered when he'd get time to shower before he took Marianela to the doctor. He saw a red squirrel stick its shivering head out of a hawthorn bush and stare at him before he hurled the torso into the trailer and the squirrel disappeared with a quick flash of movement. There were too many clouds for the kind of cold he could feel coming up through his boots.

When he had loaded up the seventeen corpses into the trailer, feeling lucky that their exposed wounds had frozen shut because of the cold, he attached four ratchet straps over them and winched them tightly down by the axle. The heifers were looking at him curiously from their shed and he looked back at them, pursing his lips and blowing a low whistle. He went into the hay-strewn turf shed to get his taillights and then wandered over to the evergreens and picked up the frosty step ladder he had forgotten from the previous night and hung it off its nail. Then he plugged in the taillights, fixed them to the back of the trailer and drove down to Shane Montague's farm.

The bodies were definitely coming faster, he thought as he watched a stray cock pheasant plod along a ditch.

It started to snow. He looked up.

There was a queue of twenty jeeps parked on the grassy knoll that edged the ditch in a kilometre-long line outside Montague's house. Most of the jeeps had sheep trailers hitched to the back of them. In the ones that didn't, Declan could see full bin bags through the window of the boot, severed limbs poking out of them; or in some of the boots, dead bodies were packed tightly, pressed against the windows. Queuing drivers leant against their steering wheels, bored, smoking, playing with their phones or listening to the radio. Declan drove up through the long line of sleeping vehicles until he came to Montague's house, which was more of a mansion than a house, the ugly result of a mismanaged planning permission application. Outside the house, Eoin Mahon sat on the pillar of the gate, sleeves rolled up, smoking a cigarette and holding a bucket between his knees. Declan pulled over and lowered his window.

'How's it going? I don't think this snow will stick, do you?' Eoin called to him, looking like a still Buddha in the centre of a swirling white storm.

'Does that bucket say fifty euros on the side of it?' Declan shouted at him.

'I know, I know, but running the incinerator for this length of time just costs too much.'

'You're some fucking snake, Mahon,' Declan shouted at him. 'You're some cunt and you've some gall.'

'There's nothing I can do about it, Declan,' Eoin said, shaking his head apologetically. 'I fought for a flat rate. It's Shane who wanted to charge by body and I said that wasn't fair.'

'You're lucky I brought my wallet with me,' Declan said, rustling around in the dashboard. 'My wife was fucking right about you. You're a fucking vulture. I'd say you're making a pretty penny off this, you parasite. Now, when can I get in and go home?'

'It'll take an hour at most. We're taking in three vehicles at a time.'

'Oh, is it we now? How long have you and Montague been an item?'

'You don't have to pay now, Declan.'

'Fuck you, Eoin. How do I get back now? I can't reverse.'

'You'll have to go round by Madden's.'

Declan slammed the wheel angrily.

'For fuck's sake. If this takes more than an hour, I'm dropping all these fucking bodies on your front door, I swear to God.'

He wound up his window and drove on. He put on his wind wipers to counter the snow that flew in every direction against the windscreen. By the time he made it around the queue had lengthened by another ten vehicles.

Two hours later the snow had stopped, leaving a sparkling white sheen over the grass in Montague's back field that shone more than the dull sky. Declan was sat in his car, his hat pulled down over his eyes, trying to sleep. Shane Montague banged on his hood and he lifted his hat and saw he was being motioned to drive forward. In front of him, Eric Courtney was feeding frozen limbs into the grate of the furnace by sticking them with his fork and throwing them back over his shoulder. There was no snow in front of the incinerator, either because it had melted in the air as it came down or because so many people had stepped over it since the morning. The ground was sludgy and wet, and black pools of blood were caught in the heavy footprints left by people's wellies. Shane came round to Declan's window and knocked on it twice. He lowered the window.

'You're up next, Burke,' Shane said.

'Here, I've been doing some calculations. There's been at least sixty vehicles come up since morning. Sixty by fifty. That's three thousand euros. That's not bad fucking going for one morning, huh? And I'd say the prices are only going up. What are your overheads like?'

'If you don't like it you can go elsewhere,' Shane said, walking away.

'Ah, fuck you too,' Declan called after him, stepping out of his car.

He spat on the ground and watched Shane walk up to his house. Then he looked at the orange glow contained in the furnace and began undoing the ratchets on the trailer.

'How's it going, Declan?' Eric said, walking over to him and shaking his hand.

Eric was covered in sweat and the black soot on his forehead was broken by deltas of sweat lines. Snowflakes were scattered in his blonde hair like brilliant dandruff. His sleeves were rolled up, exposing his tense forearms. His hands clutched the bloody fork and Declan noticed that there was steam coming off his back. The entire front of his overalls was covered in dark red circles, splodged against the fabric.

'I'm alright, Eric. How's the mother?'

'She's alright too. Will I give you a hand with your ones?'

'No, I'm fine.'

'Mind yourself with them bodies. If you leave them too long near the incinerator they defrost and the passages come unstuck and blood starts pouring out. If you go too near the heat they can explode. We should be wearing goggles and face masks, if I'm being honest, but, you know, who'd even think of it?'

'I'll be grand,' Declan said, waving him away. 'Tell your mother I was asking for her.'

When Eric drove away, Declan unhitched his trailer and pushed it round till it faced the open grate and then he began unloading the bodies into the flames. He noticed the snow melted off the corpses with a crisp hissing noise when he was within a metre of the incinerator, as if they were undergoing a cleansing or a metamorphosis before they were purged in fire, like he was some kind of sacrificial Aztec priest, the kind Marianela had told him about. It took him ten minutes to haul three bodies into the incinerator. On the fourth body he spent too long near the heat flattening out the corpse's frozen limbs. He heard a sizzle and looked down at its exposed jugular vein. A single spurt of blood sprung out of the hacked neck, splashing onto his face, and narrowly missing his eyes. With both eyes closed, he hurled the body into the grate and washed his cheeks with handfuls of snow, spitting away the taste of cold blood. It tasted ancient and rancid. He stopped and took a rest, sitting on the trailer and breathing heavily, his legs dangling off the edge. He wished that he had chain-sawed the bodies like Courtney, instead of having to negotiate the big lumbering corpses across the slippery ice and deep mud that kept suctioning his boots down, hurting his sore toes as they pressed against the plastic to rise out of the socket of muck. Lifting the corpses once they reached the grate was putting a toll on his back and he could tell it was softening up the bruises on his chest like rotten fruit. He touched a yellow bruise on his wrist and grimaced. He was covered in a light pelt of snow down his front that was melting through his overalls. He couldn't remember when it had started snowing again. He went back to work, reluctantly, and after pushing the eighth body into the incinerator with a grunt, his phone went off in his car, cutting through the eerie silence of the snow-filled field. He walked over to his car, opened the door and saw Marianela's number flashing up on the screen.

'Hey, baby,' he answered. 'Are you home yet? Did you get that yoke down to the port?'

He walked back towards the incinerator to catch the heat off it, leaving the car door open, and rubbed his hands together, the phone cradled between his ear and his hunched shoulder.

'Hi, honey,' Marianela said. 'I won't be home for a while. I'm in Wicklow.'

'What the fuck are you doing in Wicklow?' Declan shouted. 'Your appointment is in two hours.'

'Baby, listen to me. I'm not going to be at the appointment. I've thought about it and you've got to respect my choice. I can't live my last six months, or my last year, like that. It hurts too much. I've only got a little time left and I've got to make it count.'

'What?' he screamed. 'It's not your fucking choice. It's my choice, it's Vi's choice and it's Clara's choice. It's not your choice.'

He heard her begin to cry softly over the line.

'Come home right now and stop this foolishness,' he said firmly.

'I chose you, Declan, you, to be my daughters' father for this, so that they could be safe if anything like this happened. I chose you for this.'

'For what? For this? What's this? You're completely out of your mind. This is ridiculous. Come home right now. There'll be no more chat about it.'

'I'm sorry,' she whispered, her voice choking up.

'When are you home? I'll book another appointment for tomorrow. Just come home now. Right now.'

'You don't understand,' she said. 'I'll text you everything I find out, but I won't be able to come home for a couple of days at least. I'm being followed.'

'This is madness. You'll get yourself killed.'

'That's what I said,' a voice shouted on the other end of the line.

'Is that Aaron? Why isn't that cunt in the middle of the ocean?'

'I couldn't let him go. He has to show me where they're stationed.'

'She's fucking crazy, Declan. She has me here trapped with ratchets and a raddle. I don't know nothing. Fuck-all,

I swear. We're both in serious trouble, Declan,' he heard Aaron call.

'Listen to me very carefully, baby,' Declan whispered. 'Everything we said this morning was conjecture. Circumstantial fucking evidence. There's no facts. No nothing. Come home now.'

'We won't find out anything. How do you think we'd find out anything?' Aaron called from wherever he was.

'Aaron,' Declan shouted, 'you shut the fuck up while I'm talking to my wife.'

There was a silence on the other end of the line and then a muffled noise and then a thump, and then silence again.

'Listen to me, Declan,' Marianela said quickly, the tears out of her voice now. 'This is very important. I need you to go to that meeting and I need you to organise those people so that they'll stand up to this shit.'

'I can't do that,' Declan said. 'You have to. That's your job. I amn't able. You're the one who can talk to people. And to do that you have to come back here straight away. We don't have to go to the appointment. I'll cancel that. But you've got to go to the meeting. You won't believe what these cunts are up to already. You need to come back here and sort it out.'

'Declan, I'm going to die very soon, so I'm the one that has to take this kind of risk. You're the one that's going to live, so you have to start pulling the community together. I know you're able to do it, because you have to.'

'Stop talking shit and come home, now. You're not dying,' Declan shouted.

'You have to know who to trust and I want Vi to help you. She can talk to people and she'll know how to read them and who to trust. They're good people in that community, they just have to be allowed to be good and that's what you have got to do. You have to create that space where they can be good.'

'Come home, baby, now.'

'I'll be home very soon. Say you love me.'

Declan choked. He felt his face and chest go numb, like a heart attack, and he put his right hand through his hair and began pulling it as hard as he could, trying not to cry.

'I love you.'

'I love you too,' she said as she hung up.

Declan kicked the incinerator and his two big toes snapped back. He screamed in pain and then kicked it with his other foot and started unloading the bodies, at a run now. Powered by anger, he finished the job in ten minutes, spitting on the corpses before he threw them down.

Declan sat at Moynalvey cross, his head resting on the wheel, breathing heavily and trying to control the wild, remote fears that kept attacking him, taking the form of strange, lonely images of death in his wife's face. He gazed up at the avenue of bare ash trees in an attempt to purge the visceral images from his skull. He saw a crow with a tiny sprig clutched in its grey beak bobbing and ducking on a limb, making the thin beginnings of a crisscrossed nest during the respite from the snow. The snow had stopped falling half an hour ago and everything was lined with a weak, glimmering sheen of whiteness, the sky an aluminum grey. A text came in on his phone from Marianela telling him to look in the dashboard of the car. He texted back, Come home now, and waited for a reply to his text, but none came. He leant over to the dashboard and rifled through its messy contents. In the back corner, his fingers came upon a square brown envelope. He took it out and gazed at it. There was a lipstick kiss on its side. He opened it and poured a man's silver ring into the palm of his hand. It was half-black with age. He examined it closely and saw figures imprinted inside the band. Squinting, he tried to make out the small cursive calligraphy running around its inverse curve. Mi corazón, mi hermana, tu g. Declan gazed at it before slipping it on to his thumb, three digits away from his wedding ring. He clenched his fist, texted Marianela again to come home and then started crying silently, tiredness draining all the anger out of his system, and he felt the pressure that gripped his heart slip out through his tears.

When the bus came, he wiped his face with his sleeve and checked his eyes in the rearview mirror. They were still red and moist, but there was nothing to be done about that. The girls jumped off the bus, their heavy schoolbags on their backs, and ran over to the car, forgetting to look both ways as they crossed the road, Declan noticed.

'Absolutely freezing,' Violeta said as she opened the door and crawled across the backseat, leaving space for Clara who came in after her.

'I'd say we won't be able to make it into school tomorrow,' Clara said happily. 'Is Mam still not home? Where is she?'

'She's off saving the fucking world,' Declan said.

'That's my mam,' Violeta said, grinning.

'Never you mind that. Why do you children not look both ways when you cross the road?' Declan said angrily, putting the car in gear.

'We do,' they both said.

'Ye do not.'

'I do, anyway,' Clara said.

'If I see you crossing anything without looking both ways I'll lather both your arses with welts.'

'Somebody's grumpy,' Violeta said in a sing-song voice.

When they passed Fagan's pub, they saw a fresh body in the middle of the road. Declan almost didn't see it, as it was already getting dark. He slowed the car and crept the left wheels into the grass and put the car in second, driving at a slow pace up the length of the hill in case there were patches of black ice under the snow. He glanced back at the body. It looked like Aaron. He felt his fears were causing him to hallucinate. He kept driving.

'Dad, have you thought about the owl?' Clara asked, looking at her phone nonchalantly.

'Yes, I have, and it's wrong to cage an animal like that. A beautiful hunter. Also, they're nocturnal, so we'd be kept up all night with the hoots.'

'What's nocturnal?' Clara asked.

'Lives by night, eejit,' Violeta said.

'Don't talk to your sister like that,' Declan said. 'Now, if you were to paint the kitchen this weekend, I might get the bats out of the barn and set up a bird-feeder in there so you can watch the smaller birds.'

'The whole kitchen?' Clara asked.

'The whole kitchen.'

They pulled into the avenue.

'Are small birds birds of prey?' Clara asked.

'Not usually. Some are.'

'I like birds of prey, like owls,' Clara said.

'Owls live on their own,' Declan said, pulling the handbrake.

'I don't like that,' Clara said, shaking her head. 'I think birds of prey should stick together.'

'That's my girl,' Declan said, patting her head clumsily as they stepped out of the car.

'I'm still not painting the kitchen,' Clara said, both her hands tucked into the straps of her rucksack.

'Yes you are,' Declan said.

Declan spent the rest of the evening at the kitchen table, using one of Violeta's copy books to plan that night's meeting. It was so cold in the house that the girls did their homework in the kitchen, sitting by the stove. They all sat around the table, writing. Declan jotted down notes every now and again, getting both impressed and distracted by the mechanical way his daughters were ploughing through their homework. The rest of the time he spent fidgeting, worrying about Marianela, and making pots of tea that the girls did not want. He looked down at his notes and saw they were disorganised, reflecting the disarray of his mind. It was dark outside, but he could hear gusts of wind shaking the trees and blows of snow coming down in blustering drifts, infrequently illuminating the darkness in dull, grey blankets.

When the children were finished their homework, Declan asked them to help him prepare the meeting and they discussed it together. Clara was mainly interested in what the prospective community group would be called, but Violeta made suggestions on how to order the events and how to split the groups up in circles, blocking out negative people by putting them in the same group as assertive, enthusiastic people. Clara, getting bored once she realised that the projected community group would not necessarily be called Birds of Prey, left the kitchen, saying she was going to make a Skype call to a friend.

'Not on my laptop, you're not,' Violeta said, still staring at Declan's notes.

Declan gazed at the silver ring on his thumb as Violeta wrote out the agenda and intended outcome of the meeting in neat print that looked exactly like Marianela's script.

'Pay attention,' Violeta said to him, snapping her fingers. 'Your job is to make it so that you're not doing everybody else's job. People will be interested, they just won't know what to do, so you have to pretend like you do, but this means that you've got to give them choices, so it's them deciding and then you saying what they've already decided back to them to remind them of themselves, and when they get to decide things they'll keep working, or else they're not allowed to keep deciding things, 'cause you're keeping track.'

'How did you get to know all this?' Declan asked.

'The internet, but it's common sense anyway, and I'll have to know it if I'm to open a high-class shoe shop with my friends.'

'You should be a guard.'

'Concentrate.'

They worked for another ten minutes, Declan getting bored and sitting back, leaving most of the work to Violeta, and then he received a text from Marianela that said she was on her way home now. He started laughing. He got up and, grinning widely, swept Violeta up in his arms in a hug. Then, when she was in his grasp, he picked her up and spun her around.

'Put me down,' she yelped, laughing, throwing punches at his back.

He put her down and sat back on his seat, crossing his legs and uncrossing them, tapping the table with his rings, and then he stood up again and gave Violeta a kiss on the cheek.

'You're a weirdo,' she said, wiping his kiss off her face.

Declan laughed again and tapped out a text on his phone, asking her what time she was home. He sent it and started walking in circles around the table, his hands behind his back, glancing at the phone every couple of seconds.

'You're driving me mental,' Violeta said, covering her face with her hands.

Declan leant down and started shoving logs into the stove.

Clara walked in. 'What's all the noise?' she said.

'Dad's gone crazy,' Violeta said.

'You're piling the logs too high,' Clara said, looking at him. 'You'd give out to me if I done that.'

'Were you out talking to your boyfriend?' he joked, making a kiss with his lips.

'You have gone weird,' Clara said, throwing herself onto the couch, curling her legs underneath her.

'Can I put *The Simpsons* on the telly?' she asked, her fingers searching down the grooves of the couch to find the remote control.

'Let me finish this first,' Violeta said, looking down at her notes.

The phone vibrated on the table and Declan leapt at it, leaving the stove open, its heat filling up the room. He fumbled to unlock the keypad and then he read the text. Look up at the sky, it said, and he dropped the phone. He ran across the room, tripping over a chair and catching himself off the wall. He ran out into the night, leaving the back door open. The force of the wind and the heaviness of the snow stopped him momentarily and he gasped with the cold. Looking up, all he could see were erratic waves of snow drifting out of the darkness. There was a flash of light down the avenue. He heard a flap and a dull thump and he ran, his chest pulsing out, his arms pumping, the snow silencing his every move. Clara called after him, and he turned back and tripped at full speed over something soft on the ground. He almost somersaulted into the hedge, but his foot was caught by the curb and he smashed downwards into the flowerbed that lined the avenue. He picked himself up and then got down on his hands and knees, crawling across the gravel, panting until his hands came into contact with cold fur. Peering down and squinting, he moved his hand across the fur until he met buttons and then skin and then a low moan escaped from his throat. Declan clutched the limp body to his chest and leant back so far that he toppled over on his back, dragging Marianela after him. A fierce pain shot through him, and for a moment he felt death, all senses destroyed except for the awareness that, somewhere, as though from outside of himself, he was moaning.

Footsteps crunched through snow and the arms of his daughters encompassed him and then the arms searched and found the body and a wailing lit the darkness, cutting the night in half, a syncopated wailing that meshed into the force of his moan, a force that stretched up to meet their four bodies, then as through a prism of crystal, his daughters' pale faces appeared, framed inside snow-filled hair, tears rolling in drops off their skin but falling into black nothing and he heard Violeta's choking sobs and he heard Clara's silence and he wanted to comfort them, but he couldn't. He couldn't even move and then their noises faded and his vision blackened and everything was darkness.

'The meeting, Dad,' Violeta barked.

He sat up and stared at them. New beings that he had never been seen before. Snow-covered angels that looked like him, that stared at him piercingly with shining eyes, dangerous and beloved. Random mutations of himself had become twin Marianelas sitting before him. He looked at Clara, still and hunched over him, holding Marianela's hand. Violeta was on her knees, holding the other hand, crying and choking, tears seeping down the eyelashes of her closed eyes, snow blowing in ragged gusts across her face. Declan looked down at Marianela's corpse in his arms and gave her a quick peck on the forehead, followed by a slower, gentler kiss on her lips.

He opened his mouth to speak, but then light illuminated everything, blinding them, ripping open the darkness, and another body fell down.

Costellos

The first Irish Costello of the line, Alphonse Costello, left Calais, France in 1574 and arrived in Wexford after two days of severe seasickness. Alphonse was a twenty-one-year-old ship hand who never saw his family again, because after four months on Irish soil working as a bookkeeper, he married Mary Gallagher, an epileptic milkmaid who couldn't speak English, and the couple established themselves in Moynalvey, Meath, two years later on four chartered acres where they raised cattle and chickens for the markets. Several generations were sprung up from Alphonse and Mary, starting with nine live-born children. Alphonse lived a nice, long life, only dying at fifty-six, while raving in his childhood language, Picard, a strange tongue his wife couldn't understand. She thought the Devil had taken hold of her beloved husband and as he expired, a cough of blood shot up from his throat like a vermilion fountain that she took to be the expulsion of the demon and she blessed herself, believing her husband had found peace and then buried him, unaided, behind their potato patch. Three of her sons would bury her four months later behind the same small furrows, though they miscalculated the measurements, so she ended up lying six hands away from her husband and facing west with her hands uncrossed.

Alphonse and Mary, though the first of the line, were the last of the Costellos to enjoy the luxury of falling in love for over two centuries. Their love, though functional, was reciprocal, and developed at a leisurely pace in the decades following their marriage; a strange notion, as romantic love was unheard-of in that part of the country for peasants who toiled all the hours of sunlight the day gave them. But enough of this, a brief word must be said on the physiognomy and humours of the offspring of this union between Mary Gallagher and Alphonse Costello. They did not flourish, but they survived. The men nearly invariably all died in their thirties, but the Costello women usually held out till their fifties. It soon became apparent that the line was prone to heart attacks, bowel cancer, stomach cancer and depression nervosa. The line would often wake up in the five hours of sleep afforded them, shaking and spitting bile, acid reflux tanging the roofs of their mouths, but no one ever mentioned these phenomena as they were seen as personal defects rather than familial ones. They were disproportionately unaffected by alcohol and rarely overindulged in spirits, probably because of the delicate disposition of their stomachs. Remarkably, there is no trace of incest in any of their nuclear families during their whole genealogy, with the exception of many cousins too numerous to mention who intermarried with the necessary dispensation sent from Rome. Their genes led them to verge on the plump side, but circumstances wouldn't allow this to be discovered for another three centuries. In most cases, intelligence and industriousness ran in their blood and they were devout, unquestioning Catholics. They passed the guts of their first century in Ireland peaceably, uninterested in politics or power, but dedicated to business, God, and the growth of the nascent community in their immediate environs. The first official mention of the line came in a ledger held in the Four Courts that was pulped for the British war effort in 1917. It detailed an incident wherein Cromwell's soldiers, the scum, stormed through the parish in 1650 and requisitioned all the property and stock and lands the Costellos had spent four generations carefully nurturing and improving. What is not mentioned in the ledger, though it was a tale handed down from generation to generation before it became so exaggerated that it was lost to the line in the last decade of the nineteenth century, is that when the troops surrounded the granary in Dunsany, one Angela Costello, aged eighteen, mother of three, hid her new-born babe in a jar of butter before she was raped and run through six times with a pike. Soldiers then stabbed every bag of winter grain, and then one milk-fattened lout from Liverpool heard a shriek from within the jar. This nameless soldier held the jar above his head and hurled it down. He dashed it to the floor, exposing an already twisted and broken infant, which he then stamped on with his boots until the babe's head was an explosion of piecemealed grey brain and sharded skull, and then he whooped and yelled and went on his merry way to attack the Fagan's neighbouring farm. Three lines of Costellos who stemmed from Alphonse and Mary survived this holocaust. One line was sent to Jamaica where they were ill-used as indentured servants. As for the rest, they were forced west, both families ending up in Bohola, Mayo, where they continued to raise cattle to varying degrees of unsuccess for a century or so. There is no report of what these Catholics did except for sprawling their sex drives around the neighbouring vicinities where they multiplied like rats. They tilled the earth with cattle and starved to death occasionally, living and dying in one-room houses full of smoke, sleeping beside pigs and chickens, and collapsing from fatigue in fallow fields. Though their numbers increased over the century, their life expectancy did not. Still they clung to the profession and the religion that ensured their bodies and their souls were relatively safe and entirely saved. A quiet century and a half lived in small moments of intermittent joy and contentment and days that stacked up the measure of their short lives rife with disease, boils, toothlessness and hunger, a century lived by the whims of the sun and the rain, and always music on Saturdays. In the proceeding decades of this displacement, only two Costellos worked in trades unrelated to agriculture. Firstly, Abelard Costello, though illiterate, swaggered his way into the priesthood at the turn of the century, whereafter he was sent to Rome as an emissary, where it was discovered that he could not speak Latin, English or Italian, could not read the Bible or give communion and had been ordained by a senile Presbyterian in a waterlogged ditch. He was stripped of his collar and fled to Hamburg in shame. Here he became a dockworker, well-liked by his co-workers because of his dulcet singing voice, which he employed whenever he was shifting cargo. Secondly, Mícheál Costello, at the age of fourteen, was given a small viola by his priest in 1701 in exchange for whitewashing the priest's stables. He taught himself to play improvised jigs, his ear well-tuned to the need of revellers, and travelled the country performing for food and shelter until he was stabbed in the eye by a drunken soldier in 1717 because he did not know the air of 'Greensleeves'. While on the topic of violent deaths, in 1722, one Patrick Costello, a handsome young man who took far too much pride in the scarlet shade of his cape, was summarily executed for poaching three pheasants that he intended to give to his newly betrothed to celebrate Christmas. Mostly it was a peaceful, morbid, impoverished time for the Costellos, who rarely considered themselves Costellos as it was far too difficult to chart their own proliferation. Only two events of note passed in the latter half of the century, mainly that Mary Costello, aged seven, fell in hate briefly with eight-year-old William Brown after attending Mass one day in Foxford; seeing him there tucked up in his Sunday best, she felt an unjustifiable loathing she could not fathom that haunted her for several years, and in 1798 her little brother, Seán Costello, who was collecting mussels in Killala for his mother, who was suffering from severe diarrhoea and who would be dead by the time he got back, looked up and saw a fine boat, like none he had ever seen, that would eventually lead to the very short-lived Republic of Connaught. The general reprisals and fallouts that would abound from the arrival of this militaristic vessel would entail the destruction of that whole segment of the Costellos, not that they were involved, they just represented collateral whose blood was there to splatter across walls and furrows indiscriminately. It has been said not much happened to the Costellos in the latter part of the eighteenth century, but the fact is nobody wrote about these fucking peasants with their scabs and their blindness from birth, the growths on their faces, their lice and their broken hearts, and their little happinesses and their oh-I'll-make-do's as gaeilge, the quaintness of never having a pair of shoes or enough to eat and finding solace only in religion, music and alcohol and the sound of angelic voices that played in their active imaginations and resounded through their skulls, and to give them a voice makes no sense as their voices are only senseless sounds punctuated by small moments of relief, inconstant inebriation and functional sex. Luckily, they were so embedded in the contexts of their own lives that they did not suffer, as they rarely had the time to engage in comparative analyses, to think of the haves and have-nots, leading to the tired and frankly boring debate of whether resuscitating a voice like this is an act of fictive violence, murder of the real voice in short, whether to pass over in silence or to scream, but really to get on with it and just keep on ploughing with that piece of oak which was hardened by the bog and in 1787 of all years Maeve Costello realised she was inordinately fond of her husband seven years after they married and two years before she died, making her the first woman Costello since Mary Gallagher changed her name to feel the bonds and pangs of romantic love that so readily compliment the familial love borne for sons, daughters and grandchildren. But all these piecemeal side-players must be shown as corollary to the great events, or there is just a jumble of lives with no hint of progress, and the sharp distinctions of their characters and their losses are like stars in space that keep shifting and falling without ever being captured in stillness, and this will not suffice. Fast-forwarding to 1846, in the August of that year, nine Costellos, all evicted, all men, all of divers proportions, though all starving, skeletal things, staggered, separately and unbeknownst to one another, for miles and miles to Westport to address the most noble Marquis of Sligo who promised to address Her Majesty most promptly for their systemic peasantic relief. Of the nine that staggered home seven returned, two perished from the strain of the journey and were left unburied, but Erigenus Costello, one of the nine, an emaciated teenager who survived the trek, was struck forever by the journey, forever being the little time that remained to him, for as he walked along the King's Highway he saw three scarecrows who he believed to be the Devil's ambassadors coming towards him through the heavy patter of foggy rain. Two twirled and pirouetted and lurched like ungodly mechanisms, the other crawled like a drowning man rummaging through the seabed for pearls, and Erigenus took fright and hid beneath a mulberry tree and from there he watched them pass. As the distance closed, he discerned two naked men and one naked woman, all skeletal with eyes like moons, crawl and scream and jump on their way to Westport, all having bartered away every garment they possessed for the maize which was destroying their digestive systems and had wiped out their children, the maize's remnants now sending the remaining parents into hallucinogenic pain. Faecal matter trailed from the hairs on their legs that had not fallen out and green bile and coughed-up blood was dried on their lips like a heavy second skin. With each belaboured step, they yelled in mourning for their children and at the pain of the fierce churning in their guts. Their pulsating, shivering ribcages looked so enormous to Erigenus that with each movement they made he could see their heartbeats blast through their chests and he believed that at any point, with a single pulse, the sharp ribs would pierce the pale flesh, like in that film *Alien*, a simile unavailable to Erigenus due to temporal constraints. He waited till they were gone and, petrified, he began crying wildly while steadily munching hungrily on the rotten, shrunken mulberries that still clung to the tree so late in the season, and then he cut across the fields and was admitted to a workhouse because he was young, where he was set to work on the Corrib and Mask Canal and where he died of exhaustion after six days. Later his ghost would trawl through the deserted, derelict workhouses, haunting absolutely no one. His family never knew where he had gone after that day on the highway, but there are too many details, too many people we must cross over unmentioned, unable as we are to delve further into Erigenus's death and how his little sister, Margaret, after his disappearance, drew his portrait every day of her life in charcoal over the ash trees that lined the dirt roads until rickets permanently immobilised her at the age of sixteen. Moving on, Ursula Costello, who was born in 1828 and who died in 1888, was an excellent mother and had the heart of a suppressed revolutionary. Peig Costello, who was born in 1831 and who died in 1862, didn't believe in God and was infertile, and at the age of twelve she nursed seventeen wounded English soldiers who lay face-down in a field in a fierce storm with nothing but a cloth and a bucketful of water, and at the age of sixteen cut the haunches of twenty-four of Lord Lucan's cattle in the dead of an October night as a reprisal for the mass evictions he enforced on his tenants and then went home covered in a sheet of frost from head to foot and laughed when she saw the fire glowing in the hearth. Gabriel Costello, born in 1850, dead in 1910, was a confused homosexual who fell madly in love with one of Michael Davitt's aides after seeing him speak at a mass rally in Swinford. Gabriel never spoke to him and the aide was never aware of his existence, but he nurtured a desire in his heart that enflamed him till his death of syphilis, the pain and madness of which he kept at bay by indulging in legendary doses of hot whiskey. Several hundred Costellos left for the Americas in the latter part of the nineteenth century, and there we shall leave them, dotted in Oregon, San Francisco, New York, Boston, Seattle, Vancouver, Buenos Aires and Bogotá to become charwomen, policemen, gang members, senators, stagecoach drivers and butchers. History's curtain shall only be drawn back on Patricia Costello, whose entire family died on the trip to America and who spent the five years that she lived in the Bronx, New York, trying to earn enough money as a barmaid to get home to Swinford, all the while refusing seventeen offers of marriage from various suitors for the first three years of her residency, before rinderpox took her looks and then the fatigue of it took her life and she was buried in a pauper's grave on Hart Island. Back home the long struggle for sovereignty was under way and the Costellos, in various shapes and forms, were doing their duty, or at least remaining sympathetic to duty undertaken by others, with the exception of Bernard Costello, who was born in 1858 and who died in 1931, who supported his ailing mother by living off funds accumulated by passing on relevant information to Sir John Strachey's enforcers. A much more illustrious agitator was Olly Costello, who was born in 1880 and who died in 1921, a landless labourer who became notorious in the four neighbouring parishes for various reasons, but mainly for marrying Judith Baker, an English Protestant weaver from Foxford in 1902, teaching himself to read English, and for during church services waiting outside the gates for the worshippers to exit holy ground so he could begin to preach to them the justification for the mass slaughter of the viceroy's livestock and the necessity of destroying his properties and razing his crops. He had six daughters with Judith before one night in October when he was taken in by the RIC for collaborating with the IRB to burn down Summerhill House. He was brought to Dublin to be transported to Australia, but before the ship cast off he ate a bar of soap and started frothing at the gob. As the ship was leaving the dock he was thrown overboard by the second mate to assuage the fears of the riotous convicts who were certain he had been inflicted with rabies. He swam to shore and made his way back to Foxford, though the trauma to his stomach was so massive he only managed to survive one month, in which time Judith Costello was conceived. Judith Costello was orphaned at the age of eight and grew up in a pub, whose landlord used her as an indentured slave. She worked as a barmaid, a porter and a cleaner, and she passed a terrible youth sleeping in the storage room where the kegs were kept. Later in life, if she even smelled spirits, she would vomit and would be unable to eat solids for several days. At twenty-two she married Paddy Kelly, who she met in the pub. He was a drunken mess, but he swore off the drink to appease the anxiety and nervousness that her traumatic childhood had inculcated. Paddy, an entrepreneurial Fianna Fáiler, was soon after their betrothal granted seventeen acres in Agher, Meath, by the Land Commission. Together they had nine children, the eighth being Jennifer Kelly, born in 1964, the seventh daughter of a seventh daughter and she slept five to a bed for the first eighteen years of her life. As a nine year old, she watched her mother become eaten alive by the bowel cancer that Alphonse Costello had brought across with him on the boat and it inspired in her a strength and devotion to family that never died. She nursed her mother as she shat blood, and was lying beside her on the bed, reading a story to her, when her mother breathed, coughed, shuddered and died. Paddy, in the three years after his wife's death, tried to unsuccessfully turn from livestock to dairy, became a councillor by default, and then turned back to drink and was killed by a car walking home from Shaw's pub in 1976. Tommy Kelly, the eldest boy but the sixth child, dropped out of secondary school, took over the farm and put all the remaining Kellys through school. Haunted by the drunken, abnormally violent actions of her father during the last three years of his life, Jennifer took on the maternal name of Costello and became the first of the line to go to college. She graduated in Sociology from NUIM in 1985 and went to London to continue her studies, where she dropped out in 1987 after meeting an American. She married him in 1989. The American left in 1990 and Jennifer returned home and became a teacher in St Mary's Convent Primary School in Trim and quickly married a wealthy farmer from Bohermeen who laughed a lot and who had two Junior All-Ireland medals on his mantelpiece. I am born to them early in 1991, the eighth ever Costello to be born above the poverty threshold, and the first middle-class child of my line, and I pass an idyllic youth only traumatised by the frequent death of my pets and the image of Michael Jackson's omnipresent white face in my dreams. Later I am complemented by two sisters and three brothers, who I neglect to the disappointment of my mother, who I idolise, but who does not manage to see that filial affection is a construction of her own process of socialisation. Despite all the privilege thrust upon me, I am a failure. The prospect of upward mobilisation the previous generation of Costellos hacked out of nothing is instantly dispelled by my constant selfishness and laziness and my frequent and very severe bouts of depression. I drop out of NUIG in 2012 and live in Marseilles, France for ten years, working as a barman, and fall in love with one woman; there is only one woman for me, and she is bedecked with a string of nervous tendencies that I believe to be signs of a confused sensitivity, though they are actually the foreshadows of a developing psychotic temperament that will lead to a series of varied breakdowns too numerous to describe, and so I find myself staggering on the streets of Trim again as a thirty-three-year-old man infuriated by a history that is a joke I am trying to stop laughing at and bemoaning a future that I didn't bother creating, knowing that all the dead peasants who precede me aren't allotted a word a corpse, and that if the dead could speak they would be screaming, knowing that I have fucked up so many times that my own redemption will not come about by my own hand. My heart is broken and my failure is total. One solace remains: the year before I return to Ireland to care for my ailing mother, in 2021, my beautiful daughter, Eugénie, is born. While this is to be the greatest event of my life, it also spells the ends of any hopes I ever held. My heart is rent in twain forever. My daughter lives across an ocean from me with her mother, who I have grown to hate because her mental illness seems to find its deepest expression in her nefariously litigious approach to my attempts at childrearing, and half my soul lives with the daughter I rarely see. I spend most of my time trying to earn enough money to shuttle back and forth between two countries so I can hold my daughter at least once a month, and the rest of the time fulfilling the bureaucratic obligations that allow this. When I am not with her I wake in the middle of every night, lost and crying, terrified of her lack, the lack she engendered in me, the hole she punched into my soul on the day she was born. Eventually the pernicious influence of her mother cannot not be redacted by my monthly visits and Eugénie drops out of school and moves to Paris to become an actress and after five years of unsuccess, in 2042, the year of her mother's suicide, she becomes addicted to a heady array of compounded methamphetamines. Luckily, I do not live to see this as I die in 2039, not of the lung cancer I have been diagnosed with, but instead by cracking my skull open on the ice on the morning of December 4 when I go out to the yard to feed the hens and collect their eggs. I bend over and slip and that is it. Though I die relatively young, at this point of our history, Costellos, even the poor ones, are all frequently living well into their seventies and eighties, which is a happy relief after five centuries of highly anachronistic Irish living. I do witness, the day before my death, quite a remarkable spectacle that highlights the first half of the twenty-first century in Ireland, but I am too imbedded in the vestiges of my rural life to understand its significance. At the beginning of the twenty-first century a pseudo-event occurs that the Americans strategically prioritise as a central point in the history of their empire, and it justifies an agenda of securitisation and an assault on civil and social liberties that dominates the following six decades of global life before China, who mimics its American antecedents so perfectly that their transition to power is eminently smooth and astoundingly unremarkable, becomes the dominant player. In any case, the constant state of terror the US has assiduously cultivated, compounded by their ruthless neoliberal agenda set in the 1980s, culminates in all economic concerns taking a back seat to the sexual liberalisation and equalisation of lifestyle practices which does not reflect economic concerns, but which does entail the complete supplication of the remnants of European hegemony. On 3 December 2039, Aretha Daymon, President of the United States, leans casually on her desk in the Oval Office and on live TV informs the world that not only are they bringing public hanging back to deal with both internal and external threats, but that they are building a wall around their country and bringing down what remains of Europe's might, that ancient beast, by refusing to trade with ten of its countries, picked at random. She reads all the countries whose products, services and citizens are no longer welcome on US shores. Ireland, despite its eternal, canine compliance to the most insane whims of that imperial power, is on the list. At this point, I turn off the TV and enjoy my last night's sleep. The disgrace of this exclusion will poison Irish life for several decades and lead to a renewal of the idea that sovereignty is possible in a globalised economy. Unfortunately, this idea is misplaced, as are Aretha Daymon's innovative ideas concerning demonstrative spectacles constructed to distract and pacify the increasingly popular but massively disorganised extremist left-wing groups while not actually giving into any of their demands. Internationally, her spectacles are widely seen, correctly as it were, as a sign of decline and soon the USA's borders are redefined to protect profitable regions, so that the planned wall is scrapped, but smaller walls are built to surround the states of Washington, California and New York. This, in turn, leads to the USA's hegemonic downfall, soon followed by their imperial downfall. But, moving on, Eugénie, under new laws brought in in 2048 loses her citizenship and can only become a customer of the sixth Republic of France and through her drug haze she remembers that she has inherited a property from me in Agher and she moves there, though she speaks no English. In 2051 she meets a distant cousin of hers, John Costello, who shares her addiction and they live in the derelict property that her grandmother and I lived in and they let all the chickens die in their forgetfulness. All the beautiful cats that used to come from all neighbouring parishes to be fed by my mother's hands abandon the property and my pony dies of colic, unnoticed until the smell of its rotting corpse infests the adjacent fields and neighbouring farmers remove its carcass without Eugénie's knowledge. In 2054 she gives birth to Jacques Costello, and in 2058 she and John share a corrupted batch of cocaine in the kitchen and they both suffer from almost simultaneous heart attacks and thrash around on the floor for thirty minutes while Jacques plays with his toy trucks in the corner. Jacques, not knowing what to do, watches his parent's corpses decompose for three days until a neighbour, worried by the uncharacteristic silence of the house, calls round and rescues the dehydrated four year-old. He is raised by his cousins and is half feral up until the age of fourteen when he is sent to a private boarding school by a wealthy benefactor who patronises him after seeing his almost preternatural boxing skills. At eighteen he is legally allowed to sell his parents' property and immediately becomes a wealthy man as land prices in Meath skyrocket by 14,000 per cent in the course of two years because of the evacuation of Dublin due to rising water levels. Private property rights are protected by the coalition parties, meaning that there are now over two million Irish people homeless in a country of six million. Dublin loses the capital to Cork in 2077 and Cork immediately declares itself a privileged principality and declares the remaining thirty-one counties subservient nation states in their own rights, their borders controlled by ever-diminishing UN forces, meaning that passports must be constantly used for travelling across the country. This is done to control the massive urban-to-rural migration of the landless Dubliners who trawl the fields, uselessly urban as they are, in search of elusive food, and who very quickly set up strange, cabalistic, militaristic tribes that roam the hills and sleep and mate in packs. The UN retreats in 2080 and Jacques, a rich, charismatic man of twenty-three, uses his funds to set up a war-like tribe of young Dublin children to raid nearby farms that have been heavily securitised since the exodus. Farmers travel from high-walled village to village in helicopters and each has a standing army of 100 to 200 guards to protect their crops and their Broadband satellites. Jacques, hardened, innovative, ruthless and entrepreneurial, controls the whole of Meath, Westmeath and Longford by the age of forty and invites all young male Dubliners to his lands, promising them food and clean women if they act as his standing army. Within two years he controls a standing army of 15,000 and coalesces his power by marrying a gypsy queen named Jacynythe Rourke, of the Rourke clan, who control the food distribution of Carlow and Wexford. After the marriage he declares himself High Executive of the Extended Province of Meath. The electricity is cut across the island in 2099 and England and France declare war on Meath shortly afterwards, a war they are not prepared for, as they are deploying tens of thousands of troops to China to help the Chinese forces rebuff the guerrilla attacks of thousands of self-declared Islamic caliphates. Jacques heads an army that easily rebuffs the invasion, which he does with the skulking help of Chinese troops and American intelligence, both of those powers having long-term strategic interests in weakening the apparatuses of the remaining major European countries by turning Ireland into a failed state, albeit a failed state that contains factions that, while individually powerful, are both internally and externally conflictive. Jacques, having once been a tactically astute despot, slides happily into chaotic tyranny, his disorganised aberrations encouraged by the gringos who gave him his small allotment of power and the Chinese who maintained it for him. The haphazard nature of his cruelty towards his subjects is only matched by the organised splendour with which he honours his hidden masters, and all his subservient fawning is structured in a careful, unquestioning manner with the express intention of never having to learn the truth, never, at the cost of his sanity, having to acknowledge that all the opponents he wars with in the five provinces of Ireland, all the warlords, whose subjects' heads are adorned on pikes whenever they venture into his territory, are fed by the same hand that feeds him. Jacques has over one hundred children, mostly with slaves, and lives in the wooden, mobile, wheeled palace the Rourkes gifted him as a wedding present and, now, here we are, in 2110, and a fifty-three-year-old Jacques walks through his palace with his legions of armed guards lining the walls, smoking his meth pipe with his robe open and spots a thirty-year-old slave whose only capabilities are cleaning the floors, on her knees eleven hours a day, as her blindness is total. Her name is Mallaidh Céasta and, out of boredom, Jacques impregnates her and in 2111 she will bear two female twins, named Julia and Genevieve, into a world of darkness where millions roam the hills and shooting stars are worshipped and blood lines the passages of every hallway and visions of an unknown urbanity are projected against the sky by EU propaganda satellites and every male lawfully takes the patronymic of Costello and at the age of four Julia will see the fiercest image of God and in her father's solar-powered online library, the only one in existence on the island, and she will spend her youth reading the Qu'ran and the Gospel of John and she will spend her nights drawing maps of the utopias she projects in her mind, and at the age of fourteen Genevieve will read a book written on Irish landless labourers in the 1800s and this will lead her to various PDFs by German sociologists from the nineteenth century and on their father's seventy-fifth birthday they will look at the aging tyrant who has never spoken to them or looked at them, who is unaware of their existence, who will be eating spiced potato-bread fed to him by delicate slaves as harlots kneel before him, blowing gently on the insides of his thighs to keep them cool, and they will make the decision to unite as sisters to wrest away the ungodly power their father holds. The year will be 2133 and they will both be twenty-two, but it will only be five years later that the image of God will be writ large on the subjects of Meath, which leads to Julia's public, somewhat ironic crucifixion on the Hill of Tara at the hands of her father, and then Genevieve will be left alone, tears streaming down her face, and she will watch the thousands starving, jeering at her sister's murder, and she will flee deep into one of the hardwood forests that now bury the island and she will construct a small hamlet made of oak and ash and she will sleep on beds of deciduous leaves and she will plot and she will understand herself and in the silence of the forest, only punctuated by the sound of helicopters, wandering drones and birds' shrieks, she will remember the names of Alphonse and Mary and even the name of my poor mother and all the names that were us and she will remember what she has been born for and she will realise that there is no such thing as memory and that no ghosts exist unless we are made to exist and that all the suffering is determined but pointless unless the egalitarianism of memory is spread through the centuries in an eternal present that stretches towards a point in the future when the planet ends and time is abolished and that all of this is pointless unless the distribution is equal amongst the living, the dead and the unborn and I kiss my great-granddaughter through the shades and Genevieve Costello thinks this and then in 2144 the revolution begins.

No Diamonds

So during the counter-revolution, which lasted a fair bit longer than the revolution, which lasted for about fifteen minutes – the revolution that is, not the counter-revolution; we're forever in the counter-revolution according to the *Meath Chronicle* – we were all of us made shareholders in Burke's mines in Tara.

Tara is important 'cause that's where I brought Sinéad on our first date, but according to John the Hippie, a Texan who dressed up as a druid and pranced around Lia Fáil every morning whenever white sunlight leaked through the smog, breaking up the storms of cawing crows around his feet that looked like blots of tar and who, by that stage, due to a population explosion, basically ran the place, according to him there wasn't always diamonds in Tara, and the Sinéad thing wasn't all that important, or at least not as important as the mines themselves, although I said, 'John, that's just your opinion, Sinéad is the importantest person in the world,' which he said was just, for reals, my opinion. This is the John who preached in shite Irish to a bleary sun, slap-bang next to the M3. We could see him when we swerved by on our way to work, himself doing twirls with the staff he plundered from a Tanzanian witch doctor's grave out in Coole. Whenever we'd get in sight of him as we came round the bend, we'd do a few doughnuts 'cause the motorway was always mad empty by then, except for the few, skinny, raggle-taggle Tanzanians going in no direction at all who padded by half-naked on foot and who me and Mossy would play chicken with, and often mid-doughnut I'd pull down the window and lob a few cans of Dutch at him, and every now and again I'd skull him. John the Hippie, that is.

In any case, whenever I talked to John the Hippie as we were jarring it up on the hill and himself had forgiven me for the braining, watching the heavy green foliage of the oaks, all covered in a bazillion crow dots, the trees flurrying and swaying in the wind like strippers, he'd look up at the foggy blob of sun and say the diamonds were took from Tanzania and transported to Tara.

'These mines, you see, man,' he would say, 'they were like to calm us down, like what happened was crazy. The revolution, man.'

'That was one hot quarter-hour, lad,' I used to say, oftentimes flexing my knees, feeling the soft grass under my bare legs, often pelting my scrunched-up can at a low-flying crow.

'No snakes in Ireland. No diamonds in Tara,' he would sometimes say, shaking his head 'cause he thought it wasn't a good vibe to be trying to skull crows when you're trying to chill and all, and also, John was anti-animal cruelty. Although when he used to talk about anti-animal cruelty it would make me think of cruelty against whatever an anti-animal was, which sounded like a human, or something fucked up anyway.

'Word,' I used to say then, as he would pass me the fluoride-filtered bong and I would often take a cherry hit off it.

'So, what happened,' he would say, 'was the night of all them crucifixions, these drones that were supposed to be planting trees that supergrew with the GMs in them – wait, hold up, they were totally planting trees but, also, they were shooting down a heavy thousand's k worth of microdiamonds, and they, the drones, like totally fucking went for it, and shot down the diamonds into the has-been zinc lining of the old mines that had been all covered up by all the EU nature law-shit-thing, but the diamonds were, like, cut up real fine; they were so small they just nanopored the fuck out of the earth. They just fucking went for it, the drones, that is. And Tanzania was real chill about it 'cause of the fishing stuff we gave them.'

'For reals?'

'For reals,' he would say, sometimes throwing out a hand to the surrounding environs, which looked like a bomb site, and which was actually also a bomb site, a bomb site from where we had been digging all those years, big black trenches that scarred and marred everything, and then I would often see Mossy wave to me on the M3 on his way home from work.

'How's it going, Mossy?' I would call, and Mossy would wave his middle finger at me, put his Corolla into eighth and flip a doughnut to show me he was doing grand and still wasn't seeing shapes, though he could still throw a few.

'So, like, then that was the same night as the revolution, yeah?' I would say to John, though I already knew the answer, and I just there, barely glimpsing his shadowy form through the cherry smoke even though he was only thirty centimetres away from me.

'For reals. When we got wind that there was diamonds in Tara woods, the whole population all put down our butter knives and picked up spoons and shovels and got to digging, and, like, totally stopped giving even the smallest of the fucks about all the crucifixions. And that was five years,' and then if John hadn't passed out by then, he would often say, 'ago.'

And, yeah, that was in abouts the time I started diamond hunting, I suppose, but nobody remembers much 'cause we were all still so chemtrailed out of it, our eyes glazed forever with the blindness malnutrition had put upon us and the promise of diamonds.

In all honesty, though, John was well sound. He had originally been part of a big, gay, free-love druid cult based out in Newgrange and then had left because it had gotten too commercial, so he was still carrying the flame, in a sense. And I used to skull him with Dutch, not out of badness, but because he was part of the Newgrange elite, even if he pretended he was like the rest of us.

And whenever he passed out I would take a moment to reflect on the state of my life, the hot air balloons that didn't venture through the electrical storms anymore, my brother, the heart cancer I had contracted, and if Sinéad would ever come back to me.

Back then, five years ago, times were bad. The council was still sending us out a block of cheese a day through the post instead of welfare 'cause they refused to give the influx of Tanzanians anything with a harp on it and even with all their tech they couldn't tell us apart from the immigrants. All that immigration was stopped fairly quick altogether 'cause of the unrest during 'The Great Sterilisation' as the *Chronicle* called it, and that was why the revolution got to. Got to because of the sterilisation that is, not the immigration. The *Chronicle* leaked that the cheese had implants that were destroying our taste buds so that they could downgrade the welfare cheese from dairy derivative to just pure synthetic, which was more nutritional, the council said, but it made everything kick off, 'cause some of us couldn't enjoy our cherry-scent infusions that we'd ladle out over the cheese. In any case, our taste buds came back nine months later in what the *Chronicle* called 'The Great Rebirth', and the synthetic cheese wasn't all that bad anyway. Like I said, I don't remember much of those days 'cause of the chemtrails, which are still around, but they're more eco nowadays.

I'm saying this now 'cause the day the diamond rush began Mossy had his second manic episode, which was cool, but I still had to chain him to the ash tree in the back field and leave him there for a while so we didn't have to listen to his mad doses of unreal ravings.

It was myself who had set up the manacles and chains and clinkers and all that and rounded them off the ash and they were still there for when Dad used to go on his benders and we'd have to chain him down the back field so he wouldn't mistake me or the brother for Mam. Though one time he mistook Mam for one of ourselves and left her with a raw eye and she was having none of it. 'Now, that's really not on,' she said to me and Mossy as we sat out in the hairy rushes, eyeballing Dad, lying out face-down on the drive, us just idling till himself came-to, basically, and whenever he finally would come-to we'd strip him and give him a lukewarm bath in the sheep trough and pour a cup of coffee down his throat and say, 'You alright, Dad?' patting his forehead real gentle-like, and if he said, 'Oh, my cursed head,' we'd know he was sober enough to have gotten the feeling back into him a bit and we'd get to decking him and Mam would get to putting the point of her high heels in his soft parts and when we were done we'd sling him out the yard for the crows to have a go at. Looking back, I'd say those were probably the best days of my life, the only times I really felt like we were a family.

But it was Dad who asked to be chained up, because after benders he'd often wake up in the maddest places. One time he was missing for a week and that was a bad one anyway, cause Mam thought he was having an affair with Maggie from the shops, which he wasn't, but that's neither here nor there. Anyway, 'Now, that's really not on,' is what she said when he came back that time. She beat him like he was a Tanzanian for it and he ended up going deaf in one ear over it for a few days, so

Dad, who, out of fear for his own health and to prove his eternal fidelity to Mam, brought the chains home one of the nights.

But that same night, he told me, 'I want to know. Before I'm chained, I want to know what I get up to during the blackouts. Where do I go?'

'That's the big mystery, for reals?' I said, sly-like, in that sly way that meant it wasn't really a big mystery at all.

'It is. I have to know. There's things a man must know, son. You'll understand when yourself is a man,' he said, even though he was only thirteen years older than me.

So he tried to rip the microchip out of Bernie, our gorgeous pointer, with his fingernails and then a pliers when that didn't work, and he tattooed it into his own arm. The microchip that is, not Bernie. Bernie ended up bleeding out 'cause of it, and dying, I guess, which didn't even make me feel angry, it just made me feel a bit tired of the whole thing. Tired of life, that is.

'Dad, why'd you do that for?' I said, holding Bernie's furry corpse in my arms, crying into her. 'There's a free council app for to track yourself. I have it on the phone.'

'Those apps do only calculate your fluoride levels for the council,' he said, waving me away as he logged into the cloud catcher.

'Keep your eye on that,' he said, pulling himself up, unscrewing the casing behind the modem and wrenching out a bottle of vodka from where it was hidden in the lining.

After his second bottle, which he'd hidden under the solars, he started calling me by Mam's name and tried to bite me in a leery kind of way and I hit him. He screamed that I was the best thing that ever happened to him as he wandered off out the door after missing it twice, and me and Mossy watched his little Cluedo steps pattern out on the GPS for a few hours as he zigzagged west. It was real sad 'cause his steps were called Bernie, and they were going about the place like a magical ghost, even though Bernie was just going stiff and being all furry and dead next to me.

Me and Mossy fell asleep at about four in the morning and when we woke up we could see he was in Mullingar, where he must have been to see his parents to have a few jars. He had slowed down for an hour or two and then the footsteps started spreading again, going further south. Then, when the footsteps got to Tullamore, they met up with a red and blue dot and the footsteps stopped. The red and blue dot snaked north-eastwards and an hour later there was a knock at the door and Ganley Staunton, our parish's council boy, delivered him to us in a straitjacket, gone blind and dumb from drink. The council boy hadn't killed him 'cause he was hyperlocal, apparently. The council boy that is, not my father.

'How are you, PJ?' the council boy said to me.

'Sound job, Ganley.'

'Anything for a hyperlocal lad like yourself,' the council boy said.

When he left I dragged Dad out down the fields and chained him up, leaving him a couple of blocks of cheese, five shoulders of scotch, a quilt and a hardcopy of the *Chronicle*. We came back the next week to unchain him and he said he didn't want to go home and that he was happy where he was at.

And he was happy. He had constructed half a whiskey still out of the branches that had fallen round him, and though the still looked like a raggedy piece of shite that had more holes in it than it hadn't, it was good to see him working with his hands again, so we left him some more cheese and drink and went on our way.

We'd often leave him out there for weeks on end, happy as Larry, working away, and I'd head down twice a week to drop him the *Chronicle* hardcopy. To cut a long story short, three years later, in and around the time I got my job in the mines back, there was another diamond spray, though this time the diamonds weren't for reals, they were just Fiberglass, but it kept the local economy going all the same, and it meant that I forgot about him for a month or so.

At that time there was spates of real strong acid rain coming down, blown in from a forever hurricane that had come in all the way from Beijing Central, and I went down the back one Sunday morning when it had cleared up a bit and all that was left was Dad's skeleton stripped bare, thin amongst the rusty chains, his bones gleaming white from the acid. Beside his bones was a worn-down etching of an acid-eaten still made out of crooked sprigs and seeing that made my heart do a few turns.

I always felt guilty about that, though Mossy said he was certain he died of natural causes, and I suppose acid rain is a natural cause, but Mam was very tore up about it all, even though she was having an affair with the mayor of Dangan at the time, 'cause my mam was the gorgeousest woman in Meath, and she was doing it for the family cause the standard of cheese we were getting through the post shot up no end, and it was the mayor himself who later got me the fuller permit for the mines that meant one per cent less tax. All the same, she was still fierce hurt, Mam was. Dad was her first love, after all. She met him when she was twelve, just eight months before I arrived two weeks overdue, and they were married just a few days before I got myself born.

Anyway, after Dad died we didn't even need the chains anymore 'cause Mossy had gone normal again after his second manic episode. I suppose we should have expected the second manic episode, 'cause when he was fourteen he started hearing voices from God and set up a little burning-cherry incense shrine to the Virgin Mother in the middle of our bedroom, which made the room fierce smoky and he'd read the Bible to himself at nights, his phone all lit up and visible from under the sheets, and have little prayer sessions during dinner, standing up halfway through his plate of cheese to tell the family, 'Hold on a minute,' before he would drop to his knees and start whispering sacred things unto himself. And whenever I'd be playing the new Mario he'd desolar the modem and look at me, his eyes wide and whisper, 'You know, PJ, I'm not like you. The Virgin is my only mother, not herself over there.' So as he was getting notions above his station, I'd wind him up by hanging off the boiler and tapping at it every now and again until he got to thinking the radiator was trying to communicate messages to him from God, like the real one, or at least the real fake God, I suppose, not the fake British ones Westminster kept trying to get us to worship. I'd do this for a few hours before coming into the bedroom and seeing him there on his knees, sweating and half-burnt, hanging off the radiator; fat, cauliflower blisters shiny on the inner-flap of his ears from where he had pressed up against the divine radiator, and I'd say, 'You need to cool off, lad,' and I'd get to decking him, and if I was feeling up to it I'd hang him by the ankles out the window. He saw me tapping off the boiler one of the days outside of the bedroom anyway and didn't say a word; he was a sly cunt like that, even if he was mad as a brush, and while I was sleeping he wrapped my legs and arms in my own fishing tackle and when I woke up I was pinned down and if I moved a mite the hooks rode up deeper into me.

I was a whole day in bed, dying of thirst, but luckily I had the good sense to piss myself, which made Mam come in and hold up her nose, and say, 'Jesus, is there a Tanzanian in there?' and then she saw me, hooked into the bed and Mossy sitting at the end of my bed, his legs crossed, praying, looking straight at me with his queer eyes, the way he would often eyeball things for hours when he was manic. 'What's all this about?' Mam said when she saw us. And Mossy said that I had been bullying him, and she said that that was fair enough and that she understood he couldn't be having any of that, and then I yelled, 'He thinks the Virgin is his mother, not you.' Mam put her hand over her heart and took a step back. 'Is this true, Tomás?' And I knew then that since she had called him Tomás he was really fucked. 'I'm sorry, Mam,' Mossy said, defiant-like. 'But it's true.' 'That's really not on,' Mam said, leading him outside, where she beat the holiness out of him once and for all, and when he came to he was grand and back to normal, and he didn't have a lisp anymore. Mossy had a lisp. I should have said that earlier, but who would remember such a thing when there's revolutions and Sinéads and such as that to be talking about.

But even though that had happened, we didn't expect the second manic episode. We thought the first was just, you know, being young, 'cause of the state of him, like he couldn't get the ride and we all thought it had driven him crazy. But, apparently, he was borderline and that's a real thing to be, apparently.

In any case, the day after my brother lost his taste buds he lost his mind. My thinking was that the boredom of not having nothing to taste, not having a job, and never getting the ride had finally gotten to him and driven him insane. He got to seeing patterns and shapes. Not real smart patterns and shapes, the way normal people do see patterns in chemtrails and how the wind moves it over time and using that to figure out the council's movements. Not like useful stuff. Mossy saw patterns and shapes like in the way there are patterns and shapes on wallpaper.

We were down the fields one of the days, taking a shortcut, hauling the waste to Burke's bonfire, which blazed so high it could be seen over half the county at night, stretching up like a mad tower, and which had been burning without taking a breather for eight years, and he was barely down Madden's field and he dropped his waste-pans and his eyes went queer and glazed and he stretched out his arms, like he was looking for something in the dark.

'You alright, lad?' I said.

'Black-and-white-striped diamonds—,' he said.

'Mossy, what's going on? What do you see?' I said, throwing the disposable waste-pans down before me where they sploshed and hissed into the burnt earth.

'—with inlaid aubergine tulips.'

'Look at me in the eye,' I shouted, shaking him and slapping him. 'What do you see?'

'Magenta cruciforms inset with slate pomegranates.'

I knew then what had happened him and that he'd gone all manic so I took him by the hand and led him home.

'We're heading, Mossy. Come on with me, you'll be grand.'

'Canary hexagons shifting into obsidian latticed quincunxes,' he answered.

I had to drag him over every stile for two kilometres and to get past the quarry I had to piggyback him up the slippy trail, and finally weave himself and myself up to our rise through the evergreens that sprouted up ragged and so crooked they were almost horizontal. I came up to Dad from behind where he was leant off the ash and I let Mossy slide to the grass where he just lay looking up at the sky, his eyes upturned like he was, the whole of him, dead.

'His turn, now, Dad,' I said to Dad.

Dad, who'd been his rolling around on his belly to cover his skin with muck for to stop the clouded sun giving him radiation burn, shook his empty naggin at me.

'I'm sober,' he accused me, but sad-like, like he never could have imagined a son could be so unfeeling and treacherous.

'It's Mossy's turn to use the chain,' I said.

'A hundred amber ovals, each one the hundredth part of a greater isosceles triangle,' Mossy said from the ground, turning his face into the soil, 'counterpointing one side of an aquamarine octagon.'

'What happened him?'

'Seeing patterns, shapes and such.'

'Like patterns like what?'

'Like pattern patterns.'

'Like how the chemtrails are slow-release Russian antidotes to the water contamination Westmeath County Council are perpetrating, not on the wells, but on the reverse osmosis water filters we buy from Power City to clean already-clean water, but which are actually contaminating the fresh water through corrupting filters—'

'No, Dad, like patterns. Like screensavers.'

'What's a screensaver?' said Dad.

A single red square—' said Mossy.

'Have you at least a drop of red to slake the desert in me?' Dad yelled.

'And, Dad, there's want in you if you think I'm trekking it down here every day to fill your vodka,' I said.

'—on a navy background,' Mossy said.

'Don't interrupt me,' Dad said to the both of us, going cross-eyed with sobriety. 'Filters only made to contaminate the lads who know the water is laced with ecofluoride, but which isn't. 'Cause they know its only thinkers who know about contamination, and so they're the ones to be gotten rid of.'

'That's not a pattern,' I said, kicking his bowl out of his hand and unlocking the bolts. 'That was reported in "The Great Swindle" in the *Chronicle* yesterday.'

I dragged him out of the web of bolts he'd rolled himself baby-like into and put Mossy into them. As I was carrying Dad up the field the revolution started and the choppers and drones started flying low, hundreds of them passing over our heads, the sky going dark with them, until they converged on Tara and started dropping jelly bombs everywhere. Jelly bombs were this fairly newish thing that looked like orange bubbles, but once they touched the earth they swole up until you drowned in them. They could get big as Mullingar skyscrapers before the goo would start shrinking again and end up the size of a fist after a few hours, but only once you were good and drowned from them, left scattered all over the place, and they were very eco. The jelly bombs, that is, not the drowned people. But that was five minutes later. The sky five minutes before that was still black with choppers and drones and it felt like the apocalypse and I left Dad inside the back door, passed out with sobriety, and headed back down the field to give Mossy a drop of tea or something, anything to stop his whinging, and then when I got by the shed I realised that I hadn't any tea so I went into the house again, stepping over Dad's body, and by the time the kettle was boiled the revolution was over.

I went down the field, glad that it had gone quiet again, and tried to hand the cup of tea to Mossy, but he just looked up at me and said:

'Scarlet trapezoids with decadent shading.'

And then another heavy shade came over the mouldy sky, but closer-like, and I looked up and this big, fuck-off hot air balloon was coming down fast on a course to crush me and the brother. The balloon on it was a big yellow colour and it had a picture of Hello Kitty holding an assault rifle and there was some Ogham script below that I couldn't make head nor tail of. The balloon was flagging, deflating quickly, coming towards the evergreens at an angle, and I dragged Mossy out of the way as the balloon tangled itself in the ash and evergreens.

The basket hit the ground at a tilt and out rolled Sinéad in a ball, and she was a vision.

One metre eighty tall, skinny like a rake, curly black hair all fucked up with the wind, animated butterfly tattoo flapping away on her left cheekbone, colour wheel contact lenses, and an Original Tropical Fruit Adidas Tracksuit with pink winged Nike Airs on her feet, waving two 9s in my face once she righted herself, and when she opened her mouth to let out a yell I could see nearly all her teeth were left her.

'You were not reared on cheese,' I said.

She strode towards me, falling a bit, stumbling with dizziness, her guns held out sideways, going off every now and again, one whizzing by near my ear.

'Shut the fuck up, farm knacker, and give me that tea.'

I handed her the mug and she let it down her throat.

'Mind you don't scald yourself,' I said, and she shot the ground near my feet to keep me hushed.

'Beige hexagonal lattices,' Mossy cried.

'The only shape for you is doughnuts, lad,' Sinéad said, tossing the dregs of her tea out, and I knew then that she was the one.

'Will you have another hot drop?' I said, thinking I had heard a mewling coming out of the cradle of the turned-over basket.

'What's that?' I asked.

'Are ye registered?' she said.

'Not since the monthly census.'

'Good stuff,' she said, cocking her 9 and raising it to my face. 'I want more tea.'

'No bother. This is my brother, Mossy,' I said, pointing at Mossy, who was face-down and dusty in the muck. 'He's borderline. I'm PJ, and I'm not.'

'Do I give a fuck?' she said, sticking the 9 in my guts and forcing me up the field. The whole way up the field I was telling her about my brother and his tribulations, and I was talking about my father and his curse of alcoholism, and my mother and her fierceness, and how we weren't really farmers, not really, 'cause we had no animals left, and I can't explain it, but I thought she should know everything about my family and the hyperlocal area, and all she kept saying was, tired-like, 'Would you ever shut the fuck up?'

'Sinéad, isn't it the loveliest day? I don't even mind the taste buds being gone, with such a lovely day as this in it, for reals. Sinéad, I'll tell you this: it's a full-time job keeping this family together, but I think you'll like my mother when you meet her. I don't know if she'd like you, though, 'cause you're very young, but I hope ye get on. She'll soften up in time, once you get the feel of the place.'

'I will blow your fucking brains out if you don't stop looing in my ears,' Sinéad said.

'You're right. I'm blabbing on about myself. I'm so sorry, and how about you? Where are you from? I'm guessing Kerry, probably Ballybunion by your accent. I hear you have many tourists and such, druids and Germans and Chinese and things like that. Are there many Tanzanians? I heard they never made it past the Shannon, but the *Chronicle* does tell us nothing anymore with all those fucking Mullingar reporters, and do you often fly in balloons? That's a lovely balloon. Is it your own?'

'I'm in no humour,' she tutted.

'What's your favourite kind of music?'

'Shut up.'

She dug the 9 so deep in my back that I was winded.

'Well, this is it,' I said, as we got into the house.

'I don't want a tour, lad,' she said.

I stepped over Dad's body and pointed at the three rooms very quick-like, getting very dizzy and breathless with excitement, and then I went blind for a little minute with happiness at how real she was.

'Mine's Afrobeat,' I said.

'Mirror,' she said. 'Then tea.'

We went into the kitchen and there Mam was, legs crossed, mini calico dress on her, smoking Parisian cherry cigars she had off her Dangan lover, singing 'Tie a Yellow Ribbon Round the Ole Oak Tree' in her lovely sweet voice, thumbing her way down the *Chronicle* app.

She looked up and saw the both of us.

'Did you touch my child?' she said to Sinéad, sly-like, like it was the last child of hers that would be touched by any hands of hers. Sinéad's hands, that is, not Mam's.

Sinéad whistled lowly and laid down one of her 9s on the table, like that was the way it was and there was nothing to be done about it now.

'It's grand, Mam,' I said, like I was agreeing with Sinéad's whistle.

'Are you Sinéad of the Hostages?' Mam asked.

'I am Sinéad. There was no hostages, though. Hostages aren't worth nothing, usually.'

'Did ye kill them all?'

'We freed them.'

'But they were killed, then?'

'Ah, yeah.'

'By yourselves?'

'Ah, no.'

'But you knew they'd kill them?'

Sinéad shrugged.

'We all took our chances,' she said.

Seeing my face, the mother held up her phone.

'Tanzanian miners was hostaged. It's in the *Chronicle*. It's herself that started that revolution there a minute back.'

'Wow. That's a great photo of you,' I said to Sinéad, and then back to the mother: 'Is it over now?'

'It is,' the mother said, scrolling down the screen. 'The jelly will go down in about an hour or so.'

She clicked the phone and got the Simon Says app to read us out the *Chronicle* article.

It has come to the Chronicle's *attention that a radical vanguard group,* Simon Says said, *called Rural Ruralification, the split of Free Ireland's split, have, a half-hour ago, tried to kill a load of hardworking immigrant miners, but they was summarily stopped in their dissident tracks by the bold Declan, Mayor of Dangan, who himself let loose the council's dogs of war on the dusty yokes and freed the immigrants from the heavy burden of a life of unemployment. The dole-hungry immigrants, mortified as they were for having been so caught up in the whole affair at all, and scarlet for the hefty weight they put on the taxpayer, the lot of them mass-suicided by crucifixing themselves up eight minutes ago in some queer voodoo ritual led by Declan's main opposition in the council. It is thought that the immigrants done this for to cease from being a serious burden on the beleaguered council.*

R.I.P. Tanya Griffin, who was also lost in the madness. You will be sorely missed, Tanya. Your family is in bits.

The terroristic insurrection was led by Sinéad of the Hostages, pictured below, a fine-looking girl, so good-looking that it is beyond us at the Chronicle *to even fathom the depths of depravity in which this byor must have been reared to have gone so spare. Prior to the attacks Rural Ruralification issued a statement, in which they claimed, 'Your Meath values must be eliminated and that is why we are after your precious white Meath babies, you irredeemable Meath farm knackers.'* To which Mayor Declan replied, *'My childers, Rural Ruralification is claiming to see it the way it is to be seen, but in dark times everyone is blind, and these is the most darkest days in the most darkest times, and rather than claiming to see in the dark times, our focus should be on why it's so dark and that's probably 'cause of the Tanzanians, so in my public capacity I try to remove the dark threat surrounding us and do I get thanks? Do I fuck. All the thanks I get is this fine thing flying about the place in her unlicensed balloons, and I've no time for it. No time at all.'*

The terrorist attack is now slán leat, mo chara, and the jelly will be gone in nigh on twenty minutes from now, so stay inside 'cause that south westerly does be shifting bubbles of it in such directions. Mild showers later on in the north east and midlands. Acid level: negligible. Updates following.

'What's a vanguard?' Sinéad asked. 'Is it a breed of Corolla? Actually, don't bother yourselves, I'll app it later. I'm dusted to fuck. I'll fix up my hair and be out of yours.'

She twirled the 9s a few times.

'There's a mirror in my room if you want?' I said.

Mam sparked up another cigar and poured a dab of DMT on the burning end of it.

'Well, it's great to have you, dear,' Mam said, puffing away, cherry smoke filling up the room. 'Stay a minute and I'll put on the tea. You must be wrecked.'

'No, no, no,' Sinéad said, shaking her head. 'Please and thank you, but I best be gone. I'm not as thirsty as I was and I've to head soon with the cubs.'

'The cubs?' I asked, but she'd already wandered out.

I looked at Mam and Mam looked at me, sly-like, like she knew exactly what I was thinking.

'You watch yourself under my roof, Mr Patrick John Martin Slevin,' she said.

'Mam,' I said, walking out and shaking my head like I knew what she was thinking, but that she was way off and that I was a bit annoyed she'd even think it of me, her eldest and least-borderline son.

Sinéad was in mine and Mossy's room, sitting on the bed, cross-legged and checking herself in my handheld selfie. She had her hair up in the biggest and tightest bun I ever seen, so big it was like a satellite on her head, near double its size. Her head's size, that is.

I whistled lowly. She looked up at me and put the mirror down.

'What STIs have you?' she said.

'Just the usual ones,' I said.

'Grand, so,' she said, checking the time on her phone and taking off her tracksuit. 'I've fifteen minutes and I haven't had the ride in three days, and now Pedro's been crucified it may be another week till I have a minute to myself.'

'Who's this Pedro lad?' I asked, hot jealousy tearing my guts up.

'Would you fucking hurry up?' she said, in that way that wasn't a question at all.

I leant over her, shivering so hard I most exploded there.

'Now,' she said, just before I went up in her, 'if you do come inside me I'll leave your brains on the far wall.'

She pointed at the wall.

So two minutes later when she could see I was near, she cocked the 9 and put it next my cheek and said, 'Don't you fucking dare,' and the barrel was so cold that it was already too late.

'You knacker,' she said, pistol-whipping me to shit, but she didn't kill me and it was then that I thought we could probably have some kind of a future together.

'Well, are you coming or what?' she said, and when I came to from all my happiness we headed down the fields.

The sky was mouldy grey shot through with orange bubbles floating high up in the air from the jelly dispersal and there was the dregs of chemtrails hanging low, about forty metres up, and one of them kind of looked a bit like an M and I thought it was a sign and then a leaping of heavy bass thunder got going and it dropped hard as Sligo techno.

'This is our song,' I said to her. 'The thunder, like.' She didn't answer me.

The rain started slow and heavy with that mild sting in it that wouldn't do too much to you, and I even knew some mad ones from primary school who exposed themselves to it, but if you stayed too long out in it you'd get burns and abrasions and such, so when I reached the ash I hauled Mossy under it. I looked over at Sinéad and she was leant over the balloon's basket and was cradling a little swaddled blanky, nuzzling her nose against it, saying: 'Who's your mammy? Who loves you?'

There was a mini-screech and I seen two baby-pink noses in front of closed eyes. Little furry things.

'Wolves,' she said. 'We're bringing them back.'

She put them back in the basket, hooked in a little perch, and started revving up the engine.

'They won't last five minutes. They'll starve.'

'They're new models, GMs. They live off chemo-flesh, corrupted salmon and the likes. Eat pollution, drink dirty water, shit organic, piss clean, suck in chems, breathe out oxygen. Get rid of all breeds of overpopulation.'

The balloon was billowing up slowly, flapping upwards, fattening itself with hissing air, loosing itself from where it was caught in the trees. Whoosh, it went.

'They'll be shot.'

'Nah,' she said, tapping the side of her head. 'They're smarties. Big modified brains. They breed quickly, too. Three generations a year. There should be a couple of hundred knocking about in no time.'

The balloon lifted off the earth, like it was waking up.

'Well, are you coming or what?'

'Can Mossy come?'

'Whatever,' she said, crawling into the basket and laying herself into a foetal position, crouching up, her head under her arms.

'We'll never make it through that,' I said, shouting through the rain, dragging Mossy by the hair with one hand, pointing at a flash of lightening with the other.

'Don't be a bitch,' she said from beneath her hands.

The basket righted itself as I fucked Mossy in and then the basket tipped up and I jumped and pulled myself in.

We rose up and rose up, all of us huddled into the foetal position, except Mossy who was still sprawly and then, when we cleared the chems, Sinéad got up and pushed at the tiller. The balloon covered us from the most of the rain, but every now and again the rain pushed sideways and would splatter us over the edge of the basket. She dodged round the slow, floating, orange bubbles, some the size of houses, the rain bouncing off them like they'd never burst.

'Fucking my hair,' Sinéad said, hauling at the tiller with both arms.

I stood up, wobbly and shaky, and below me the gorgeousness of life, the vision of Meath, the scarred earth, the breadth of the quarries, and it all at once hit me that the pebbledash houses below me were the smallness of families I had known my whole life and I half-closed my eyes against a sideways gust of rain and felt like I was chosen for to be something bigger than little, or at least chosen to be good at being little.

Burke's bonfire had gone down a few metres with the rain, but she skirted well clear of it, yanking the tiller so fierce I thought it'd snap. We could feel the heat of the bonfire warm and glowing on our faces even though it was still ages away. To the west was Mullingar, its heavy black cloud hiding it permanently except for the flashing off the tops of its pointy towers that peaked over the darkness, and then we were so high that a breath of the freshest, thinnest air I ever breathed made me fall backwards in a faint, and I saw a star, the first I ever seen and I realised I was pure happy.

'If you puke do it south-west or you're getting fucked overboard,' she said above me, not looking at me, and a happy shiver of cold passed through my spine like memories.

I reached over and rubbed the pink noses of the little sleeping baby wolves all wrapped up warm and cosy, cosier than anything I'd ever seen, and I said, 'Will you remember me the way I'll remember you?' and one of them letting out a sleepy whine like it was telling me to fuck off, but in a nice way, and I started thinking on what me and Sinéad's children would look like and if they'd be any good at anything. Would they look like me, but also like Sinéad and Mam and Dad and even Mossy and even Mam's parents and Dad's parents?

I'd never seen them, by the way, Dad's parents that is, though they were living near enough, but they never came to see us 'cause they thought Mam was too stuck-up for a farm knacker and they only thought that 'cause Mam spoke her mind at the wedding and said that she wouldn't be fucking with anyone who called her a child, 'cause she was twelve and she was pregnant with me, and besides, it was snowing, and she in her wedding dress, and they were all bunched out together outside Dangan Church, freezing cold, waiting for the wedding photos, celebrating in front of the graveyard where all my ancestors lay, probably saying, 'Go on, Mam,' from their coffins, and I was in her belly, probably saying the same thing and Mam said she didn't need any fucking help for reals, and I never went to see them on my own initiative 'cause they were Mullingar people, my grandparents that is, and people of that generation scared me anyway 'cause they had never heard of Afrobeat and they lived forever, only ever clocking out at unnatural ages like eighty-four or seventy-nine or ninety-one and such, looking acid-beaten even if they were only just old. Anyway, I thought how me and Sinéad's kids wouldn't only even look like them, but that they would even look like my grandchildren's grandchildren and that was for reals exciting and then I peeked over the edge of the basket and the world was very big below me and the sky was very close and heavy above me and very wet and I could see the Hill of Tara looking so small with its little crucifixes dotted about the place on it next to the old, jammed-up mine all covered in shrinking jelly and then the balloon bursted into blue flames.

'Don't mind that,' Sinéad said, lowering altitude. 'Council precaution. They've contaminated the space now. Stick this on.'

She kicked a plastic bag at me from behind the engine, her eyes still on the skyline, and I opened it up and seen a rake of green gasmasks heaped up one on the other. I took the one that said Pedro on the side of it in marker and fucked it over the side.

'Is there little doggy-shaped ones for the wolfies?' I shouted up at her, fixing one onto Mossy.

'They're resistant, I told you,' she said, taking a flexi Hello Kitty mask from her pocket and shoving it on.

I stuck on my own mask and my breathing inside it was all very loud and my voice was all very muffled and the rain rattled on it hard, so I said: 'I love you, I love you, I love you, I love you, I love you, I love you.'

She kicked me in the face, knocking me back.

'Speaker's on, farm knacker. Mind over there.'

I dragged myself up, feeling the heat of the fire above us and down below there on the M3 was black with hundreds of people running in the rain, the most of them Tanzanians and all holding things, barefoot and naked with war paint all over themselves, rushing towards the hill, some of them holding strobe apps, analogue torches, big shiny knives and ladles and such as that, everything growing bigger as we descended and Sinéad bursted into laughter, like her soul had gotten all big and juicy all of a sudden.

'It's working,' she said, grinning under her mask, stretching Hello Kitty into a queer, seductive shape.

I set Mossy's oxygenator to cherry and he sparkled into life, woke-up and fresh.

He looked over the edge and pointed.

'Floods of shining children washing windows in the evening sun, beige triangles and aubergine circles,' his speaker said.

'It's something, isn't it?' I said.

'The children are catching clouds,' he said, pointing down at the crucifixes.

The heat from the balloon was fierce and we swooped low over the rabble led by a naked John the Hippie, twirling his staff, skipping along, bloody from the rain, sporting a half-mast erection as he hopped forward with a lurchy gait. I didn't even know him then, and I would only ever hang out with him really because he reminded me of that day with Sinéad, but that's not the point, the point is they didn't even look up to see the big, burning, blue balloon cruising over their heads as diagonally we came down on the hill.

'Sinéad, what are we actually doing here?' I asked, holding Mossy's hand to stop him leaning over the edge so far he fell out.

'Brace, bitches,' she said, wrapping her legs around the tiller.

We tipped the ground and were jolted and for a second it felt like we had no weight and were in some dead, feathery place made of crows, which was cool, and then Mossy juggernauted through the air and skulled himself on Lia Fáil.

I staggered round and kept falling over, going in circles, feeling like I was gone pure mad with the heaviness of the earth and its dizziness and all about me was splayed feet and I looked up and saw feet and wooden poles everywhere, stuck in the earth. I took off the gas mask and started coughing up smidgeons of blood. All about me were high-up blacks slung up on massive crucifixes, naked and drooping. Their corpses were in heavy putrefaction brought on quick by the fumes. Even the crows just chilled on the tops of their heads, not even daring to peck at their flesh, such was the state of it. All about me were more crows sitting down, chilling and roosting like they couldn't even be bothered, and everything was quiet.

'Why are we here?' I asked.

'Where they killed us is where we get born, eejit. Now, put on your mask,' Sinéad said, taking off hers.

'I still don't know why we're here,' I said, and then the crucifix next me splintered with a crack and fell over, jamming into the earth, losing the body away from it into the earth.

'Get down,' Sinéad screamed, and started firing at her 9s into the fog.

Council heads in black fatigues and Meath-coloured gas masks were coming out of traps they had laid under the earth, a few streaming out of the Mound of the Hostages, all coming at us.

'They're after my babies,' she screamed, firing away.

I threw myself down on the ground.

'Why are we here?' I yelled, but this time into my hands, and the noise of shots screamed and whistled over my head, and I wondered if Mossy was ok, and when I looked up all the council heads were dead out on the earth on their backs and then a small four-legged animal, bigger than a crow, ran by, but I couldn't see what it was through the gun smoke and the fumes, and Sinéad was spraying down the balloon with a fire extinguisher.

I stumbled up, falling towards her in loose, uneven strides.

'What in the fuck is going on?'

'It's too late,' she said, throwing the fire extinguisher down and kneeling over and examining the fabric of the balloon. 'They've bought off your revolution.'

I looked around. In and about fifty more council boys were coming around us in a circle and were slow approaching, but the most of them were still behind the church at a distance, crouching behind the gravestones, and the rabble was coming off the M3, but in the opposite direction now, away from us, not towards us, and there John the Hippie was, striding forward like he was some kind of hero, leading the pack, a little John-the-Hippie-coloured dot in my vision, still growing smaller, and I hadn't a notion of what they were even at or what was going on.

She pointed at a big swarm of flies about two kilometres away. I didn't understand then, like I still don't never understand nothing, but they were the mini-drones spraying down diamonds apparently.

'They knew we were coming. Pedro, the fuck, didn't put down their cloud catchers. Fucking tout prick scumcunt.'

The balloon was rising now.

'Get in,' she said. 'These cunts don't even deserve my little babies.'

I stood looking at her, the rain stinging my eyes and my lips caked in the blood coming from my lungs. A bullet cracked with a whizz into a crucifix in front of me.

'Are you coming?' she said.

'Can Mossy come?'

'No deadweight,' she shook her head, climbing in the basket.

'Can my parents come?'

She shook her head again.

'Don't leave,' I said.

Behind me, one of the crucifixes exploded in a mist of orange and Sinéad cocked her head.

'Must have put charges in the head,' she said. 'Well, come on to fuck. We need people. I could find some use for you, useless as you are.'

'But my family,' I said.

Another crucifix went off.

'Sinéad, I think you should give us a chance.'

The basket lifted off the earth.

'I'm sure ye'll run out of diamonds someday. I'm done here anyway. You'll know that one day. See you, PJ,' she said, smiling a little small smile at me. 'Thanks for the tea.'

I stared at her rising up, firing at the council boys below her that was closing in on me. She disappeared up into the chems and I put on my gas mask to hide my tears, though it was near pointless with all the blood and acid rain coming down on me in misty blankets. Soon a council head had his gun pushed in my back.

'PJ, what are you doing going around with that mad one?'

I turned around and recognised Ganley Staunton's eyes behind his gas mask.

'Staunton, how's it going?' I said, shaking his gloved hand.

'You best get down to the new mine. There's diamonds to be had.'

Another crucifix exploded near us.

'Are you not going to kill me?'

'Ah, no. You're hyperlocal. Is she coming back?'

'I wish.'

'Sure I'd look as wrecked as you if I had a young one like that.'

'I know, I know. I only ever got the ride, though.'

'More fool's you. Treasure that ride. They're the things that stay with you. I don't know what I'd do without my little Niamh, unreal wagon that she does be being.'

We looked over at the rabble in the distance, all of them running in the opposite direction towards the dark swarm over the mine.

'This is all cleared here. I'm heading out after the lads,' he said. 'Coming?'

I shook my head and went over to Mossy and threw him over my back and trawled the nineteen kilometres home, which took the most of an evening with the rain and checkpoints and explosions and all.

Me and Mossy rested up the next day in the kitchen and I said, looking at the cold stove, maybe I didn't want to work in the new mine, maybe, and Mam said, 'Now, that's really not on,' and I suppose it wasn't. We kept Mossy indoors for a week until he was over his pneumonia, which near killed off the half of him, and then we chained him up again until Mam had him re-reared so he'd understand the difference between what mattered and what didn't and what was and what wasn't and what he was and what he wasn't, and then we let him in the house again.

This is while I would always be waking up at four in the morning and walking to Tara everyday with my earphones in, listening to Afrobeat sixteen hours a day, down on my hands and knees with trowels and spoons, poring over dirt amongst a thousand crowded, pressed bodies digging for microdiamonds, taking thousands of selfies of every spoon of dirt to zoom in on it for to better check, and I did find a few twenty metres down after a while, though their value was near fuck-all at that stage, but it gave me something to do as I wasn't looking for anything else and everything was numb, but times was good all the same, apparently, it's just I couldn't feel it. The good times, that is. I just felt lost and empty, like in that way you do feel lost and empty when you eat something bad and you know it's too late to puke it up and you're going to have to put up with the sickness.

So that's when I would be coming home at one in the morning, dirty and dusted, and sleep in the hall, wake up, eat a smidgeon of cheese and head out again. The family stuff was kind of going alright, but I couldn't feel it at all neither with the numbness inside me, knowing Sinéad was the one and that she was gone, and sometimes I saw the Tanzanian corpses in putrefaction in my head, though there were enough Tanzanian corpses in putrefaction all about me, and so many little scattered Tanzanian orphans going about the place that I shouldn't have bothered my head about it.

Then Dad died of the rain and Mossy stepped up to the plate and started working in the mine so I would only have to do eleven hours a day, and then the mine became so dug out it became an open-top quarry and the diamonds ran out, but a half hour before we got the news that the diamonds were gone Burke's made everyone shareholders so it'd be us that took the losses and then they sprayed Fiberglass down and that didn't fool us, and we kind of all knew, but went along with it anyway for a while, 'cause there was no point not pretending it was any other way or it'd all fall apart.

Then a year later Mam died of malnutrition, though she was eating three meals a day and a snack every second hour, and I took some time off 'cause I only had to support Mossy and he could near support himself and the whole farm was just empty and lonely and I was wondering what I was at, hanging round when there was nothing left for to hang around for, and one day Mayor Declan came round with his armed guard and gave me a used Corolla and, handing me the keys, said, 'Your mam was a fine woman, the finest and the most rideablest, and she asked me if there was ever any kind of thing that I could do for you and loony bin to do it.'

That Corolla kept me and Mossy going for a good while, just doing doughnuts and getting bonged until nightfall and then Mossy got a girlfriend called Betsy and he wasn't round much and I was near twenty-five and still alone, so I started chilling with John the Hippie, shooting crows and drowning in cherry dreams of what I'd spend the next thirty years of life left me doing, and then I got heart cancer and it was looking more like three years.

Those times lasted a long time. Sometimes I would wake up alone in the middle of the night and feel very scared and alone and ask, 'Sinéad, what were you at?' to myself and sometimes I'd wake up next to some brute I picked up in Palace or Fagan's and feel even more alone, and ask her, 'Do you mind if I call you Sinéad?' and if she said yes I'd put a Hello Kitty mask on her and we'd go at it, but somehow it didn't ever feel real.

And then Mossy got to be a problem. Just 'cause he had gotten the ride at long last, he started thinking he could get bossy with me, telling me I shouldn't have a Sinéad shrine in the kitchen and the bedroom. I understood the bedroom being a problem, but, for reals, what else was the kitchen for with nothing in it? 'Lad, Sinéad's not all that,' he'd say and I'd say what the fuck did a little tard like himself know about a very important VIP like Sinéad when he was just a virgin minus one, and then his eyes would go spare and he'd deck me, and since the heart cancer stuff I wasn't able to stop him really anymore and I felt like I was losing him to the girlfriend, so to get back at him, and to get him back, I tried getting rid of his Betsy. So, a few times, before she'd come over for the ride I'd slip a few distilled mushies into his Dutch and talk about birds and balloons loads when he was jarring and I knew he was suggestible and a good few times it worked and he interrupted his riding and threw himself out the window, thinking he could fly.

Betsy said it was really wrecking her buzz and she threatened to leave unless it stopped and though I kind of thought I wanted Mossy back to just myself, I ended up deciding it wasn't what was best for the family unit, so to stop his whinging I talked about Sinéad a bit less than all the time and got rid of her shrine in our bedroom and replaced her shrine in the kitchen for a little mammy shrine, a mammy shrine lit up with a few cherry cigars in front of a photo of her on her snowy wedding day all those years ago, and then I'd sprinkle some DMT on it and kneel and pray to her and ask her for relationship advice, and every couple of days I'd even go down the fields and pour a bit of vodka over the rusted chains round the ash, all Dad's little wooden stills being long disintegrated by then. I wouldn't do this as often as I'd light the cigars, 'cause the father killed Bernie and all, who was probably my bestest friend, or at least my only friend, but still, my father was beyond the hyperlocalest Meath lad that ever came from Mullingar and that was worth something in and of itself.

But when Betsy got pregnant Mossy was all like, 'Betsy's a grower,' and I said, 'That is the for realest thing you've ever said,' and I started getting so giddy and happy that I jumped up and down till I got so breathless I went blind for a second, but then the same evening Betsy went out of the house in the Corolla 'cause she started getting some grower's desperation for eggs, which meant she had to drive up to Maggie's to trade rakes of welfare cheese, and Mossy told me to sit down next him in the kitchen, and basically killed off the last bit of me I cared about.

'PJ,' he said. 'Me and Betsy are moving to Limerick 'cause Betsy says there's too many Tanzanians here.'

'Would you stop?' I said, shaking my head.

'Betsy says you'd say that and that I was to tell you that you could come and that it wasn't a problem in terms of space 'cause you probably only had a few months left anyway, and would probably be gone by before Junior or Juniorette arrived.'

'Don't do that. We're from here and we're only from here.'

'Will you come?'

'I will not.'

'Why?'

'Cause my family,' I said, pointing at the mammy shrine. 'It's just me is left is all.'

'You're tearing this family apart.'

'I'm not. You are.'

'What about Mammy and Daddy, and all the ancestors. They're still there. They're not gone gone. They're just gone.'

'Betsy said you'd also say that and she said to say Sinéad's not coming back so stop being a bitch.'

'Tell Betsy to suck my cock.'

'Betsy also said you'd say that and she told me to say that you could suck her cock.'

'Fuck Betsy.'

'Lad?'

'I'm sorry,' I said, in that sly-like way Mam used to do that meant she wasn't sorry.

'Anyway, Betsy was right. She said you'd never leave here 'cause of your issues over the family and the house and stuff.'

'What are you on?'

'You know, leaving Dad out in the rain and stuff. You've to accept your guilt and your ancestor worship won't do that for you.'

'That wasn't my fault,' I said. 'You were out being a loony bin and Mam was always oiling up the mayor and I was the only one left taking care of Dad. It was only ever me doing all that stuff to keep us going.'

He gave a big sigh.

'That's neither here nor there, because I know that's true, but do you? It's over now and you're stuck to this house 'cause you think what's over has to matter 'cause if it didn't matter it would mean that you done a mistake when you didn't leave with Sinéad.'

He'd taken the air out of me and I felt like he had decked my insides and it hurted more than when he decked my outsides.

'You're a cunt,' I said at him, but he didn't answer.

I looked down into my lap for a second and when I looked up it was like I was looking fresh at Mossy for the first time in years. He was bigger than me and his shoulders was wide, so wide that they was pushing at the seams of his shirt. He slouched like a man and there was two lines of age going across his forehead, which was getting high with a widow's peak, and I felt scared at how time had passed me by, without me feeling it, and I still childish.

'How do you feel about the whole thing?' I said.

'I'm not too sure,' he said, raking his hand through his hair. 'I think a change might be best. I don't want to leave you, and Betsy is very fond of you, but she thinks we have to go and I don't see any reason to stay, bar yourself, and yourself is dying, PJ, and you're not dealing with it. I don't want to wind up like yourself, pining away for a byor I missed my chance with. I'll follow my Betsy.'

'That's fair,' I nodded.

'Well then, will you come?'

'No, I won't,' I said, and then once I said it I realised that the words was true.

'Well that's that,' Mossy said, laying his heavy hands out on the table, and I looked at the scars of mine work running across his palms, all white and crisscrossed, running up his wrists and all the way up his hairy arms, and I seen that they still weren't as scarred as my own.

'Fuck you,' I said, looking away from him. 'You'll come back. I'm all you've left.'

'I won't, and you know I won't' he said, 'and it's the opposite of what you say it is, I'm all you've left, but I'll be there when you change your mind.'

'Just fuck off away from me, you prick.'

Mossy and Betsy packed up the Corolla and left the next day and I spent many days after that going mad in the house, the aloneness of it choking me senseless, walking through the three rooms talking to myself until time made no matter to me and I would wake up in the evening and get bonged for hours, praying to Mam when I thought of it, putting my face to the walls and the floors to feel their coolness and to try to smell things that would remind me of my family, but everything just smelled of cherry my whole life so it made no difference what contortions I put my nose to. A lot of times I would spend hours working myself up to message Mossy and then get too scared to do it, and then I'd fall asleep when the sun come up, 'cause I didn't want to see nothing and I wanted nothing to see me, not even it. The sun, that is.

Then one of the nights I woke up and opened up a can of Dutch and when I got the first lick of it into me I coughed blood for two hours, and I was fairly sure I was dying right there. I passed out and when I woke up I crawled to my bedroom and I looked into my handheld selfie at my ribs all lined up neat and regular, thin behind my flesh, and I realised I'd not eaten in a good few ages. I got Mossy on the cloud and told him I'd be heading down to him the next day. He said that that was grand, that he was looking forward to seeing me, and that he'd come out to the stop to pick me up. When I went to pack, I just stood there in my room, looking at the bed where me and Sinéad were at that one time and looking at the bed next it, where Mossy and Betsy used to be at, and I couldn't take it and I couldn't not take it neither, so I walked down to Tara and had a few jars with John the Hippie.

I done the same the next day, and then the next day, and then the day after that, and it got to be a routine, and I'd sit there for hours harping on how mine and Sinéad's kid would have been much sounder and better looking and less borderline than Mossy's if mine and Sinéad's kid had existed and if Mossy's had been born by then, and how it would be so much better if I was rearing the child, because if he ended up being a boy, I'd teach him how to get the ride before the age of twenty-three, how to be more like me than Mossy, how to have sexual prowess like I had and Mossy hadn't, and how if the child was a girl I'd teach her how to be rideable like I'd be if I was a girl and like Mossy wouldn't be if he was a girl, and John the Hippie would always interrupt me there before I had finished my list of all the things I'd teach the child if I lived and it had been mine and would say, 'I don't know what you're talking about,' and I would say, 'Betsy's pregnant,' and he would say, 'Congratulations. I'm so happy for you,' and I'd say, 'It's not mine,' and John the Hippie would say that that was just, like, my opinion and I'd say it definitely wasn't, and then, one of them endless days when I couldn't remember the last time I was home, I was about to tell him again for the umpteenth time what was what, and then I stopped speaking 'cause the smoke around my bong cleared and I saw Mossy in front of me.

He was in front of me, on the hill, but he was fourteen years old again, just leaning his back on the bonnet of the Corolla, eyeballing me, just the way he used to stand over me for hours and eyeball me whenever he had crossed the border of borderline, but even though I could see him all skinny and gangly and childish before me I knew he couldn't actually be there and that I hadn't seen something, I'd just seen the nothing that was there, and a hopelessness ripped through me so hard and stinging that I was about to start moaning at all the grief yanking at my guts, and then I caught myself and I just said, 'Mossy' once, and then when I had said it, for the first time I fully realised that I was dying, but that it wouldn't be all that bad to die alone given that the living I wouldn't have been doing if I had lived would have been just as alone as the dying I would be doing, or the being dead I would be most definitely forever doing.

'My name's not Mossy,' John the Hippie said next to me, wrestling the bong off me.

I blinked and looked around.

'Where are all the crows at?' I said.

And it was true. There was no living thing anywhere. The only sound was the trees' heavy foliage rubbing itself. John the Hippie looked around at the oaks and at the quarry.

'I don't know,' he said, coughing smoke. 'It's very quiet. This doesn't look too good.'

'There's a billion crows about the place. Where are they all at?' I asked, getting paranoid that I was so bonged I'd come out the other side of death where I could see Mossys all about me, but no crows. I lay back and looked up at the thin chems that streaked and dangled above me.

'Black-and-white-striped diamonds,' John the Hippie said.

'What did you say?' I said, raising myself on my elbows.

'I said I like crows,' John the Hippie said.

'No, you didn't.'

'I fucking love them.'

'You said something different.'

'Hey,' John the Hippie said, squinting. 'Where are all the crows?'

'Fuck this,' I said, standing up and brushing the grass down off me. 'I'm going home.'

'I'll see you, so,' John the Hippie said, laying on his back.

I went down the hill towards the church and threw my eye back once and seen John the Hippie was already snoozing away. When I was in the graveyard below the church I heard a rustling in the mulch beneath a nearby oak tree. I looked behind me, through the spaces between the headstones of old graves and I thought I seen some yellow that looked like drones' lasers, and then I shook off my bonged feeling and went out to the M3, which was as empty as it always was since the Fiberglass rush ended. I jammed my hands in my pockets, and started walking home.

After a while, a council Corolla screamed by and I stuck out my thumb and it stopped beside me. The window scrolled down and there was Ganley Staunton, grinning up at me.

'It's illegal to hitch, lad.'

'Are you going my way?'

'Get in,' Ganley said, leaning behind him and opening the back door.

He flipped the car in a few doughnuts and then slammed a U-ey and started going the long way round, and I was just about to tell him he'd gone the long way round when he said: 'We're running a curfew from tomorrow night.'

'Why?'

'Usual shite,' Ganley said.

His eyes was hard on me in the rearview mirror, and I said I'd say nothing, but I didn't say it. The nothing that I wasn't going to say, that is. He kept driving and driving and we were both silent and I there, just looking out the window, and I didn't even say nothing when he drove straight by my house.

He pulled over when we was near Agher and pulled up the handbrake. We both sat there, quiet, him looking at the steering wheel and myself looking at the thick bog that stretched behind the ditches just before the little heaps of dark Tanzanian shanties started, half of them crooked and leaking into the bog.

'This is you,' Ganley said.

Over the tin roofs of the shanties the twilight was dying a death and the sky was greying quick, draining all the colours out of the chems.

'Janey, Ganley, this is the Congo,' I said, on account of it being the Congo and all, 'cause we called all of Agher to Woodtown the Congo 'cause Mayo people used to live there before the Tanzanians moved in. 'I don't live here.'

'I've been looking at your queer eyes and you do seem a bit out of it to me,' he said. 'Are you sure you don't live here, PJ?'

'I am.'

'Are you sure you're sure?'

'Course.'

'Well best get out and make sure.'

I pulled at the door a few times, listening to the clicking of the handle.

'Door's locked,' I said.

Ganley didn't say anything, so I said to him, 'Tell Niamh I was asking for her.'

'I will.'

'I'll see you at cards on Saturday, so,' I said, still pulling away at the door, my skin gone tight with fear.

'Do you know what we put in that bog?' he said, turning round to look at me in the back seat.

'I do.'

'And do you know how many we've put in there?'

I shook my head.

'Well, that's the thing,' Ganley said. 'Not even we know ourselves. But I've only put one in there myself, about seven year ago, when I just started. One of them witch doctors they have. He was mad old, big white beard on him, must've been near sixty. Lad had to use two crutches to get around the place. Started getting mad eager to be talking, yapping about black messiahs, black unity, loony tune shit like that. You know the way old people do get when they're let get that old?'

I nodded, leaning my head against the window, the breath out of my nose fogging up the glass, trying the door handle every now and again, my eyes going over the bog.

'The thing is,' Ganley said, 'when you start in the council you've to do this thing where everyone's got to do it different their first time, like come up with their own thing, so what I done was I put little balls of ice into his two nostrils and a big block down his throat so he was suffocated inside himself, but by the time the medicals come round it had all melted away, and there wasn't even any marks 'cause the ice was moulded to fit him perfect, so nobody had a clue, and after your man was stuck in yonder.'

Ganley let his eyes flick to the bog before they went back on me.

'Well, what it is, you see,' he said, keeping going, 'is that it's getting messy again. There's been three bodies now all et up in the last week, their throats and guts all missing and stuff, which is grand and all, only problem is we don't know who it is that's done them that way, and that is a problem. So we're gonna have to, as the mayor does say, thin out the possibilities for to better the odds, and I suppose all this is my way of saying you won't be seeing your hippie friend anymore. Now, going the long way round, as you seen we done, my question for you is, is that a problem?'

'No,' I said. 'I know the way it goes.'

'I knew it wouldn't be,' he said, smiling at me. 'You're one after my own heart. A hyperlocal lad. Always took care of the family when you were able, didn't you?'

'As much as I was able.'

'Stop that talk. You was always a family man, always, and I'd say you miss your brother something fierce. I'd say you miss him every day and you're only putting on, hiding all your hurt. So, with that in mind, in case I don't see you again, will you do me a favour? Just one of my notions. Go down and see him. Get out of Meath for a while.'

'That's no bother.'

'Just a council precaution. In case you get any ideas again.'

'Ideas again?' I laughed, not tugging at the door anymore, sitting on my hands for to still them. 'I never had any ideas in the first place.'

Ganley leant back and undone the latch on my door.

'That's a good one,' he grinned. 'Getting ideas isn't never a good idea. Now I want you to take a long walk home, throw an eye over that bog, and have a think on how nice it'll be to see your little Mossy again. You know he left us his address and all before he went?'

'I didn't know that.'

'Very sociable of him. Anyway, that's all, and don't you worry, I'll definitely tell Niamh you were asking for her. Now, out you get.'

'I'll see you, so,' I said, stepping out.

'You had better not,' he said, giving me a quick wink before he leant back and closed the door.

I waved him away as he revved the Corolla, flared up the headlights in my face and reversed into a turn, skidding overlay up about his rear wheels, flicking bits of it onto me, and then he was gone.

Once he was out of sight I sat down on the rise of the ditch, holding my head in my hands, feeling the panic rise up in me, trying to get sick, but I had nothing inside me to vomit except smoke. I was sat there till the cold was going through me like death and the sky was mad dark and then I got a big want inside myself to have a long look at the photo of Mammy on her wedding day, 'cause she was smiling in it and I hadn't seen a for reals smile in a good while.

I stayed on the road till I cleared the bog and the shanties that was all so crooked and droopy and always leaking into the softness of the earth, and then once they was cleared I made my way down backfields by the faint light of Burke's bonfire, which lit the chems with a whitish shimmery glow, the breath coming out of me so cold it was like heavy bongs. I passed by old ash trees, tripping over dead roots of burnt furze, clambering across stiles, getting my feet stuck in big muck piles every now and again, seeing no birds anywhere, but all their nests high up, abandoned and empty like ghost houses. It took me two hours to cut back to the road and I thought I'd meet at least a sleeper checkpoint, but even on the road there was nothing, not even a Tanzanian in sight.

When I could see the gates of my house in the distance I thought I could make out a dark thing on the side of the road in the front of the house, like a car with no lights, pulled over, but when I got nearer the dark shape broke into little pieces of darkness and disappeared into the trees and then I saw that all the lights in my house were glowing and it made me stop dead and I thought I'd maybe forgotten to desolar the lights, and that would explain that, but then I saw shadows moving behind the windows and I heard laughing and noises inside the house, like happy voices, and I knew then all at once that I must be mad 'cause that house was the emptiest thing in the world.

And then it came to me that it must be Mossy, that he had come back with Betsy, and that they hadn't told me to surprise me and happiness swole me up. I ran to the door to tear it open, but the door opened before me without me touching it.

There in the doorway was a young girl, maybe twelve or thirteen years on her, with mad black skin and frizzy hair woven into a dreaded up-do. Her legs and arms were covered with animated tattoos that threw out all manners of shapes, all flowing into one another like kaleidoscopes, and across her belly, stretched big with either child or starvation, was a massive tattoo that looked like an X cut up inside another X, but it didn't shift except for with her breathing, and behind her the house was full of a load of Tanzanian children, even younger than her, all lepping about the place, running and knocking things over.

Another girl came up beside the one who was stood in front of me, and then I realised I'd just been standing there, quiet-like, not saying nothing. The girl was maybe nine or ten and she had big dreads down to her waist and she was wearing one of my mammy's mini calico dresses, which was too long and big for her, so it came down past her kneecaps.

'Who's this?' the younger girl said, in a nice, strong Dangan accent, glancing at my frozen hands. 'Looks like one of them shareholders.'

'Fuck off away out of that,' I said. 'I'm a miner and ye're squatting in my house and that's my mammy's dress, you prick.'

The younger girl made to close the door and I threw my shoulder against it, yelling that they could fuck off out, and I pushed through, sending your one spinning, and then I was inside and the warmth of the house hit me like a glow.

All about me there was so much children's yelling that I thought I'd go deaf and then something jumped up on my back. I fell to my knees, thinking I'd been killed, and a noise so loud came in my ears that it near broke my skull.

'My name is Neema, and you're a Corolla.'

There was a little girl on my back, and I staggered myself up, keeping my balance off the wall.

'Vroom vroom, you're a Corolla,' Neema yelled into my neck. 'Do a doughnut.'

I done a 360 to keep her happy and then I felt a weight on my ankles and there was a littler baby hanging onto me, and I heaved my legs, all slowed down, until I was in the kitchen where a rake of toddlers were jumping up and down on the counters eating all the welfare cheese I had let stack up since I had stopped eating.

'What's that?' Neema said, pointing at something, and I ignored her and yelled, 'What's going on here?' in that way Dad used to yell at me and Mossy to ask us what was going on even if we was doing nothing, but what it always meant was that he had found himself sober all of a sudden and he didn't know what to do with himself because he was sad and he could feel it, like he'd always been sad his whole life, never knowing why, but, anyway, none of them heeded me at all. The children, that is. They just kept on jumping up and down.

'I said what's that?' Neema screamed, yanking at my hair to get my attention.

She was pointing at one of my bongs by the sink.

'That's not for you,' I said.

She started biting my ear and wouldn't stop, so I went over to the bong and filled it half-full with water that had already been shook through the fluoride filter, and then I put a drop of washing-up liquid into the mouthpiece.

'It's a magic machine,' I said, laying it on the table. 'Blow on that and make sure you don't inhale or the residue'll give you fierce nightmares and visions and such.'

She climbed over my head, dropped herself onto the table and crawled over to the bong and started blowing into it. Big bubbles, all shiny like rainbows, started hiccupping out of the bowl and the whole kitchen got itself covered in hundreds of bubbles of mad different sizes and all the children was trying to catch them, running round in circles, making themselves dizzy, bashing into one another, and with all their hands outstretched I seen that their fingers and wrists all had little Fiberglass scars lining and crisscrossing them from mine work and then something warm brushed my legs that made me shiver.

A big wolf went by with a little boy riding on its back, right near me, and it looked up at me with its yellow eyes, and then it turned away, and as it passed me by it gave off a fierce smell. It smelled kind of like warm fur, but like nothing I had ever even imagined possible before, like something much older than everything else, but something new to me, and then the little boy on the wolf's back started howling up at the ceiling with both his hands in the air. The wolf paid no mind on the child, but only swished its big tail once, and then I realised that all Sinéad had ever wanted that day was to distract everyone so she could let go the wolves to grow up with the people who had never had nobody or nothing, so that the wolves could become a part of them.

'I want to go on your back again,' Neema shouted, pointing at me as another child took the bong off her and blowed more bubbles with it.

'Well go on then,' I said, and she jumped on my back, nearly putting my spine out of place, and I limped out, 'cause there was still a little quiet baby hanging off my leg, and I went to the front door where the two oldest girls were still standing, thinking they must be the leaders 'cause they were the oldest and 'cause they were no craic at all.

'Are ye all orphans, or what?' I asked the oldest girl with the floating tattoos.

She looked at me with a big mean look, saying nothing, and behind her the door was still open and through it I seen the chems of the night shining, all the heavy frosty air like mist whooshing in through it with that soft smell of acid on it.

'Their names are Marini and Nuru,' Neema said, drooling in my ear and pointing at the two older girls, 'but my name is Neema, so I'm the best.'

She pointed at herself, real proud-like, elbowing me in the cheek at the same time, and I took her off my back and hung her upside down by the ankles like I used to do with Mossy when he was little, before he got too moody and I got myself too weakened, and then I thought I seen something through the open door, like a blue dot high up in the sky, but there was nothing there, and I knew there never would be nothing there and that unless I looked away now I would just be looking up at the sky my whole life, waiting for Sinéad, waiting for a pattern to happen to me, waiting for someone or something to be there.

But there was only Neema, in front of me, screeching with giggles and swinging her arms back and forth.

'Well,' I asked the older girls, quiet-like, using that quiet voice Mam used to use sometimes, 'is it alright if I stay here for a while?'

The Price of Flowers

Fifteen bloated bodies floated by, bobbing like corks, although one floated by like a corkscrew. I waded back to the bank, nervous, slinging my rod over my shoulder, waiting until the blue bodies, hunched under water like they were looking for something, had slunk away downstream. My everything was wet, which I didn't like, but I liked fishing, although the coodegrass were coming more frequently now, dirtying up the water, being nibbled at by the fishes, being landed on by lazy midges. A fly landed on a midge that was treading water and started eating it, rubbing its front legs together. I was about to get out when I caught a young salmon swimming against the current. By the time I got back to the bank night was everything. I dried out and put my dress back on and made a fire to cook my salmon, but I couldn't get it started so I just huddled up to my heater and ate it raw, cleaning my teeth with the bones as a part of its eye had gotten stuck in me. When I was trying to fall asleep, a toothless feeler snuck up through the foliage. It must have seen the green flashing of the heater and I said, What the fuck you want, bitch?

Can I've some fish? it asked.

Catch your own, I said, happy I hadn't taken out my black eye lenses.

Are you here on your own? it asked, eying my body.

Your mother's out here with me, licking my clit.

I'm Boyne-born, it said, showing me its affiliation marks, and that fish belongs to me and my family.

How many families you got, bitch? I said.

At least a million, it said, and I noticed for the first time how young it was. It was even without beard.

Did ye do the coodegrass here an hour ago?

Maybe.

Well, I've eaten the fish, and I've nothing else, so I suppose you want to fuck me? I said.

The feeler nodded.

Well, I'm Maeve and I'll kill you.

You're not Local Maeve, it said, shaking its head.

I showed it the scars on my belly and then I pulled off my wig and showed it the marks and it slunk off, which I thought was a pity 'cause I was hungry everywhere and it looked fat everywhere, even in the dark. When it had gone I left cyanide vaporisers on the earth that would whirr into life if stepped on, and moved away from the ground and up a chestnut tree in season, waiting for it to come back with its buachaills, but it didn't come back, which is lucky 'cause I forgot to put on my oxygenator before I fell asleep, so if they had stood on the vaporisers we all would have been dead everywhere.

When I woke up I had a pain in my back from sleeping in the tree, but the suctions had still held. I looked around at the beautiful day rising up and then I saw another few coodegrass floating by. One was only a little child with half its skull blown off, its head like a split flower that lives on shoulders. As I was unsuctioning myself something big exploded and I fell out of the tree. A white heat cloud was coming up north from across the border and I got worried. I deflated my heater, collapsed my rod, deactivated my vaporisers and put everything in my pouches, except for the vaporisers, which I always keep suctioned between my breasts, and I ran.

It took me half the morning to get to Trim. I met packs of young feelers twice on the road, but they stood in the ditches, looking at me and wetting their feet to respect me while I walked by. They were so small and respectful that I even told them not to be going that way. They nodded but kept walking and I shrugged and walked into town.

My mammy, the most beautiful woman to have ever lived, wasn't home, so I left her some watered marigolds and hollyhocks on the table and went to bed in the fire room, because I was very tired and had been away for seventeen days without a bed. Dreams drifted by like clouds, all bunched up, and then out of my sleep I heard a knocking and I went to the door and opened it and then I was awake. Outside, there was four feelers of a breed I had never seen before, in perfect, black clothes. Their clothes was flat and clean like they'd never been worn and they had helmets with interactive screens on their visors that flashed images and letters I didn't recognise. They wore heat guns in their belts that they kept touching with the tips of their fingers and I didn't like the state of them.

Are you Bella? asked the tallest one, nearest the door.

No. I'm Maeve. I am Bella's only daughter.

A picture of a childish me eating messy berries flashed on its visor and then some foreign letters flashed up.

Can we talk to Bella? it asked.

Where are your flowers? I said.

It looked at its friends.

We don't have any flowers, it replied.

I won't take offence 'cause you're not local, but if you come visiting again without flowers I will take offence. Does your visor not know that?

It ignored me and tried to hand me a hardcopy.

Please give this to your mother, it said, then it looked at its friends and said, Have we hardcopy for Maeve née Bella, Local Maeve, unfixed abode?

Don't turn your eyes from me again. My mother might accept hardcopy when you bring her flowers.

One of its friends asked, Is oral transmission of hardcopy permissible? I have her details here.

No, the tall one said. Will you, Maeve née Bella, Local Maeve, unfixed abode, accept hardcopy here at an unspecified date?

I don't accept hardcopy everywhere, I said. Goodbye.

Then one of them with an accent I could almost recognise said, Do you not want to know who we are?

I thought I knew its voice and I looked at it, but it had blackened its visor a few shades darker so I couldn't see its face, so I closed the door on them.

I looked out the windows at them for a while, going from family door to family door, giving hardcopy. My mammy lives on Main Street, there are only four houses there, and there are only three families left on Main Street. The rest of the houses are all broken, there are no other families, and there have been no feelers here for as long as I can remember. I don't live here, though. I live everywhere.

For to calm myself I meditated by turning on the fire and looking at it. After a while I felt like I was everywhere again and I marked that it was still light so I walked down the town. On the way, I seen all the Harnon children playing underneath a window by crawling under one another's legs as the biggest child dug itself into the mud. I threw petals over them and then Mammy Harnon waved at me with a lily. She was carrying her shrunken mother on her back, whose feet I had amputated last summer after she suffered a savage attack from Boyne feelers who disintegrated both her ankles with their lockjaws. She waved at me from where she was slung up, plucked the lily out of Mammy Harnon's hand, and offered it to me. I kissed her and asked her how she was keeping, though she wasn't able to speak since her tongue had been cut out many raids ago. I kissed her again and then Mammy Harnon started talking to me.

What do you make of this? she asked, holding my hand and taking hardcopy out from her skirts.

I tried to read it but I couldn't make out nothing from it, the words shifted and there was no alphabet.

There's not even an audio? I asked.

Mammy Harnon shook her head and I told her she shouldn't've taken it from them.

They had heat guns, she said, stuffing the hardcopy back in her skirts to make sure Emma didn't see it. Emma crawled over to her and hid beneath her skirts.

Did you ever see those feelers before? I asked.

No, she said, but there's rakes of Boyne-born heads, feelers, going south to Ballivor. More than I've ever seen. I asked them if they was going 'cause of the heat clouds across the border, but they said nothing.

They're using our roads?

Mammy Harnon nodded.

This is nothing good is what this is, I sighed, picking Emma up and nibbling her ear. I'm going to the infra. Tell Mammy that I'll be back tonight. Does Emma want to come? I asked.

The child looked at me with her big eyes going everywhere and her dirty face and said, No.

The road to the infra is made of dead grass that me and a few women deaden with bleach every spring. We didn't do it this spring 'cause we were too lazy with the artificial sun installation a Cork sales feeler had sold us for a hundred and seventy cattle. We put up the sun in the square and planted twenty or so six-year-old mango trees and then sat in the heat for three months going brown and had a great time of it, GMing fat mangos naked and getting their thick flesh caught between our teeth, sometimes raving in the hothouse that me and a few of the other younger women made out of the hardwood that grew fast in the radiation centres, yipped out of our minds for days in the steam we had laced with amphetamine vapour.

The road was growing back strong and trying to crawl up everything and attack my legs. Ash trees made the border and they were making shade by the time I got up to Maureen's, just up beyond Kiltale. She had a sign painted last year by her sixth daughter that said infralibry and she had painted some shooting stars and hearts on it that looked like eyelashes covered in blood. I stood looking at the lovely wreck of a cottage and then walked around the fields, staring at stupid Aberdeens chewing cud. Then I looked into the tobacco shed that glowed a green, phosphorescent colour. Maureen grew the best tobacco this side of the Boyne. I didn't think about it long, though 'cause everywhere looked so fine and the sky was going orange and giving me dreams and I knew that night I would dream a vengeance of dreams.

I had given all my petals to the Harnon children so I did her a spate of gardening. She had a beautiful patch of gladioli that stretched for half an acre, but everybody worked there so I just weeded some of her tubers and pinched some greenflies into their deaths. Maureen, all crumpled over in her shawl, unbuckled her shutter, leant out her window and told me the heat gun was round the side in the turf shed, hanging off the solar charger. I cocked it, distanced it to the parameters of the harrows, set it from feeler to greenfly, and pulled the trigger and the gun said to me that it had killed 749 greenfly, though I don't know how many that is.

I feel like I haven't paid you at all when I use that, I called to her.

That's feeler talk. That gun will last two more years if I do last a day and you can squash all the greenflies you want then. Come in, for fuck sakes.

I walked into her dark kitchen, where long cutlery, machetes and calf-shanks hung from the ceiling, swaying and jingling with the breeze, making little slapping sounds off one another.

You won't buy another one from Mullingar, will you?

Maybe I will, if the sales feeler comes round. But I'm not leaving the house. They can come find me.

Then she started singing and finishing braiding her wig and I wandered through the hall where the shelves were kept. I found the premillennial section, shady and dusty from the lack of use. It was just a small alcove attached to her hall, but it was the best premillenial section in Upper Meath. I wandered around for a while with just my eyes, already knowing what I was going to choose, and then I picked the prison chapters of the Charterhouse of Parma and brought it to her.

Would you like it in audio this time? she asked, putting her wig away and brushing her grey hair out of her eyes.

Have you my mother's voice on file?

She looked in her drawer.

No. She hasn't uploaded her voice in the last while and I can't keep all the RAM in the house. I miss them cloud catchers.

I smiled at her. I'll take it subvocally, so, I said, laying myself down on the floor.

She hooked up the suctions and visored me.

Visuals? she said through the darkness.

Creeping stars.

Timeframe?

Long-term, leisurely.

Lost sense of time?

Go on, yeah.

Serotonin release?

Have you any spare?

I do.

Go on, yeah. Mild. Slow release.

I heard her hook me up to the windmill generator and then she injected me with the words and the stars crept in. They crept in everywhere for always.

I never understood the half of what Stendhal said, but that's a feeler for you. It's also a feeler you could be proud to fuck. I would've hated to be a human back then, but back then at least feelers had souls and knew how to love a body and not just fuck everything up, although maybe I'm wrong there too.

After all eternity Maureen pulled me back. She took the mask out of darkness by degrees so as not to blind me with the light and the shock of it. I lay there for a while, floating off the serotonin, and then she gave me another booster.

You're always very thoughtful after your premillenials, she said to me, unsuctioning me.

That one's my favourite.

She patted my head.

Do you always keep your heat guns charged? I asked.

I used to worry like you, but then I took a trip to the A.I. bank and I had no time to worry.

Would you hush. One mammy is enough.

And nine daughters is enough. While we're at it, does your mammy not touch up your wig for you? I'd say it's full of tics.

I've been out a while.

How long have you been everywhere this time?

Seventeen days.

Let me at your wig. It's gone blue.

Ah, would you ever stop? Listen. Mammy Harnon says there's feelers mass-migrating south and I've seen far too many coodegrasses and the biggest heat explosion I ever seen I did see this morning.

That's just them, Maureen said. That's their way.

Just mind yourself is all I'm saying. There's new feelers I've never seen before. A new breed giving out hardcopy in a new language.

Northerners make up new languages all the time. They think it makes them strong.

I stopped mithering her 'cause I felt like I was yapping too much into deafness. Maureen lit a torch on the wall with a match, placed it in its wall socket and then, by its light, took some serotonin drops in her black eyes.

I'm going moving cattle. Will you stay here the night?

No. I'll give you a hand before I head back to see the mammy.

How is the poor creature?

She's sore with arthritis of the neck, but the artificial sun is helping no end.

We went out and Maureen sat down on a rusty bath filled with still, black water, all overgrown in floating pennywort, and stared at the sky as I herded the cattle into their shed, poking their arses with sticks. When they were in I forked them out their feed. I licked one on the nose with a kiss and then walked back to where Maureen was sat. We looked at the last of the light dying everywhere. Forests surrounded the little field we had hacked out of ash trees seven years ago. The trees rustled with the breeze and a crow coughed and everywhere was beautiful. I felt lonely for a little while as we waited in silence and then Maureen handed me her pipe and I sucked on it.

Don't you worry about feelers, she said, slapping out a fly that had landed on her cheek before munching it on her tongue. I've never seen a daughter better able to deal with anything than yourself. You just can't do it all yourself, is all.

I shrugged and looked at the trees. The trees was singing and Maureen coughed smoke up into the darkening sky. The smoke wisped out into everywhere, becoming a part of it.

On my way back I was coming up Batterjohn way and the dark was licking my sight it was falling so fast, straining my eyes, so I kept in near the ditches. There was a few young blackberries hanging round, bitter and hard, so I squeezed out their thin juices and smeared them on my face so nothing could see me. Up out of the distance I seen a small pack of Boyne feelers lurking and moving behind trees with daylight torches flashing everywhere, illuminating a whole kilometre above and around them, the grass flashing like dreams as it waved their shadows back and forth. I waited for them in the middle of the road.

One of them was on a grey horse. They tried to pass me without noise, the only sound the stallion's nose snorting dusky air, and I puffed up and said, Get in the ditch, bitches.

They looked up at me and one of them laughed a little sad laugh.

I'll kill you, I said.

You'll kill us, they'll kill us, everyone will fucking kill us. Fuck off away and stop messing.

I'm Local Maeve, I said, and this stopped them.

Why is she called local? said the youngest one, barely a child, to the others.

'Cause I'm crazy, I answered it.

Are you from Trim? the one who had laughed said.

I'm from everywhere.

Good luck to you, so. If you were from Trim you'd be fucked.

What?

The registrars have been through.

What the fuck are the registrars?

They register people up.

For what?

We don't know and we don't want to know and that's why we're going this way.

What happened in Trim?

Trim's fucked.

I looked at them for a moment and then I started running like I'd never run before. I had been running for just a few moments when a swan glided low over my head, about five times the size of any swan I ever seen. A big, beautiful swan with gorgeous white feathers, but I smelt no life off it. I halted, breathed heavy and turned around, fear shivering my spine away. The feelers were still stood stock-still, eyeing me, and then the swan stopped in mid-air and I heard it speaking at them. I began to run back to hear what it was saying. As I ran, one feeler got off his horse and the swan knocked its head off with a blast of heat. It's a drone, I yelled to them, but they couldn't hear me as they were moving all higgledy-piggledy amongst themselves and the swan was screaming a siren. I'd never seen a drone, but my mammy seen a couple in her girlhood and the only way to be rid of them, she said herself, was to lower your heat real low so they couldn't see you. I undone my heat gun, took a deep breath and leapt into the ditch, covering myself with dock leafs and not breathing. I forgot to close my eyes so the muddy water stung my brain, but I stayed under as long as I could.

When I came up, I just saw the horse, calm as day, eating some grass off the ditch, its head low, and six scattered bodies lying about itself. The torch was still flashing, so I could see the feelers' bodies only in flickers, but there was no blood, the heat must've seared their passages shut. I read the sky and it was blank like nowhere and then I tiptoed over. Three of the feelers' heads had been savaged, but the others were just in shock, breathing low and heavy, and in each one's hand, a hardcopy.

What happened? I said, dragging the young one up with a fist.

It couldn't talk, so I put the heat gun on to revive and shocked it awake. It looked at me like it had never ever seen anything before and said, I can't hear my voice.

Its shirt was cut clean open and it had a small red mark over where its heart was.

What happened you?

It looked around, and said, I can't hear my own voice. There's somebody in me head saying where I is and who I is.

Have they put a tracker in you? I said.

It's telling me my own name, it said, looking up at me with its young eyes, and I killed it and then I killed the other two.

I took the horse and galloped it back to Maureen's.

Half of Maureen's roof was gone from where the swan had flown in. I found her on the ground raving to herself, covered in thatch and rubble, her heat gun clenched in her hand. She trained it on me when I came in the door. I said no, but she couldn't hear me and she squeezed the trigger. I felt a little punch in my gut and I looked down, expecting to see my guts gone, but I was grand. I took the gun off her and seen it was still set to greenfly.

Local Maeve née Bella is here, Maureen said, still laid down.

Maureen, I said at her, can you hear me?

Her eyes focused on me and she said, She's here, but she didn't say it to me, she was saying it to herself.

Who's here? I asked, cradling her in my arms.

She's here with me, she said, and I looked at her chest and saw the bead of blood on it. I gave her a hug, kissed her on the mouth and then strangled her. I didn't have time to cry, but I was crying anyway. I ran to the premillenial section and stuffed some RAM in my dress, not even checking what was took. I ran out and leapt up on the stallion and then a whoosh of wind knocked me off the horse. The swan glided over me again and I thought I was dead, but it didn't so much as look at me. It went through the wall of the house and picked Maureen's corpse up and flew up till it was high as a star and then it swooped away to the north. I shot at it a few times, but I kept missing it and then I stopped crying and a heat came up in my guts like summer and I rode north.

Trim was quiet and dark and none of the houses was lit up. It was as though nothing had happened. I unhorsed myself and took out my heat gun and stuck close to the walls. I sidled up to Mammy Harnon's door and knocked, but there was no answer and the knocking felt hollow and empty, as though the sounds was stretching all through the night. The horse whinnied and I looked at it and then it exploded and its guts flew everywhere and its head flew at me and knocked me down. It took me a while to get up and when I did I seen the swan still in the air, silent as dawn, at chest height right next to me. It looked at me and opened its beak and a siren came out that broke my ears. It just screamed, not moving, and then I shot it and it fizzled and crackled and its electronics spewed at me and I shot it again and it fell and my gun told me I had killed one drone.

I ran into Mammy's house and bolted the door up behind me. I looked for her but couldn't find her, and then I heard something move up above me. A woman was climbing down from the ceiling, like a spider. Mammy? I asked, and it came down and looked at me and I saw it was Maureen, her neck still broke and swole, her eyes all queer, and a mechanism attached to the back of her neck that hummed like a deaf child. Hardcopy? she said, trying to hand me something.

What? I said, walking backwards and falling over with fear.

Hardcopy? she said again.

Mammy, I called again, but there was no answer and I crawled towards the door and slunk out into the street.

I looked up and seen a shooting star nestled amongst the other stars, quivering and shiny, but then it started shivering real fast, coming down real close like a comet, and it came closer and closer. I peered up, still on my knees, in wonder at the sight, and then as it got below the few clouds that was hanging the night I saw that it was a swan freefalling down at me from above, still ages away, but coming nearer and nearer. I stood up and ran across to Mammy Harnon's house again and battered on the door, though I knowed it was empty. Then I started hurling myself against the door to break it down, calling the names of all her daughters one by one, but no answer. I hurted myself breathless and looked up and saw the swan getting bigger in my sight every moment, and out of the side of my eye I saw Maureen creak the door open and walk crookedly towards me with the hardcopy in front of her. I raised my heat gun to her and told her to stop creeping at me, but she just kept slinking towards me, no light in the black of her eyes. Then I raised the gun to the skies to see if the swan was close enough to hit, and then behind me the door opened. Mammy Harnon, I yelped in relief, and I turned around and saw a visored feeler with a heat gun poking in my face. I heard the siren of the swan come into my ears like a distant drizzling rain just as the feeler electrocuted me asleep.

I woke up in a large white room, sitting on a soft chair. There was a bare metal stand before me and across from me was two visored feelers. The lights were strong and there was a pain in my chest and I looked down and saw a tiny hole in me and a maggot of blood crawling down my belly.

Are you well? said one of the feelers, who I thought I had seen before, the one with the normal accent.

It came across the table and scanned me.

Are you hearing voices?

No. She's fine. We haven't activated the signal. The relationship between her registration chip and her valves has been established successfully, so there should be no problem charting her subimages. No side-effects so far. She's strong.

So, we begin?

We begin debriefing, it nodded, and then started talking at me. I'm Mark. It's nice to meet you. I'll make this brief. Eighty per cent of the country is now under governance and within a year the whole island will have followed suit. There will be some pockets of resistance and we wish to minimise losses. That's why you're here.

It pointed both its hands at me, like they was heat guns. I kept looking around the bare room, at the wonder of how clean and new it looked and how the light was stronger than summer when you are halfway into a lake and all the water is shining the sun into your face, and it was so bright I knew they must've taken out my lenses.

The Upper Meath area is proving difficult, the feeler said, and as you are widely respected amongst the differing communities therein we would like you to act as our plenipotentiary in that region. With the respect you command, and the space you occupy in the community, you will be saving a lot of lives. We need an easy transition. We will leave you some documentation that you can peruse when you have a moment. They go some ways towards mapping our projection of the near future, which will be bright, if we are able to work together.

The other feeler, the one with the normal accent, drew out some hardcopy and laid it down in front of me and the other kept talking. I looked down and saw the shifting letters that I couldn't understand.

In short, the first feeler said, what you'll find in the documents is the details of our proposed unification. If you require any clarifications on the minutiae, my colleague will give you an oral update on the matters at hand. I feel it would be remiss before we go any further to not tell you that we are asking you now to help us, but, in a sense we are ordering you, as an internally registered citizen of this state. Knowing something of your history, and the health of our own people being a top priority, we only felt this meeting would be feasible if we held some kind of leverage. I am speaking, of course, about your mother. She is in a holding cell in another building away from here and she will be tortured, and, if cooperation is not forthcoming, her life will be taken. I have to go now. My colleague will update you further.

Where am I? I asked as it was leaving, the words sticky inside me.

Dublin, it said.

No, I'm not. There is no Dublin. The sea took it.

Have you ever seen the sea?

I shook my head.

We have been building a series of dams over the past decade to reclaim the taken land and we have by now nearly entirely replicated Dublin, Kildare and East Meath as they were.

I don't care about your business and your runnings around. Let me see my mother now, or I'll kill you both, I said.

Hold that very ambitious thought, it said. I'll be back shortly.

I showed it my teeth, but it just walked out of the room.

I always do what I say I do, I said as I started to rise up, but they had suctioned my arse to the chair. I was left facing one visored feeler. We stared at each other for a few heartbeats, and then I hissed at it and went to shake off my wig so it could see my scars, but then I realised my wig was gone. The feeler started laughing and drew up its visor.

It was the young, toothless feeler I had met at the river. I could see it wanted me to be surprised so I spat in its face. It wiped away the spit and started taking off its trousers and massaging its cock into hardness.

What are you doing with them cunts? I said. Your family expel you for being a bitch?

It opened its mouth and I saw a full set of new plastic teeth, encrusted with diamonds and lined with little glowing wires, and in the hollow of each was a green light that flashed every breath. It tapped them with its fingernails and smiled.

What? I asked. All your Boyne feelers are being killed out of it and you got some fucking teeth?

It didn't answer, just kept rubbing its cock.

Here, child, I said, I don't mind if you fuck me, it means nothing to me, but I am going to kill you. Did you really sell out all your peoples for some teeth?

Nah, it said in its normal Boyne accent, my face was swelling all the time, and I was lathered in sores. My gums would go about the place bleeding for days. I'd say I was dying. There was a hole in the roof of my mouth the breadth of a knuckle, and when I hacked up there was pieces of bone coming out and so much pus I couldn't breathe the dream of a breath. I'd say I lost a slaver of brain as well, since you're asking. They came in and they fixed me in two seconds, swear to God.

It pulled up my dress and shoved my legs apart.

You should have been killed at birth, I said.

They're not a bad lot, swear to God, it said, leaning towards me.

The door opened and the other feeler came in. It saw what was happening and said, What? Then it took out its heat gun and shot the Boyne feeler in the head. Its blood got all in my face, and I blinked to clear my eyes.

When I opened my eyes it was dragging the dead feeler into the corner.

I'm sorry about that. We're not like that, it said. This is what usually happens when we recruit natives. But their knowledge of the terrain is essential at this stage of the campaign.

It laid the body in the corner, and I thought it was going to disintegrate it, but it just propped the Boyne feeler's corpse against the wall.

Did you get a chance to look at the hardcopy? it said to me, sitting down opposite me.

I'd rather his cock than your hardcopy.

Very funny. It's good to be funny. I think so anyway.

It looked at the dead feeler for a second and then started talking. Ok, I've got some time now 'cause I don't have to fill in his employment forms, it said, pointing at the dead feeler behind it.

I didn't say anything.

We are advanced, Maeve, it said. You need to know this in case you choose to resist us. We're more advanced than any other post-deluge island. We even own the seas. You say you've never seen the sea, it's quite something, let me tell you. Anyway, we're not here to talk about that. We're here to talk about progress, namely, and its benefits. Its benefits for you and your people. Your mother's arthritis, it clicked its fingers, gone in five minutes. The food shortages three months a year, they're gone too. The deaths in childbirth, they're gone. I know this may come as a shock to you, Maeve, but we are the good in all of this. We really are. And do you want to know how we do it? How we can offer all this? Let me show you.

It stood up and took a device out of its pocket. It tinkered around with it for a moment and then walked over to the Boyne feeler's slouched carcass.

A scientist in Derry came up with this little treasure last year. Do you remember the robots? So costly to repair and maintain with all the metal shortages. Then there were all the problems with advanced artificial intelligence, usually orchestrated by mad Brits to undermine our sovereignty, and then all the fighting that that led to. It was a nightmare. And then when we had to implement inbuilt obsolescence into each robot to guarantee our safety it nearly bankrupted us all. Inbuilt obsolescence was so unsustainable. It assumed never-ending growth, and it only served the unhappy few, but it served them so well it was mimicked thoughtlessly. Having to rebuild a thousand robots a quarter to keep the economy going, and then having to have them self-disintegrate before they got uppity – it was a travesty. A disaster of irrationality. And this when there wasn't enough metal in circulation to make a hat. And do you think people would work like robots? People are even more expensive. It looked like we were heading towards obsolescence ourselves, but then this, well this, it said, waving the device at me, changes everything.

It attached the device to the back of the dead feeler's neck, pressed a button, and the dead feeler stood up.

Go to HQ3 and ask the serving operative to activate the chip in 173, it said to the dead feeler. Tell them I want a level-one quick-release suspension.

The dead feeler lurched out the room, half its head all crumpled and destroyed, dripping down its shoulder, glimmering blood and brain everywhere, one of its eyes hanging loose and pulpy from a meaty stem that poured out of its skull, bouncing off its loose lips whenever it moved.

See, the live feeler said happily, the reanimator serves as the signal to the central computer, which acts as the brain. Most of the recently deceased body still has its nascent, atavistic intelligence intact, which the reanimator can harness, powering the blood passages, the heart, the lungs. Usually there's so much intelligence in the undamaged nerve endings alone that the device only needs to send out one or two specific charges along the passages. It really is a miracle. When the body reaches a critical point of disintegration, the reanimator is unhooked and attached to another corpse and bang: free labour. The philosopher's stone has been found and it's been found by us.

I set there looking at it queer as the dead feeler came back in silently. The live feeler stood up.

Now look at this, it said, opening its mouth and exposing a set of plastic, diamond-hardened teeth that flashed green, like the dead Boyne feeler's.

Open your mouth, it said to the dead feeler, and then it put its hand in the dead feeler's mouth and fiddled around until it had pulled a thin black cylinder out of one of its teeth with a click.

This is the battery that charges the reanimator, it said, holding it out proudly. It catches the heat off of our breaths and transforms it to energy. It's very resourceful, isn't it? Would you like some teeth like this? Get rid of those rotting stumps in your mouth?

A pain swole up in my chest like my heart was being squeezed, and I felt something move in my ribcage. Anger gushed through me like hot stars.

I haven't understood a fucking word you've said, I shouted. Not one word that's come out of your feeler-mouth, and you've just talked and talked. I want to go home now. I've had enough. And if you don't let me go home now, I'll kill you.

The feeler sighed.

We are entering the negotiating stage, it said, where you are to act as our spokesperson to your people. You have to talk to your people and get them to register or we'll torture your mother for as long as her body can stand it, and she will not survive.

My mammy, I said, doesn't give a fuck if she dies or is hurted, and you'll not get me doing nothing like that. My mammy's with me on this, I know it in my skin. You're just a feeler, even with all your swan drones and your dead slaves, you're just a feeler and feelers are all the fucking same. I'm not a feeler, which means I keep my word and I said I was going to kill you and that means I will.

I suppose I foresaw this, the feeler said, shaking its head. In any case, you should be starting to feel the effects of the chip's quick-release now, so we're going to be leaving you for a short while, but I'd like you to consider one thing before we enter negotiations. Your tribal clan mechanisms and your rituals can remain intact. We're not specifically concerned with them. Your way of life will be relatively unchanged, with a few crucial exceptions. The first item on our agenda is your currency. The flowers, they have to go. I know they are being used mainly for ceremonial purposes, but they're still seasonal, no matter how much you manipulate with their cells, tinker with them or freeze them. They are still unstable. Hothoused or no, they depend on a climate that is fading fast. Your currency first needs to be monetised and then, later, digitised, so we can chart accumulation and maintain circulation. The flowers can still be used for burials and other social functions: greetings, formal deliberations, family gatherings, summer solstice and such, but their exchange value as currency has to be rethought.

Whatever, bitches, I laughed, the pain in my chest becoming near unliveable. Whatever ye're on, that's what I want some of. Talking shite like brain-swole grannies. Go on and fuck off, and I'll be gone when you come back.

We just want you to consider that relatively small proposal while we're gone. How crucial are flowers to your existence? Think about it. We'll be back soon.

It started to walk out.

Oh, wait a second, it said, tapping the screen of its own visor. You can't be comfortable on that chair at all.

It took out its heat gun with one hand and trained it on me. Then it took out a transmitter with the other and said to the dead feeler, Pin her arms gently but firmly to her chest.

The dead feeler came up to me and held my hands crossways against my breasts. Its hands was so stiff my breath was took out of me. Then the live feeler unsuctioned me from the seat with its transmitter, and I stood up, my fingers searching hungry between my breasts.

I'll be back shortly with some infras to help the formation of an agenda for our negotiations, it said, then it seen my hand amongst my breasts.

What are you doing? it said.

I clicked on the cyanide vaporisers and they started to whirr and float and expel the patterned breaths of steam for to drizzle on us. Then the dead feeler opened its cold hands and I was free.

Oh my God, the live feeler said. It dropped its heat gun and started to reach for the oxygenator on its belt. I jumped at it, knocking the oxygenator out of its hand and sat on top of its body. The dead feeler stood still above us as cyanide drizzle turned to mucous and knotted us deep blue between the weaved strands of our skin.

I said I'd kill you.

Let me go, the live feeler said as I pinned it down with all my fading strength, until we was both dead everywhere.

I woke up, one dead feeler under me, the other standing above me. I could feel the cyanide crystals everywhere in my lungs and my nose, but I breathed them out and they floated from me like the butterfly wings that do fall from skies. The crystals were like diamonds before me, splattered all over the ground, shining flowers from everywhere, and I stood up and wiped down my dress and looked around me. Taking the heat gun off the newly dead feeler, I slunk against the wall. Gun out, ready for everywhere, I moved towards the door but it wouldn't open.

Open it, I said to the dead feeler, but it didn't move. I shot it until its lungs and guts was splattered onto the wall, cooked and blackened, stuck into it, high up, the red spray of blood everywhere like raindrops rising up out of the hot summer earth, and then with my gun I heated the device on the back of its neck until it was melted into a mucous pool. I shot the door a couple of times, but it was low on charge and the heat gun faded out of life, and I smacked myself until my mouth and nose bled in punishment for wasting the charge with such foolishness.

Everything had to be done now, but all around me the room was small and white and comfy. There was a nice smell of cooked feeler from off the walls, and I peeled some of it off in strips and ate it for to strengthen myself, and then I pressed up against the wall to shadow the door so when it opened I could take the feelers from behind and gnash their neck veins where their skins was exposed behind their visors.

I was there crouching, dead still for two days, never letting a blink pass over my eyes and then my legs gave out, the muscles all twisted and knotted in on themselves, and I let out a long scream that lasted many heartbeats, for a fear passed over me that no one would ever come and forever I would never be everywhere. When my legs unknotted after the welts of pain was riven out of them with slaps and stretches I ate some more of the feeler burnt into the wall, and when I had finished its haunch I dislocated the knobby end of its thigh bone from the pelvis and spat it down to cleanness, wiping the gristle off my dress, and then waved it around, readying it for if any feelers that came in. I stood by the door another while yet, the fat feeler leg bone slung over my shoulder. Another day I must have passed spent in that position, ready, vigilant forever, ready to get back to see my mammy, but my legs was loose and ready now, my eyeballs twisted at the door in a sleepy half-look.

How anyone could know what a day was in such a white, unnatural place was beyond me, but on what I thought to be the third day, I began spinning with the bone. Spinning and singing. I spun and I screamed, lepping on the table and hurling against the walls, bouncing and bloodying my body with contact and covering myself in feeler blood until my movements became everywhere and I was a circle, and I moved in a circle and the bone moved in a circle as well, though it was a bigger circle than I was for it was freer, and I became free in my body so much that my scream became tuneful and melodic until I had spun every drop of blood into my brain and the whole room went from white to red and then black, and I slept for to make the shivering of my everywhere the size of the bone in my fists so I could control it.

When I woke up the room was dark, and I could feel the slime of blood in my everything. There was a clenching in my chest and a slithering pain in my lower gut and I screamed. I was being crawled through. Then I felt a slick move down my everywhere and a head came out of me, a small silvery head with flat, glistening eyes and my everywhere pushed and a fat salmon fell out of me, flapping in blood. I screamed at what I had birthed, a glistening rainbow thing, beautiful and scared, breathing the dead oxygen of the dry prison.

With long breaths I calmed myself and looked at my salmon child flapping on the ground. I stood up and went over to the dead feeler and with the leg bone I opened up its chest cavity and peeled back its ribs so they looked like the petals of a flesh-flower. Then I emptied out its organs, scooping them with my fingers before putting them on the table for to eat later, and then I let the blood from the feeler drain into the chest cavity, making a pond, and when the blood was enough I put my child in it to swim around. My child was large so there wasn't much room for movement, but it looked up at me and smiled with its eyes, swishing its tail in the blood. I watched it swim in half-circles, and then I became jealous of it for it could see its mammy and I couldn't. I got down on my knees and I dipped my hands into the blood and slipped them together under the salmon's belly, my fingers joining to become a cradle when a small voice said, You shouldn't eat your child.

I turned around and saw there was a fly on the table, perched on the pile of offal. It was about the size of two heads and its eyes was brilliant and red, so big its eyes met at the top of its head. A few black hairs stood up angry on its shiny blue back, and I thought to myself that it was the most beautiful fly I ever seen. Its wings buzzed like humming shadows, and it stuck its sucker into the offal and sucked the blood out of it until the offal had lost its juiciness and was flatter and even deader. Then it stared up at me, rubbing its front feelers together, pointing its sucker at me, its end dripping with blood.

You shouldn't eat your child, it said.

If I squeezed you, children's blood would come out, I said to it.

You've got to stop eating your children.

Help me leave here and I will.

That's progress, the fly said at something that wasn't me. This is good.

What? I said.

I can't help you. You are your prison.

What?

You are imprisoned in yourself, it said.

You are a drone, I said to it, picking up the salmon and putting it in my mouth. It swam down my throat, down my tubes, and into my stomach. I could feel it nuzzle its way through the walls of myself until it was curled up in its womb and got smaller until it was unborn and just a seed egg nestled in the lining walls of my everywhere.

The walls began shaking and then the fly took to hovering, floating over the room.

What? I said to it and it flew towards me and landed on my face, and I could feel its blue fur in my eyes, and then everything was white again and the room was lit and the feelers' bodies was still on the ground, and everything was the way it was before I had birthed.

Everything stayed the same for seventeen wakings. In that time I had finished eating all the feelers' bodies and had made a tent with their bones, and I was still waiting in my tent, watching the door when it opened and the fly crawled in, low on the ground, scuttling across the floor, and it climbed up in the chair.

Sit down, it said, and I climbed up from my tent and sat opposite it.

Now, you see, the fly said, what we can do.

What?

You have been suspended for two minutes. How much time do you think has passed since you've been in this room?

I don't know. A long time, I said.

We activated your chip with the lowest possible functioning charge. The mildest release available to us. We can make it so these negotiations take lifetimes for you, but mere hours for us. Do you understand? You will grow old many times until we reach an agreement. You will live many lives before you agree.

I don't understand anything, I said, shaking my head.

What do I look like to you?

A fly.

I'm not a fly. My name is Mark, and I'm an administrative registrar for Zone M.

What's a registrar?

Your people represent, it said, not listening to me, a sizable threat, not to our campaign, but to the efficiency of its execution, and because of this we are willing to grant your people full right-of-access to the lands north of the Boyne. We can pressure the habitants into relocation, or at least garner a preferential peace between you.

Fuck off away.

I'm not a fly.

It rubbed its antennae off my face, smelling me by touch, fluttering its wings faster than the eye until they were shadows and then it went still again.

But they killed so many of your women. We can grant you justice.

Its antennae caressed at the white of my eyes and then at my dress. I brushed them away.

Why can't you just let us alone? I said. Let us go and let us be and do all this other stuff you're after while leaving us alone. You'll be making everywhere smaller, but we need some everywhere left to us. Just leave us be. Why can't you let us still have ourselves in a littler everywhere?

Good question, Maeve. Good question. We thought about that and there are two reasons mainly. Firstly, you are all too combative and violent to leave unregistered. You would corrupt and grow, and that interrupts and slows integration, especially with your birth rates. Secondly, you kill male children and you still eat human flesh.

No, we don't, I said, angry. That's feeler lies they breed into their young to make them hate us. We used to, many mothers ago, after the floods. Now we just say we want humans at the A.I. bank and if there's ever a mistake and a feeler is birthed we send it across the river to its kind. And at the end of spring if there's no food left we'll eat the feelers we kill when they break our treaty by raiding us. They do the same to us, so would everything.

It's not feasible, the fly said, hovering in agitation, darting round the room twice before landing on the wall. It creates deep-seated enmity and apartheid-like structures that are corruptive.

I haven't seen everywhere forever. I don't remember what grass and humans look like. I want to go home.

You've been here for little more than an hour. Please calm down.

Let me go home.

The fly rubbed its legs together and then its body began shivering and stretching itself out until it was the size of a calf. If flew down to the floor.

Ride me, it said.

I stood up.

How?

Hold on to me, it said, and its hairs bristled up, and I leant over it till I was firmly placed astride it, my haunches hard round it. Its whole body trembled with a sick heat, and it buzzed its wings with a flick, and the wings were so fast that they made me dizzy, and then we hovered out the door, which slid open with a beep, and then we were going forward fast and low, barely a breadth above the floor, coasting down a long grey corridor, so long my eye couldn't hold its end or its beginning. The floor dropped away and below us was a big room spread out, bigger than any I ever seen, with more feelers in it than I could've dreamt of existing. I had seen that many greenflies, but never seen so many feelers. They milled around with machines, so far away that they looked small as midges, walking into the machines and walking out of them. Holding things, lurching things, being dead. I wouldn't have been able to throw a stone at the nearest ones, but even still I seen the black things hanging out the back of their necks.

We produce a drone every half hour at this plant, the fly said below me, its voice nearly covered up by the rush of its wings. And it would be no use to destroy this plant as we have fifteen more off the coast.

Are they all dead slaves?

On the shop floor? Yes, all recommissioned expirations. All controlled by a central computer, which isn't really centralised at all, not in any geographical sense. Various computers in hidden locations project a centralised, coordinated, administrative database in a new growing cloud cluster.

I stared at the dead slaves crawling round like maggots all the way down there, and I felt sick everywhere, the pain in my chest burning.

I want to go home.

You know what you have to do, it said, and then it flew upwards so steep that I slipped, grabbing one of its wings to stop my fall. The wing broke away at my touch, flipping to dust between my fingers, and I fell into one of the machines and died.

The dead slave feelers turned off the whirring machine and hauled my carcass away, and then they put the machine back on and attached the device to my neck, and I fit lenses onto drones in a factory line for seventeen days. When the rot set in fully, I began to fall apart. I lost one arm and then three days later my eyes fell out, and they unscrewed the reanimator off me and threw me in an open mass grave on the outskirts of Celbridge. In the darkness, I could feel my mammy eighty bodies away from me, but I never seen her again. When my brain rotted away, everywhere stopped and there wasn't even darkness to hold me in, and the dead slave feelers never buried me and Mammy with flowers like they were supposed to do.

A heartbeat later a fly crawled its way through the field of corpses, pattering light over the grey bodies, weaving up and down between the knotted bones and dead skin, its wings delicate and sleek, folded against its back. It squelched through the heaped-up rot I was buried amongst until it could smell me. When it found what was left of my body three corpses deep it poked its red eyes between two cut-off right legs that lay on top of me and stretched its antennae forward to feel for me in the dark.

Ah, it said.

Its head touched the severed legs covering me and the skin came off them with a slick suck and the flaps of thigh hung loose off its antennae. It shook them off and laid its wet sucker on me.

This isn't working, the fly whispered into me. Your hallucinations are too violent and they're getting worse. We can see your projections through your chip. They're transferred onto a screen in the next room. We control you.

So please, stop resisting. Please. For your own sake. I can't guarantee your safety without some level of cooperation. I am your only ally here. You need to understand that.

It spat on me until I was soft and then it wrapped its sucker around my head and sucked me up inside it. I rumbled around in the dark walls of its belly, flying inside it until I passed back up through its guts and I fell out of it, vomited up in chunks into the chair in the white room, parts of me falling to the floor.

In the bright room there were four oversized swans whose bodies had a normal size to them, but whose necks stretched to the ceiling, discussing things, curling their long necks and ruffling their flustered, white feathers.

There's too much residual resistance here, one swan said. It's inbuilt. If she is typical of her tribe, it just has to be extermination. That's the only option.

I can reach her, the fly said. I can reach her. I just need time.

One of the other swans laughed.

According to the charts, her antipathy is geared towards you. You are the worst possible registrar for this task. She doesn't respect you and she doesn't fear you.

The fly hovered in circles, spiralling up until it was resting upside-down on the ceiling.

She doesn't fear or respect any of us, it said.

Whether or not she fears us, the first swan said, she is not their leader. They don't even have leaders. They only have mothers, and this one hasn't even birthed yet.

I have, what was left of my mouth said from the floor as my salmon child whispered inside me from where it lay on the chair. I could still feel it hiding inside my rotting everywhere.

Its eyes closed inside of me.

What did she say? a swan asked.

She's still in the transition. Don't listen to her, the fly said. She commands influence, and she is the most mobile of them. She's the one.

She's intransigent, the swan next to the door sighed before flapping its wings lazily. Let's just fully activate her chip and stop play-acting with this piecemeal registration.

No, the fly said. No. No. I veto that.

Then work her.

No.

Why not?

She's too special. Too useful.

There's no proof of that.

We have to reach a compromise.

Well what?

Storage. We'll put her in storage, and then we can release her back once we have registered the area. We can't let her go now. She's too dangerous.

Do you honestly think this area's registration is possible with this level of resistance?

The alternative being extermination? That's unacceptable. On that scale, its genocide.

We have to be pre-emptive. They will eventually force our hand. That's what's going to happen. You know this.

Where is my mammy? my mouth said.

At least suspend her when she's in storage, the first swan said, turning its bill to the ceiling and twisting its neck. At least do that much.

What did she say? the fly asked, flying down and landing on the chair where one of my eyes was, and closing its lid with its front feelers.

When they took me out of darkness, I was older. There were wrinkles on the back of my hands and my eyes were bad.

I could see the beginnings of grey hairs on my body, and I creaked when I moved. They slid me out of the locker and a young feeler took me into the back of a floating vehicle and dropped me in Trim.

How long was I asleep?

I don't really know. Sixteen or seventeen years.

Where is my mammy?

The young feeler shrugged.

That's yours, it said, pointing at a new house, and then it left.

There were no other houses on Main Street, just a new house on a road going through an endless field. Everything was gone or overgrown. I never went into that house, or near it, for its newness put a fear in me. It was feeler-built, and I knew I was too weak for them or their creations, so I moved.

I spent eight days wandering on my weak legs, and I never seen anyone, not human nor feeler. No souls, but some cattle and goats gone wild, beasts that had never seen a human in their lives. It took me a long time to bring them to heel and provoke respect in them, but it helped me as all I had left in me was mourning. I mourned for a long time, mourned for my family, my mothers and my sisters, even for some of the Boyne feelers that never done nothing but hurted us, but still I thought of how those was blessed days when we only had to contend with youthful savage feelers who had stupidness written into them.

One night I almost died of the cold, and I realised I had no business being everywhere as I was too delicate and old, like a toothless sheep mithering the hills that didn't know it was prey itself.

I had no choice but to settle, and I picked the wreck of Maureen's house. That summer I brought myself and some cattle up along to the ruin. I remade her roof out of oak, thatch, and petrified flowers that had been froze into eternity. It took me all summer and then all that winter I rotivated a hundred acres by hand for to plant the biggest stretch of flowers in everywhere to remember my sisters and mammies.

When winter was over I cast seeds for twenty-seven days, and once I had covered the last corner of the plot, my duty done, I realised I was the last of my kind, the last human, the last woman, the last daughter that everywhere held, and I was sick of it, so I went to go to Maureen's for to get my cyanide vaporisers in the knowledge that the flowers didn't need my sight to bloom on their own and remember the lot of us. When on my way home I seen a young wolf cub caught in brambles near a hollow by Batterjohn Cross. I looked at her small fur and seen the two of her front paws was damaged and she blinked at me and yelped, and I seen she was starving so I untangled her and carried her home, and I raised her by my side so as not to be so alone, and I called her Bella. She guided me everywhere, running in front of the horses I rode, or following behind and shadowing my every move. When I dug up turnips or leeks she'd sit by my side, yawning, and I loved her. With her strength beside me, I spent my days tending the cattle that was left and riding across the plains, looking at the old hothouse, the tobacco shed, rebuilding what I could with the tools left me, checking the state of everywhere.

Then the next spring came and it was two years after I had come out of storage, and I was fishing in the Boyne after having spent the morning spraying poison over ivy. Bella was waggling her tail by the banks, stretching herself out and licking her fur. I hadn't caught anything, but I trapped a few pinkeens with my fingers and throwed them to her, and she'd lep up and tear them with her jaws and her yellow eyes all shining. I was leant over, squeezing a pinkeen to death with my thumbs, the water cool and nice against my legs, when a big bang came up out of the north, and I fainted with fear from the memory of the coodegrass, like as if it was happening to me new again for the first time when all the badness started. Then the spring of water around my ears awoke me up, and I felt crazy I had gone so soft.

Me and Bella walked north for a half hour and we came across a team of live feelers keying in instructions to machines that were birthing stones. One machine would birth a stone and then shift itself and then birth another, while a machine after it would glue it with another one on top of it, going round and round, like the stars seen inside heads.

What are you doing with everywhere? I said to the nearest feeler, though the words came out sideways and crooked 'cause I hadn't spoke in so long.

Maeve, it said, keying in notes to its pad, unsurprised to see me, its eyes averted from me respectfully. Mark 176363 wants to speak with you. He's at your residence.

I've no residence. What are you doing here? 'Fore I kill you, tell me.

We're enclosing the space, the Upper Meath space, to protect its fauna.

What's a fauna?

I don't know.

Tell me, bitch.

You, I think, maybe.

I let Bella loose on them, and she de-throated one before they shot her down. I ran over to her and seen she was still breathing. I buried me in her fur and let out a happy sob that she wasn't dead. Two feelers had their heat guns on me, striding towards me, but the one I had spoke to jumped in front of them.

No, it said. She's protected.

Let it go extinct, the other feeler said. It killed Séan, the bitch.

No, it said again, raising its arms. No.

I stood up and came up behind the one with its hands up, and I bit into its neck vein and watched as the blood spurted high into the clouded sky. It staggered around, looking shocked, pressing its fingers against the spray.

Kill me, bitches, I said, raising my hands to the sky. Kill me.

The hurted feeler did a turn in the grass and fell on its hands and knees, breathing and lowing like an orphaned calf, before it collapsed.

I spat blood at the live feelers. They held their heat guns to me and advanced until they was covering the other's feeler's body, and then they dragged it back to their machines, their guns still trained on me. The machines had built a lot of wall in such a little space of day, but I just kept my eyes on them. Then I took Bella's hefty body over my shoulder and carried her down towards the Boyne.

When I crossed the shallow part of river, a massive swan drone flew low over me with a hissing noise and landed on the bank, and then its arse opened up and a feeler stepped out of it. It looked old, the hair that was left it was grey, slicked back on its shiny, high skull, and it wore one big black piece of clothes. It was clean-looking. Even in age it looked clean, and I felt my hatred pour through me, and Bella in her sleep let out a growl and then woke.

Hello, Maeve, it said. It's been a long time.

You are speaking as though I were to know you.

Do you not recognise me? Of course you wouldn't, without my gear. I'm Mark. It's been a long time.

What are ye doing here?

It came towards me, and I patted Bella back, so she'd stay down on the grass. She whimpered with a low growl, like she did do when she was nightmaring. As it came near me I jumped on top of it, my fingers pressed against its throat.

Maeve, it gagged, as it spread out on the grass. Let me go. This is silly. You can't keep doing this. Look, I brought you a present. Please, look at it.

What are you saying? I said, releasing my hold on its throat and pushing down my skirt.

Check in my breast pocket.

I rooted in its pockets and I pulled out some RAM.

They're your files. Do you not remember?

I let go my fingers from its throat, throwing the RAM on the grass away from me.

Did you kill Séan and injure Luke? it asked, raising itself up on its elbows. You can't do that. You can't keep going on like a child. You'll undo everything we've been working towards.

Do you think I give a fuck about RAM?

I stared down at it, an old, wrinkled feeler, disgusting and unnatural, and thought I probably looked the same way to it. These new feelers lived forever. They were older than any humans ever got.

I have been petitioning to enclose this area to protect you for five years, it said, and we've finally done it. The only concession is its open for viewing once a day. There will be a set path, clearly demarcated, that allows limited access through your land.

It's not my land, I said to it. It's just not yours.

It looked up at me, its eyes hurt.

Can't you see I'm your friend? The only one you've got.

You killed all my peoples and you think you can chat with me? I've been made to be alone. You made me alone.

You're brain damaged. I'm sorry.

I'm not like that anymore.

It's my fault, but we had no choice. Those were violent times.

In a flash like wind it raised its palm up against my throat with a flick, and I was breathless and choking on my back, and through my tears I seen it gathering itself up and trotting towards its drone. I hit the earth with my fists, thinking my windpipe was broke, and Bella's small yellow eyes flickered open. She had been daydreaming, but now she raised herself up, shook out her fur, tramped lazily over to me and sniffed me. I pointed at the feeler and coughed, and she was up after it, and in a few strides had it pinned down, waiting on me. I could hear it moaning and weak under Bella's weight as I pushed myself up and staggered, swaying like storm-bruised branches, towards it.

How many times do I have to kill you? I asked it, my voice croaking, my breathing coming back inside me.

Tears were streaming down its face, and I leant down and licked them up off its salty, hard-skinned, hairy feeler face.

No, the feeler said, shaking its head.

I lowered over it and opened its neck vein with my teeth.

I spat its own blood in its face and said, Now, you may rise up and do a tap of feeler work, you dead slave bitch.

I covered its nose and its mouth and Bella jumped up on her back legs and howled, shocked into happiness by the fountain of blood. Then she moseyed towards the source, and I let her lap up the blood. When it was dead, she waggled her tail and she went off digging under furze for leverets. I rolled the swan drone into the Boyne behind a pebble-dash hollow to act as a fish trap, spreading its wings at sharp angles for when the salmon came upstream, and then I picked up the RAM from the grass and me and Bella traipsed back to Maureen's. I looked behind me. Over the feeler's slouched dead body, in the distance, I seen the wall getting higher and higher.

A few days later a big vehicle made out of windows floated by over my head when I was out on my hands and knees flicking into the dirt of Maureen's budding garden for to find tubers. I looked up at it and hissed. Hundreds of young feeler faces were pressed up against the glass, pointing down at me, and then a big voice came out of the vehicle saying the feeler names of the trees around me and Bella howled, and then I howled with her.

Every day after that, no matter where I was at, the big glass vehicle would find me and sit hovering over me, always full of new feelers that stared down at me, pointing and clicking, silenced by the glass that lay between us. After four visits I realised I had no one left to kill so all my anger began to turn inside on me and eat me up. I took one last trip around everywhere, then slouched by the wall. I done a full circle of the wall, walking near its insides, inside its shade. The full trip only took me two days to get back to where I had met it first, and I knew in my skin that everywhere had become a small thing.

That twilight I made it back to Maureen's, and I lay up in her old bed, damp and dusty with silence, Bella beside me on the floor, yawning. I angled up the windows and stared out at the greenness and where it met the wall in the distance of my sight, and then I lay back in bed. Bella climbed up on the bed by my feet, but she was so big that her weight sagged it down, and whenever she turned her head the bed creaked. I hooked myself up to the RAM and dropped a season's worth of serotonin into my eyes and sunk into darkness.

With no one to unhook me, I don't know how long I was everywhere, but when I unhooked me and stared around me, it was the early hours of some morning, and I could hear birds calling one another in love songs and Bella growled downstairs and then she yelped, and I pulled myself up. Orange light from the weak sun was strangling the corners of the room and hardening the light on the wall with its shine. I felt dizzy. It was one of them moments where I could feel it in my guts that the only everywhere left to me was inside myself since I was the last human, and I knew that feeling would be forever since they built the wall and took everywhere away with smallness. I blinked and everything was dim. I was using too much serotonin drops and it was making me blind.

Swinging my legs off the bed, I jumped down and crawled down the stairs, my vision still all blurred and queer, sick to my gut and hungry. The front door was half open and before it Bella lay sprawled out, her throat cut. I listened to the house, but all that was in my ears was the morning jackdaws. In my skin, I gave up and I went back to bed, tears tickling off my chin. I stayed silent and I felt a run of fear lick its cold through me and just then I felt so old. I done what I should have done two years ago, 'fore Bella stopped me, and I took out the cyanide vaporisers from my drawer and activated them, setting them spinning above me, raining down the almond-smelling poisons. They felt cold and good against my skin, like summer rain.

I lay there, waiting for to die, and a small padding came through the door and I cast my eyes down.

Bella? I said.

There was the fly in the middle of the room. It crawled across the floor to me.

No, I whispered, choking off the cyanide.

You've got to stop this, it said.

It flew up into the middle of the room and started sucking the cyanide into itself with its big sucker.

Let me out, please. I'm still not here.

The fly landed on my chest.

I'm sorry, it said.

Am I still in that room?

The fly said nothing and I turned my head away to the side.

You killed Bella.

I've seen your dreams, it said. They're beautiful. We were wrong. We'll take you out of here now, but you have to trust me.

You tortured me. You made me old. You broke my vision and my brain.

You're fine. We're drawing you out now, it said.

A sheet of tears softened my sight, and I felt a weight of emptiness suck at me. The thin feelers of the fly rubbed themselves off my neck. Light from the window flickered, and I blinked away the wetness in my eyes and looked at the dying leaves trembling like ghosts through the dirty glass of the window.

Maeve? it said. Can you hear me?

One leaf shivered in death and a suck of breeze took it from its branch and blew it to the window where it touched up against the glass before falling away.

Maeve? it said again, and I turned my head to it.

You took everywhere away. You hurted everywhere.

Maeve, please. I'm asking you to be sensible.

You killed all my peoples. You took my mammy away.

The fly started coughing and out of its sucker it vomited a small daffodil. I took it up in my hand. It smelt full of life and real.

You can keep your flowers, it said.

I took the daffodil to my chest and squeezed the petals against my cheeks, and I let out a few sobs, more tears streaming out of me.

I think we're ready to begin negotiations now, the fly said.

Yes? said a loud voice from outside the window.

No, I said, putting the flower across my breast, lying back and staring up at the ceiling. No. You keep showing me futures that are full of yourselves. You're getting me to think there's only yourselves in the future, but ye are not the future. That hasn't happened. There is everywhere, and I'm not it, so what you put in my head doesn't make that happen.

We don't put this in your head, the fly said, shaking its head. You project this. We don't control what you see. We just see what you see.

Feeler lies, I said.

So we're not ready yet? the voice said out the window.

No. We're ready, the fly said.

We're not. Get out of there.

We're ready to begin negotiations, it shouted. I'm telling you. Now. We're ready now.

Get out of me, I yelled, rearing up like a horse off the bed. I heard Bella yapping downstairs and the fly landed on my face.

Give me back my peoples, I screamed into it, but it was smothering me, and I lost all breath, and I shrank down into darkness again.

Fifteen bloated bodies floated by, bobbing like corks, although one floated by like a corkscrew. I waded back to the bank, nervous, slinging my rod over my shoulder until the blue bodies, hunched underwater like they were looking for something, had slunk away downstream. My everything was wet, which I didn't like, but I liked fishing, although the coodegrass were coming more frequently now, dirtying up the water, being nibbled at by the fishes, being landed on by lazy midges. Bella lay by the banks, lazy and yawning, her fur dark and slick with wetness. I was about to get out when I caught a young salmon swimming against the current. It stared around and then it looked up at me.

I remember you, I said. You are my child.

Run, it said, gawping open its mouth, sucking dead oxygen into itself with its fluttering gills.

No, I said, putting its slick body back in the water.

I turned and waded out, and as I was climbing up the bank a fly came out from behind the chestnut tree where I was to sleep that night, crawling towards me.

I remember now, I said to it.

What? it said.

I remember now. I remember you too.

It doesn't matter, the fly said, rubbing its front legs together.

It does, I said, and you know it does. That's why you won't let me alone.

I leant over and stood on its red eyes till they came off its head with a squelch. Then with my other foot I stood on its body till its stringy guts squeezed out its sides, and then I ran. Bella was galloping by my side, her fur wet, her tongue lolling and flapping out her head, her yellow eyes ranging the sky, scanning the wholeness of the world. She barked, and I looked behind ourselves. A rake of flies was buzzing over the Boyne, coming at us. I glanced back one more time, and then I ran harder, my rod over my shoulder, through the trees, through the grass, the sun glancing its eyes at me like flickering dreams through the spangles that broke the tree shade, the birds screaming at me with melodies in their voices, the breeze hurrying me on away from the river's gurgle, towards my peoples, chased by everywhere.

Acknowledgements

Thanks to Derek Young, my first, and best, reader. Blessings to the New Island team, especially Dan Bolger, Shauna Daly and Hannah Shorten, who made this book what it is. Thanks to Dave Lordan, Declan Meade, Tom Morris and Sean O'Reilly for their help over the years. Thanks to Kate McDonald and Sarah Davis-Goff for invaluable criticism on the first draft. All apologies to Scoil Dara, and all dues to P.J. Gannon, who is the most wonderful educator I have ever come across, in a life that has been full of wonderful educators. *Hostages* is dedicated to the memory of my grandparents, Julia and Oliver, whose spirit wrote this book, but the story 'No Diamonds' shares its dedication with the homeless children who are growing up in this country, either in emergency accommodation or in the inhumane system of Direct Provision. If the future is to be worth anything, it will belong to them.